I moved to my right behind the crest, so no movement would catch his eye, and stopped when I was directly opposite the small-caliber rifle.

I timed my lunge so that it came just as he was lifting a full shovel of sand and beginning to pivot to throw it behind him. I came down the slope in giant plunging strides. The whirling shovel caught me just below the knees and I landed face down on the hardpan at the bottom of the dune.

He wrested the gun away from me and aimed at the middle of my forehead. I could practically see the little round hole it would make where it went in.

I had to make my move now—and fast.

"MacDONALD is in top form in his latest thriller."

—*Booklist*

John D. MacDonald

The
EMPTY COPPER
SEA

FAWCETT GOLD MEDAL • NEW YORK

THE EMPTY COPPER SEA

Published by Fawcett Gold Medal Books, a unit of CBS
Publications, the Consumer Publishing Division of CBS Inc.

ISBN 0-449-14149-7

Printed in the United States of America

10 9 8 7 6 5 4 3 2 1

*Dedicated to all the shining memories
of those last two passenger ships
which flew the United States Flag,
the Monterey and the Mariposa,
and to the mariners
who sailed aboard them.*

A man needs only to be turned around once
with his eyes shut in this world to be lost.
—THOREAU

CHAPTER

1

Van Harder came aboard *The Busted Flush* on a hot bright May morning. My houseboat was at her home mooring, Slip F-18 at Bahia Mar, Fort Lauderdale. I was in the midst of one of my periodic spasms of energy born of guilt. You go along thinking you are properly maintaining your houseboat and your runabout, going by the book, keeping a watchful eye on the lines, the bilge, the brightwork, and all. But the book was written for more merciful climates than Florida, once described to the King of Spain by DeSoto as "an uninhabitable sandspit," even though at the time it was inhabited by quite a lot of Indians.

Suddenly everything starts to snap, rip, and fall out, to leak and squeal and give final gasps. Then you bend to it, or you go live ashore like a sane person.

Crabbing along, inch by inch, I was replacing the rail posts around the whole three sides of the sun deck, port, starboard, and stern, using a power drill and a power screwdriver to set the four big screws down through the stainless flange at the foot of each post. I had sore knees, a lame wrist, and a constant drip of sweat from nose and chin. I wore an old pair of tennis shorts, and the sun was eating into my tired brown back.

It had been six, maybe seven years since I'd seen Van Harder. He had owned the *Queen Bee III* in charter-boat row. He had been steady and he could find fish, and so had less trouble finding customers than a lot of the others. I knew he wasn't going to overwhelm me with a lot of conversation. I knew he'd had some bad luck, but that was a long time ago. A frugal man, he had saved his money and finally sold the *Queen Bee III* to Rance Fazzo, had acquired a shrimp boat and a large debt, and had moved around to the other coast.

I finished the post, walked over, and mopped my face on the towel. We sat on the two pilot chairs, swiveled away from the instrument panel to face astern, toward all the shops and towers of Bahia Mar, both of us shaded by the folding navy top.

Van Harder was a lean, sallow man. Tall, silent, and expressionless. I had never seen him without a greasy khaki cap with a bill. Florida born for generations back, from that tough, tireless, malnourished, merciless stock which had scared the living hell out of the troops they had faced during the War Between the States. His eyes were a pale watery blue. He was about fifty, I guessed.

"They tell me Fazzo is fishing out of Marathon now," he said.

"Doing okay, from what I hear."

Silence.

"Meyer still around?"

"Still around. He had some errands over in town today."

Silence.

"Guess you heard I lost the *Queen Bee Number Four*. Shrimp boat. Sixty-five foot."

"Yes, I remember now. Wasn't that four years or so ago?"

"Two month shy of five year. Run down by a phosphate ship headed for Tampa. Forty mile west of Naples. Three in the morning. Lost two men. One of them had the helm. No way to tell what happened."

"Insurance?"

He spat over the rail, downwind, with excellent accuracy and velocity. "Enough to pay off what I owed on her. Got a job hired captain on another shrimper. Bigger. New. Hula Marine Enterprises."

"Hula?"

"That's the *h* and *u* off the front of Hubbard and the *l* and *a* off the front of Lawless. Hubbard Lawless. Hula run six shrimp boats at the time, and seven by the time they sold out a couple of years ago. What happened was Hub seen the handwriting on the wall, and he sold out to Weldron, which is a part of Associated Foods, own markets and all. I could have stayed on with Weldron, like most of the others did, except the ones so old they would have been in retirement too quick, and Weldron wouldn't take them. But Hub Lawless, he offered me a job skipper of the *Julie*. Real nice cruiser."

"I've seen her over at Pier Sixty-six, way out at the end. Nice."

"Dutch built. Big twin diesels. Fast. Good range. White with blue trim. How'd you know it was the same *Julie?*"

"I remember that name. Lawless. I asked who the owner was."

"If it was a year ago, I was captaining her. Year ago April. Had some time to come over here and see who was around, how things were going. Didn't happen to run into you then, McGee."

"But this time you looked me up." Not quite a question, but at least a leading remark. It sailed right by him. No response. I slumped in the chair, chin on my chest, ankles crossed, staring patiently at my big brown bare feet, at some paler cleat marks on the outside of the left ankle, and at the deep curving ugly scar down the outside of my right thigh.

"Funny thing about it all," he said, "was that Hub took me on because he knowed I was steady. The captain he had before, I won't mention no names, he got into the whiskey and he took a cut for himself when he ordered supplies, and he had brought women aboard when Hub was off on business trips."

"Why do you say that's funny?"

"Funny meaning strange how it came out, is all. I become a born-again Christian when I was twenty-eight years old. Clawed my suffering way up out of the black depths of sin to walk in love and brotherhood with our good Lord Jesus. Now Hub knew that. And he respected that. Until that night he never had no women aboard except his wife and his daughter."

"What night?"

He turned and gave me a long, watery blue stare. "The night Hub Lawless got drownded! What night you think I was talking about? There wasn't a newspaper in Florida didn't have the whole thing in it."

"When did it happen?"

"March twenty-two. Fell off the *Julie* somehow."

"I've been gone since early March, Van. I got back a week ago. Duke Davis had a party down in the Grenadines on that big ketch of his, the *Antsie*, and he had a bad fall and tore up his back, and he cabled me to come down and help him bring the *Antsie* all the way home. I didn't have any time to read the papers or listen to the news."

"Thought you look darker than I remembered."

"What's this all about, Van?"

He gave it about thirty seconds of thought before answering. "I know maybe more than I should about the time you he'ped out Arthur Wilkinson when he was way down, and it was right after you he'ped him, he married Chookie McCall. What I heard that time was that if somebody lost something important to them, you'd try to get it back, and if you did, you'd keep half what it's worth."

"That's close enough. So?"

He leaned toward me, just a little. I sensed that this was something he had thought about very carefully, turning it this way and that, not certain whether he was being a fool. His wisdom was the sea. So he took onto himself more dignity.

"They is stolen from me my good name, McGee."

"I don't see how or what——"

"Now you wait a minute. I got marked down as a drunken man, a fool who lost the owner overboard and nearly lost his vessel. They had an inquiry and held I was negligent. I haven't got my papers and I can't work at my trade. I have talked it over with Eleanor Ann, who has got a nursing job there in Timber Bay, and she says if it is what I want to do, she'll help out. I would say that by and large, my good name is worth twenty thousand dollars anyway, so what I'll do, I'll give you a piece of paper. You can word it any way you want, and I'll sign it. It will say that if you can find some way to show it wasn't my fault at all, I will pay you ten thousand dollars, not all at once, but over whatever time it takes me to make it and pay it."

Everything he had was wrapped up in that request: his pride, his dignity, his seafaring career, his worth as a man. And I sensed that this was the very last thing he had been able to think of. Travis McGee, the last chance he had.

"You better tell me exactly what happened."

"You'll make the deal?"

"After you tell me what happened, I will sit around and think about it, and I will probably talk to Meyer about it. And then I will tell you if I think I can help at all. If I can't, I'm wasting your time and mine."

He thought that over slowly, pursed his lips, and gave a little nod of acceptance. And told his story.

At about four in the afternoon of March twenty-second, Hubbard Lawless had phoned the *Julie* from his country office out at the grove and asked if the cruiser was okay to take a night run on down to Clearwater. It was a pointless question because Van Harder always kept the *Julie* ready to go. Van reminded Mr. Lawless that the mate, DeeGee Walloway, had been given time off to go up to Waycross, Georgia, where his father was close to death with cancer of the throat. Lawless said there was no need for the mate. There would be four in the party, and one of them would be available to handle the lines, if necessary, and they could certainly serve their own booze and peanuts.

Harder thought it would be four businessmen; he had often made short trips up and down the Florida coast when Lawless wanted to meet with people without attracting too much attention. The boat made a good place to hold a conference. It couldn't easily be bugged, a fact that politicians seemed to appreciate.

They came aboard at nine. They came down to the marina dock in John Tuckerman's big blue Chrysler Imperial. John Tuckerman was a sort of unofficial assistant to Hub Lawless. He didn't seem to hold any particular office in any of Hub's many corporations and partnerships, but he always seemed to be around, laughing, making jokes, making sure of air reservations, hotel reservations, dockage space, hangar space, and so on. They brought two young women aboard. Half the ages of Hub and John Tuckerman. Tight pants and airline carry-ons. Perfume and giggles.

Van Harder didn't like it one bit. The *Julie* was a family boat, named after Mr. Hub's wife. Women like those two didn't belong aboard. Harder knew from what people said that Hub Lawless was very probably a womanizer, but until that moment, when the two came aboard the *Julie*, it had been just talk as far as Harder was concerned. When he had been doing charter fishing, he had been known to turn back and come roaring to the dock and refund the unused part of the charter if people started messing around aboard the *Queen Bee III*. He couldn't exactly refuse to make the run to Clearwater, but he did not want to stay on as captain of a floating whorehouse.

Still puzzling over what to do, Harder took the *Julie* on out of South Cedar Pass. It was an unseasonably chilly night, with a northwest wind and the sea foaming white across the bars that bracketed the tricky channel inshore of the sea buoy. Once he was in good water, he set the course for a point offshore of Clearwater, put the steering on automatic pilot, and watched the compass carefully to see if, in the following sea shoving against the stern starboard quarter, she would hold at that speed without too much yawing and swinging and searching.

As was their custom, when Hubbard Lawless felt the *Julie* settle into cruising speed, he built Harder's single drink, a tall bourbon and water, and brought it up to him. Harder decided it was a poor time to speak to Mr. Lawless about the women. He did not feel that the single drink was in conflict with his religious convictions. It never led to another.

"Not long after I drank it down, I remember I had a buzzy feeling in my head, and then it was like the *Julie* climbed a big black wave that curled over at the top. I woke up sick and confused. I didn't know where I was, even, but we were tied up back at the regular dock. Hack Ames, he's the Sheriff, he was kicking me awake and yelling at me. He didn't want to try to pick me up, I stank so from having throwed up on my clothes. I reached up and got hold of the rail and pulled myself up, but I was so dizzy I couldn't dare let go. I couldn't make out what all the yelling was about."

"What had happened?"

"John Tuckerman testified at the inquest. He said one of the girls felt a little sick and went topside to get some air and went hurrying below again to tell them I was unconscious on the deck. Hub and Tuckerman came up and they checked me and thought I looked pretty bad. They thought maybe I had a stroke or some damn thing, so the best thing to do would be get me to shore. They had both run the boat, but neither one of them had come back in South Cedar Pass at night with a sea running. The way they worked it out, Hub Lawless went way up on the bow while Tuckerman eased it in. They steered at first by the city lights, and then by the sea buoy, and slowed way down to hunt the next marker. The girls stayed below, out of the cold wind. The boat was rocking and pitching in the chop. Hub was hanging on and trying to spot the sandbars. Tuckerman said that all of a sudden Hub pointed to the right. Tuckerman thought he meant turn hard right, and that's what he did. The instant he hit the hard sandbar, he knew Hub Lawless had been pointing out the problem, not pointing out where to steer. The jolt tore Hub's grip loose and he went overboard off the bow. The waves were picking the bow up and dropping it back onto the bar so hard Tuckerman knew he had to back off or start to break up. He put it in hard reverse and yanked it back off, and he couldn't find the switch to turn on the overhead searchlight so he could hunt for Hub. He threw a life ring over, slinging it toward the bar, hoping Hub could find it. He didn't know how to work the ship-to-shore, and even if he did, he didn't dare leave go of the wheel and the throttles. He yelled for the women and they finally heard him and came up to help look for Hub. It was a wild dark night and the only thing

14

he could think of to do was try to find the markers and find his way in and get help. I stayed passed out through all of it and didn't come out of it even partway until, like I said, Hack Ames was aboard trying to kick me awake."

"Funny thing for him to do if he thought you were sick."

"He testified he thought I was drunk. He said I looked drunk, talked drunk, walked drunk, and smelled drunk. There was other testimony at the hearing, about how small boats had gone out hunting for Hub Lawless, and one of them found the life ring and nothing else. I testified I had that one drink that Mr. Lawless brought me like always. They asked me why I'd refused to go to a doctor, and I explained that once I started to come out of it, I felt groggy but I didn't feel sick, not in any particular place or particular way. They decided that Hub Lawless was missing and believed to be dead by . . . I can't recall the word."

"Misadventure?"

"That's the one. His body never has showed up."

"What is it you think I could do anyway?"

"There's a lot of talk around Timber Bay. People say Hubbard Lawless is alive. They say he's in Yucatan, living like a king."

"There's always talk like that when the body isn't recovered, and when the person had some money."

"But what if he *is* alive? You see what I mean?"

"Then he and Tuckerman had to plan the whole thing, and they had to knock you out."

"What I didn't tell you, I was drunk a lot when I was a sinner. I was jailed for drunk, time and again. I gave it up all the way for twenty year. Took it up again, just the one drink when Lawless would fix me one, showing myself there was no holt on me any more. They asked about that at the hearing and I told them. I told them I'd been

15

passed-out drunk and remembered it clear, and this wasn't like it."

"Why would the man fake his own death?"

"Money trouble. Woman trouble. Insurance. That's what they're saying. I got to have some help. I don't know what to do with myself. I don't know which way to turn any more. That was in March, and here it is May, and I haven't had one real good night's sleep since."

"Van, I don't want to say yes or no this minute."

"I can understand that."

"I want to walk it around a little."

"Want I should come back about evening?"

"Where can I reach you?"

"I got one day of work, crewing for Billy Maxwell tomorrow, for walk-around money. I'll bunk aboard his boat tonight. It's that thirty-eight-foot Merritt with the—"

"Down at the far end. I know the boat."

"Remember, I'll sign a paper for the money, and I'm good for it."

"I know you are. I'll be in touch tomorrow. Or why don't you come here after you get through with the charter?"

After he left I sat there and watched him walk along the pier, a big sad sallow man, with a little bit more than his share of pride and rigidity. The world had tried to hammer him into the ground a few times, but he had endured and survived. Maybe this time he could not. Maybe it was too much.

CHAPTER

2

As I drove into town with Meyer that bright evening, we got onto a familiar complaint. Back not long ago when all the action in town was located in the rectangle bounded by the Beach, Sunrise Boulevard, Andrews Avenue, and New River, you could not go into the city without seeing a few dozen people you knew. Meyer had spent a whole day doing errands without running into a single person he knew. And it depressed him. He is the sort of man who manages to know people. He knows at least six people for every person I know. His little bright blue eyes sparkle with pleasure when he meets anyone he has ever met before, and the splendid computer between his ears immediately furnishes a printout of everything they had ever confessed to him. Meyer can suffer bores without pain. He finds them interesting. He says the knack of being able to bore almost anybody is a great art. He says he studies it. So if my hairy amiable friend had been unable to find a familiar face in downtown Lauderdale, the world was in deep trouble. He is seldom depressed.

At least the tourist influx had died down to about 15

percent of peak, and we did not have to hunt for one of those places where locals go to avoid the crush. We settled for Dorsey Brannigan's pub atmosphere and Irish stew, and a couple of bottles of stout.

I knew that Van Harder's story would get Meyer over his identity crisis, and so it did.

He had followed the news story of Hubbard Lawless's untidy end in local papers and could fill me in a little on the man.

"About forty, as I remember. An achiever, Travis. One of those twenty-hours-a-day fellows. Wife and teenage daughters. A florid life-style, I believe. Lots of small corporations and partnerships. Housing, fishing, citrus, ranchland, and construction. The follow-up stories hinted that he was in very serious financial difficulties at the time of his death. And there was an enormous life insurance policy. Two million or more. I can't remember the exact amount."

"Anything about how maybe he took off, faked it all?"

"Nothing direct. Mystery surrounds the disappearance of Timber Bay tycoon. The body has not been recovered. I think it safe to assume that if the papers were hinting, then the public was talking more directly about that possibility. Then it died down, I'd guess about mid-April."

"What do you think about Van Harder's story?"

"He's a reliable man. So let's say it was a heart attack, a stroke, a savage bout of food poisoning, or somebody put something in the drink. In any event I think we can say that Lawless left the boat before it returned. He left on purpose or by accident. And in either case, he died or left town."

"I don't know what I'd do without your help."

"It's simple mathematics, Travis. Permutations and combinations. You have three sequences—of four choices, two choices, and two choices. So there are sixteen possibilities."

I stared blankly at him. "Such as?"

"It was a heart attack. Lawless fell overboard by accident. He made shore and realized what a good chance it was for him to try to disappear forever. Or—Lawless put something in the drink, went overboard on purpose, miscalculated the risk, and drowned. Do you see why I say there are—"

"I see, I see. You don't know what a help that is."

"Break it down and you can't find one of the sixteen where Harder is at fault."

"Should I try to help him, dammit?"

"Would you like to know why I am saying yes, you should?"

"Yes, I would."

"Because as you told me this heart-stirring tale, you kept loading all the dice in Van Harder's favor, so that when you came to the point of asking me, I'd say yes. Okay. Yes."

"I'll be *damned* if I will. I am not in the business of salvaging the reputations of broken-down fishermen. I visited the city of Timber Bay once upon a time. It was closed. I am sick of red-hots, of overachievers, of jollyboy Chamber of Commerce types. I've stashed enough money to last until Christmas week, and I've got work to do on the *Flush*, and when the work is done I want to ask about eight good friends and you to go on a nice little lazy cruise down to—"

"Will we need some sort of a cover story for Timber Bay?"

"We?"

"You don't think I'd let Harder down, do you?"

I stared at my friend with fond exasperation. I said, "You have a small piece of boiled onion on your underlip."

"Sorry," he said, and removed it.

"How about a bottle of Harp?"

"Splendid!"

"No, we won't need a cover story. People will want to talk about Hubbard Lawless. All we have to do is get them talking and then sort it all out."

"I'm glad you talked me into going," Meyer said. "Life has been too restful lately. And here comes somebody I *do* know. Life is improving." I looked where he was looking and saw Cindy Thorner and her husband, Bob, just leaving. They saw us at the same time and came over and sat with us for a while in one of Brannigan's big oak booths. They are South Miami people, and we had met them during a couple of skin-diving fiestas down in the Keys. Cindy is a perky soul, looking far too young to have grown kids, a blue-eyed blonde with enough energy for three ladies.

They had been in Lauderdale for some sort of bridge thing, some determined pursuit of master points about which I know less than nothing, and were about to head back. Meyer got off into his diatribe about not meeting anyone he knew all day, and how depressing it was, and how everything is changing so fast.

Then he told us all his new insight into the problem. Florida can never really come to grips with saving the environment because a very large percentage of the population at any given time just got here. So why should they fight to turn the clock back? It looks great to them the way it is. Two years later, as they are beginning to feel uneasy, a few thousand more people are just discovering it all for the first time and wouldn't change a thing. And meanwhile the people who knew what it was like twenty years ago are an ever-dwindling minority, a voice too faint to be heard.

They had to go. As Cindy got up she said, "Meyer, a Florida conservationist is a fellow who bought his waterfront property last week."

"And wants us to make room for two or three of his friends, and then shut the door forever," Meyer said.

Then she told me that the best reef for snorkeling she had ever seen was at Akumal in Yucatan, fifty miles down the coast from Cozumel. She said they were there at Easter and I should promise myself not to miss it.

After the Thorners left, Meyer said, "A person can go for months without hearing anybody say Yucatan, and now I have heard it twice in the same evening. A more primitive soul would take it as a sign."

"A sign that Hub Lawless is down there snorkeling away, drinking booze out of green coconuts, and finessing the señoritas?"

"We could go look there first, maybe?" said Meyer.

I drove back through the thinning traffic a little past ten. My ancient electric-blue Rolls pickup whispered along, silent and smooth as one of the great cats a-hunting. We decided there was no need to keep Van Harder in suspense once the decision was made, so, once I had stowed Miss Agnes in her parking slot, we walked down charter-boat row, past *Windsong* and *Dream Girl*, *Amigo* and *Eagle*, *Playtime* and *Uzelle*, *Pronto* and *Caliban*, all the way down to where Billy Maxwell's *Honcho* was moored and dark, the dockside lights slanting down into the dark cockpit.

I put one foot on the stern quarter of the *Honcho* and leaned my weight on it and let it rock back. Within seconds Van came up from below, silent and quick, a short gaff in his hand. Even though the *Honcho* was rocking a little in a fresh sea breeze that pushed against the tuna tower, that subtle change of motion was enough to bring Harder up out of sleep, instantly alert to repel boarders.

"Oh, it's you fellows," he said in a sleep-rusty voice. "Come aboard and set?"

"No thanks, Van. I stopped by to tell you we'll go over to Timber Bay and see what we can turn up."

After a long five seconds he said, "I do surely appreciate it. You fix up that paper to sign?"

"No hurry on that."

"They aren't going to care for people nosing around there."

"Who isn't?"

"Reporters came around, and all. Government people and law people and bank people. They asking questions, handing out legal papers, and so on. So the family and the people that worked for him and the people tied into it all, one way or another, they're sick of it now, even though it slacked off a lot by the middle of last month. How you, Meyer?"

"I've been fine, Van. Sorry to hear about your bad luck."

"It do seem to come at me in bunches lately."

"Forgive me for asking, Van, but did you see a doctor and get checked over?"

"Hoped he could find some reason I passed out. Doc Stuart. He said he couldn't find any evidence I'd had some kind of heart spasm or something go wrong in my head, but then again he said he couldn't find any reason to say something like that hadn't happened. But if it had, it might probably happen again, and that would help pin it down. Aside from kid stuff, I never had a sick day in my life. Not ever. How soon are you going on over there?"

"We can talk about that tomorrow," I told him. We ambled back and sat for a time on the transom of Meyer's chunky little old cruiser, the *John Maynard Keynes,* looking at the overhead stars, faint through the particulate matter which jams the air of the gold coast night and day, never dropping below twenty thousand particles per cubic centimeter, except when a hurricane sweeps it away briefly, blowing it all into somebody else's sky.

"A cover story will help. I was wrong," I said.

"I'm working on it," Meyer said. From his tone of voice I decided not to ask any more questions.

I went back alone to the *Flush*. My security system advised me I'd had no uninvited guests. I was still worn down by the weeks aboard the *Antsie*, working that ketch north into the teeth of a hard wind that never quite became a gale and never died out. Cold food and safety lines, chafing and salt rash, constant motion and noise, and the deep fatigue, like a bone bruise all over. I wanted to drift *The Busted Flush* down through glassy bays, past mangroves and pelicans and the leaping of mullet. I wanted to take her down through Biscayne Bay and Florida Bay, and up by Flamingo through Whitewater, and out the mouth of the Shark River, and up past Naples, Fort Myers, Boca Grande, Venice, Sarasota, Bradenton, Tampa Bay, Clearwater, all the way on up to Timber Bay.

Once I was in the big bed in the master stateroom, I traced the route in the Waterway Guide all the way up to Cedar Key, which would be the last overnight before Timber Bay. I hadn't run any part of the lonesome leg from Egmont Channel a hundred and fifty or so nautical miles up to Lighthouse Point beyond St. Marks in quite a few years, and so was pleased to learn they'd put in a new chain of sea buoys nine to sixteen miles off the shoreline—nineteen-foot-high dolphins with slow flashers I'd be able to see six miles away in clear weather. Timber Bay lies twenty-seven nautical miles north of Cedar Key, and that pinpointed the city halfway between the marker number 16 for Pepperfish Key and marker 18 for Deadman Bay.

I reached for scratch paper and made a rough estimate of four hundred and seventy-five statute miles from Bahia Mar to Timber Bay. Running a ten-hour day at my cruising speed of a dazzling seven knots, I could just do it in six days, if absolutely nothing went wrong. As something always does go wrong, I always add a fudge factor of 50 percent. Nine days.

The *Flush* and I used to make nine knots. Then it was eight. Now we are down to seven, even when the bottom is clean and fresh. The problem seems to be in the efficiency of the two smallish Hercules diesels. They have many, many miles thereon. They are noisier than when I won the boat long ago. Some day they will have to be replaced. I have replaced almost everything else, a bit at a time.

I checked the accommodations at Timber Bay in the Guide and found a map of the waterfront and a description of the facilities. Cedar Pass Marina looked just fine. Ten feet on the approach and ten feet alongside. They could accommodate up to seventy-foot craft, so my fifty-two feet was no problem. Everything I needed was available at the marina, from electric to diesel fuel to repairs, showers, Laundromat, groceries, restaurant, and even a motel.

I had a distant memory of its being a small and sleepy place. Like Cedar Key, it had been one of the towns supplying the timber which was barged south down the coast to build hunting and fishing lodges for gentlemen from the Midwest before the southwest Florida area was available by road and railroad. Again like Cedar Key, it had supplied the wood for a few billion lead pencils, until the wood finally ran out. Both of them were well off the main north-south tourist routes, with Timber Bay being about fifteen miles west of Route 19, down State Road 359, a long straight two-lane road through a tangle of dankness, smelling of snake.

Now, apparently, as they had found Cedar Key, the tourist and the retired had finally found Timber Bay—just as, inevitably, every square foot of the state except the state parks is going to be found and asphalted and painted with yellow parking lines.

I woke up at two in the morning with the light still on and the Guide open and face down on my chest. I stayed awake just long enough to be sure I didn't sink back into the same dream that awoke me. I had been underwater, swimming behind Van Harder, following the steady stroke of his swim fins and wondering why I had to be burdened with tanks, weights, and mask while he swam free. Then he turned and I saw small silver fish swimming in and out of his empty eye sockets.

As I faded down toward sleep I realized the dream had told me something. I should give up my rationalized cruise. When the cavalry went riding to rescue the wagon train, they never took the scenic route.

CHAPTER

3

The next morning, Wednesday, the eighteenth day of May, after I finally gave up trying to find Meyer, he found me. He was beaming with pride and satisfaction. We went into the lounge of the *Flush* and he showed me the three identical envelopes, all addressed to him, hand delivered, not mailed.

The stationery was uncommonly crisp, and it was a ribbed creamy forty-pound bond, bearing at the top the corporate logo of one of America's most successful conglomerates.

Up at the top left was printed in very small letters, "Office of the Chairman of the Board of Directors."

My dear Meyer,

This letter confirms our conversations regarding our potential interest in various enterprises and holdings large and small, which are now available or may become available in the Timber Bay area.

Knowing our long-range plans for the area, you will be able to determine if there are properties or enterprises there which should require our further attention with a view to negotiation.

In the event we do acquire anything there, with such acquisition based upon your recommendation, we both understand that you will be due remuneration on a percentage basis, just as we have operated in the past.

You are, of course, authorized to use your best judgment in showing this letter on a confidential basis to those who might have a need to know, and you are authorized to instruct them to get in touch with me personally if they should have any doubts as to your credibility.

Cordially yours,

Emmett Allbritton
Chairman of the Board

"All three are alike," Meyer said.

"How the *hell* did you manage this?"

"I had breakfast with good old Emmett aboard his little hundred-and-twenty-foot play toy at Pier Sixty-six. Back when he was CEO of his corporation, I saved him from stepping in something nasty. They were acquiring a company which had a patent infringement suit filed against it. Emmett's legal people didn't think the suit had much chance. I was doing a Eurodollar survey for them at that time, and I came across something that indicated the suit would be large and nasty and successful. I went directly

27

to him. He delayed the closing until the suit went to trial. And was very glad. So he owed me one. He had stationery aboard, and I took it to a public stenographer I know and composed the letter and took the three originals back to him for signature."

"You *do* know what you've got here?" I said.

"Travis, what I have here is a con man's dream. Emmett knows I won't misuse it, and he knows I'll destroy all three letters the instant there's no more need to use them."

"What about Van Harder? He can't lie worth a damn."

"Who says anything about lying? I am going to ask him if it meets with his approval if I kill two birds with one stone by checking into some property over there some friends might want to buy. Actually, if I do find something that looks very good, I think Emmett *would* be interested."

"Have you figured out my role in all this, pal?"

"If you are my friend, you are going to be accepted. Avarice is the longest lever in the world. Everybody is going to be very anxious to help me. Nobody will want to risk offending me. If they offend me, I won't make them independently wealthy. Of course, it would be easier if Van Harder wasn't there, giving them cause to wonder if we are what we say we are."

"Ha!" I said.

"Whyfor the Ha?"

"He could bring the *Flush* all the way around. As a favor. So we could come back home the slow way."

"Some likely people around here could fly over and help us come back the slow way," Meyer said, nodding and nodding, smiling and smiling. "How long will it take him?"

"Six to nine days."

"Do you trust his luck?"

"He's used up all the bad part."

"I stopped at Zzest Travel and had Peggy look up the best place to stay in Timber Bay. It's the North Bay Yacht and Tennis Resort. Suitable, apparently, for a man of my influence and knowhow. They should have some humble accommodations for you as well."

When he came back from the charter, Van Harder said he'd be glad to take my houseboat on around to Timber Bay, but couldn't he be more help to us in Timber Bay, telling us who everybody was?

While I fumbled the question Meyer said that maybe it was best if we went in cold; then we could tell Van our impressions by the time he arrived at the Cedar Pass Marina.

It took until noon the next day to teach Van the little eccentricities of the engines, bilge pumps, generators, two banks of batteries, automatic pilot, air conditioning, water tanks, fuel tanks, engine gauges, RDF, SSB-VHF, tape deck, marine head, freezer, bottled gas, and so on—and to lay aboard provisions enough for the trip, get the needed new charts, estimate the cash he would need, and recommend the places to hole up. He marveled most at the giant bed, the enormous shower stall, and the huge bathtub, shaking his head and saying, "My, my, my."

I showed him the security system—the concealed switches for the Radar Sentry and the Audio Alarm and the fail-safe bulbs he would find lighted if the devices had been activated when he was ashore.

Meyer kept Harder busy while I removed my working capital from the double-hull hidey-hole on the port side in the forward bilge area. After Harder left at noon—warping the *Flush* out with an offhand competence that would have erased any doubts if I'd harbored any—I put the better part of my funds into a safety-deposit box.

It was an odd feeling to be at Bahia Mar without the *Flush*—different from when I had to put her up for bottom work. This was more of a betrayal. She was burbling happily along, down toward Dania and Hollywood, and all I had left in the slip was the overpowered runabout, my T-Craft *Muñequita*, tarped and tied off, bobbing whenever the power squadron boys went by.

By six thirty that same Thursday we were settling into a two-bedroom suite on the second floor of the North Bay Yacht and Tennis Resort. We'd flown from Lauderdale to Gainesville and then caught a little feeder-line Bonanza from Gainesville to Timber Bay, with one stop at Cross City. At the trim new little Timber Bay airport I rented a light gray Dodge Dart. The girl at the rental desk gave us a map of Timber Bay. The basic layout was simple. Imagine a capital H with a backward capital C jammed up close to it: ᗡH
The interior of the C is all water. Some small islands and unusual outcroppings of limestone block the open mouth of the C, leaving South Cedar Pass at one end and North Pass at the other. The crossbar of the H is the urban continuation of State Road 359, which comes from the east and dead-ends right at the bay shore. There it intersects the western vertical line of the H—inevitably called Bay Street—where Bay follows the C curve of the bay shore for a time before straightening out. The south end of the bay is where the marinas, commercial docks, and fish houses are located. The north end of the bay is more elegant, and beyond the top of the C a lot of sand has been dredged up and imported and a lot of fill put down to make a beach development area north of North Pass. The other up-and-down line of the H is Dixie Boulevard, named after the county. When it gets out into the country, it changes to Road 351A, going north to Steinhatchee and south to Horseshoe Beach. The northern open end of the H is residential, getting more pleasant the farther you get north of the crossbar until you get too far north into an

area of shacks and junk trailers, abandoned wrecks, bed-springs, and refrigerators. South of the crossbar is mostly commercial. The crossbar itself is called Main Street. Between Dixie Boulevard and Bay Street, on Main, are the banks, office buildings, and better stores. Urban sprawl reaches out to the east, north, and south, with franchise food service, small shopping plazas, automobile dealerships, drive-ins, and housing developments.

The North Bay Yacht and Tennis Resort was just north of the top of the C, with boat basin and dredged channel, with a private slice of the handmade beach, with tennis courts, pool, children's playground, cocktail lounge (entertainment nightly—Billy Jean Bailey at the piano), Prime Western Beef, closed-circuit television movies, and a wealth of other irresistible advantages.

When I had stowed the few items of gear I had brought along, I went into our sitting room and found Meyer standing out on the shallow balcony, with the sliding doors open. I joined him and stood beside him, leaning on the concrete rail. Directly below us was a putting green, where a fat man labored mightily to improve his stroke. Off to the left was the big pool, with a few swimmers. Off to the right was a slice of the boat basin, where the bright-work winked in the last of the sunlight of the May evening. Directly ahead, beyond the putting surface, were the tennis courts. In the nearest one, two girls in pastel tennis dresses engaged in deadly combat. They looked to be about fifteen. The one on the right, a blonde in pale salmon, had a lovely style, drifting with dance steps to the right place, setting, stroking, following through. The one on the left, in pale aqua, was shorter and stockier, with cropped dark curly hair. She was a scrambler. She was often out of position. She made improbable saves. She went to the net when she shouldn't have but managed to guess right a lot of times about where the passing shot should be. When she hit it on the wood, it tended to drop in. She tried for shots that were beyond her abilities—long-range drop shots, topspin lobs—and made them pay off just often enough. She was sweaty and grim. She fell and bounded up. They had a gallery of about a dozen people. One point went on and on and on. Had it been a faster surface, the little dark-haired one couldn't have beaten the blonde. Finally she went racing to the net after an angled return of second serve. The blonde whipped it right at her, apparently trying to drive it right through her. But in desperate reflex she got the racket in the way. The ball turned the racket and rebounded, touched the tape, and fell in for the point, and the people clapped and whistled. The winner held her hand out, and the blonde looked at it and turned and strolled away. The winner went and got her big towel and mopped her face, wobbled over to the grass, and spread the towel and fell on it, gulping for air but smiling all the while. The winners smile. The losers holler "Deal!"

We went out and explored the city in the fading light of evening, drifting the gray Dodge back and forth through the social and commercial strata, snuffling the flavors of change, the plastic aromas of the new Florida superimposed on the Spanish moss, the rain-sounds of the night peepers in the marsh, the sea smell of low tides, creak of bamboo in light winds, fright cry of the cruising night birds, tiny sirens of the mosquitoes, faraway flicker of lightning silhouetting the circus parade of thunderheads on the Gulf horizon—superimposed on all these old enduring things, known when only Caloosas made their shell mounds and slipped through the sawgrass in their dugouts. Here now was the faint petrochemical stinkings, a perpetual farting of the great god Progress. And a *wang-dang* thudding of bubblegum rock from the speakers on the poles in the shopping-plaza parking lot. And screech-wheeling vans painted with western desert sunsets. And the lighted banks and the savings-and-loan buildings, looking like Bauhaus wedding cakes.

We found a place called the Captain's Galley, with a parking lot full of local cars. There was no table for two, sir, not for fifteen or twenty minutes. The smell of fried grease was so heavy we hesitated, but I looked into the dark bar and saw captains' chairs for the customers facing the pit where the barkeeps worked. And when I asked for the brand of gin we wanted the iced martinis made from, there was no confusion or hesitation. The young man in the sailor suit whipped the blue-labeled square bottle of Boodles out of the rack, poured generously, made us the driest of the dry, glacial and delicious.

I overtipped at the bar, a device useful in all such circumstances because it caused some secret signal to pass between the bartender and the fellow with the sheaf of menus. With more warmth than he had shown when we arrived, he led us to a corner booth set up for four, whipped away the extra setups, and said it would be his pleasure to go personally and come back with our second drinks if we were now ready, and we were. It is all a kind of bullshit, of course, to pry special treatment out of busy service people, but it improves taste and appetite. If you feel valued, it makes a better evening. And to busy service people everyone falls into a known category. It is enough merely to imitate the habits and mannerisms of that category which expects and gets the very best service. Hub Lawless would have expected it, gotten it, and probably tipped well, in the familiar style of the sun-belt businessman.

A pretty waitress with frosted hair told us the flounder was exceptional tonight, and yes, she would see that they picked two very nice ones to broil for us. And they were indeed splendid, as was the salad with herb dressing, hot fresh rolls with sweet butter, the carafe of house Chablis, and the espresso.

The throng had thinned out by the time we left. Meyer went out of his way to tell the manager how pleasant the evening had been. He asked if we were passing through, and Meyer said we were in town on business, looking at property, and staying at the North Bay Resort. I went on out to the car. Meyer came out in five minutes, humming happily to himself.

As I drove off he said, "That manager's name is Bellamy. Moved down here from Atlanta three years ago. He owns a piece of that place, so he works lunch and dinner seven nights a week. If we want a quiet table any time, we can phone him. Just ask for Dave Bellamy."

"And he is one of your dearest friends."

"Is that supposed to be some form of humor? Dave is a nice man. He said the best real-estate broker for commercial properties is George Glenn. Glennmore Realty. First United Plaza. I wrote it down."

He had been writing lots of things down. While I had been provisioning my houseboat and explaining her eccentricities to Van Harder, Meyer had been going through microfilm copies of the two-months-old newspapers at the library, writing down the facts he had related to me on our flight across the state.

We found a more detailed map of Timber Bay and all the rest of Dixie County in the newsstand area of a big drugstore in the Baygate Plaza Mall. We found a phone book and wrote down addresses in Meyer's pocket notebook.

We went poking around, looking. We found HULA MARINE ENTERPRISES A DIVISION OF WELDRON/ASSOCIATED FOODS (the sign read), down at the south end of the bay, with hurricane fencing closing off access to the big dock, warehouses, and processing plant. Bright lights shone down on the whole area from high poles, discouraging intrusion. We cruised slowly by the Hubbard Lawless residence at 215 South Oak Lane, a winding mile of asphalt in the northeast sector, off Dixie Boulevard, bordering the Timber Bay Country Club. It was a very long low white structure set well back behind a low concrete wall. There were dim lights on in the house. In the glow of a streetlight some distance away, the wide yard looked unkempt. The three overhead garage doors were all closed.

We found some of the other identities left behind by Mr. Lawless, like so many cocoons shed in some startling metamorphosis. Lawless Groves. Double L. Ranches. Hula Construction. Hub-Law Development Corporation. At Hula Construction the hurricane-wire gate was chained shut. A single guard light shone down on the empty area where equipment had once been parked. Grass was beginning to poke up through the thin skin of asphalt.

"How old was he in March?" I asked Meyer.

"Not quite forty-one."

I aimed us back toward the North Bay Yacht and Tennis Resort. Those birthday years that end in a zero are loaded. A time of reevaluation. Where the hell have I been and what have I been doing and how much is left for me, and what will I do with the rest of my short turn around the track? I had one of those zero years coming up, not too many birthdays from now. Maybe Hub Lawless had felt trapped in his own treadmill, hemmed in by his juggling act, tied fast to success. The most probable catalyst was the random female who had come along at the wrong time in his life.

"Can you remember the names of those two girls?" I asked Meyer.

"Felicia Ambar and Michele Burns."

"They still around this town?"

"They were both employed here in Timber Bay. Maybe they moved on. Probably you could find out about that better than me, Travis."

So I began to find out about it as soon as we got back. Meyer went on up to bed at my suggestion, and not at all reluctantly. Billy Jean Bailey was having a slow night in the lounge. It was called the Western Sky Lounge because, I suppose, of the hunk of glass the size of a basketball court standing on end, facing west. She looked no bigger than a half a minute sitting at her little pink sequined piano at the foot of that giant window. One spot shone down on her from the ceiling fifty feet overhead. She had a platinum natural, a pink sleeveless blouse which matched the piano, and silver slacks which matched the sequins. I sat at the bar, turning to watch her and listen to her. There were a few couples whispering together and groping each other in the shadowed privacy of banquettes. There were some noisy salesmen at the bar, at the far end. Billy Jean had a deep expensive-looking tan, a round and pretty face, a button mouth, an amplified piano, and a baritone voice.

She played a medley of old standards. She did a lot of flowery, tinkly improvisations, moving far away from the melody and then sneaking up on it again. I like a firmer structure, a more emphatic rhythm. Then the improvisation is supported, as with Joe Pass on that incredible guitar of his. But she did well enough. And looked good while doing it. And seemed to sigh at one point, looking around, seeming to grimace.

I got up and walked over to her. It was a long walk. She watched me arriving, her smile polite. She kept the music going with a little bit of right hand and hardly any left at all.

"Maybe 'Lush Life'?" I asked.

"My God, a thousand years ago I used to do that. I'll have to fool around with it and work into it. Sure. And?"

"And a drink with me on your break?"

"If you can hum it, I can fake it."

I went back to the bar. She found her way into "Lush

36

Life" and, with but one stumble, got the words out of the music box of memory, did it very straight, and then moved into it with enough class to silence the salesmen for all of thirty seconds. She closed it off with her theme and came over, standing small at my elbow.

"As always, Mitch," she said to the barman. "Over there," she said to me and headed for a narrow booth for two. I paid the tab and carried her drink and mine to the booth.

"Thanks, friend," she said, "for bringing that old one up. I don't know how it fell out of the repertoire. It goes back in. I am Billy Jean Bailey and you are . . . ?"

"McGee. Travis McGee. Been working this lounge long?"

"Practically forever. Hell, it's all right. Good people own and operate this place. I used to do the resort-tour thing when I was first down here. I started in Youngstown. I used to do the Maine coast thing, and the Catskills and Poconos in the summer, and down the other coast here in the winter. Lauderdale, Hollywood, Miami, and so forth. But that can kill you off before your time. Then Danny died. He was my agent and kind of boyfriend. And they wanted me back here. That was three years ago. And here I am. Still. McGee, you drive one of those shrimpers for Hula? No? I thought you looked sort of the type. Like around boats and so forth. Jesus, this is one dead night here. Been in town long?"

"Checked in here this evening. I don't know anything about the town."

"There's no action, if that's what you mean. Oh, there's a couple of discos like everywhere, mostly all kids."

"No games?"

"You've got to be kidding. Oh, they probably play for lots of money over at the Elks or maybe the Legion. But you don't mean that."

"No, I don't mean that."

"So you can look at it this way, McGee. We're right at the heart of all the Thursday-night action there is in Dixie County."

"You're all the action I need, Billy Jean Bailey."

Her mouth hardened. "If you mean what that sounds like, you are in for one hell of a sudden disappointment."

"Whoa. I meant it is nice to sit and talk and have a few drinks and listen to the piano lady."

She studied me, head cocked. "Okay. Maybe I keep my guard up too high. But you know how things are. I don't even sit with guys much. I don't know why I did this time. You dint come on strong, and I liked what you requested, I guess."

"Friends?" I asked.

"Sure."

"I'll be around for a while. I'm over here from Lauderdale with a man named Meyer. He's my best friend. He's gone to bed in the suite, but I didn't feel like folding yet. What he's here for, he's looking into property that some bank might be liquidating that belonged to a man named Lawless."

"Oh, Jesus, *another* one."

"What do you mean?"

"McGee, dear, you have no idea the people who have come to town because of that Hub Lawless thing. My God, there is the IRS and people from the Department of Agriculture, and bank examiners, and investigators from the Justice Department, and FBI people, and insurance people. It is a real mess. You have no idea what a shock it was to this town. And still is. It has really sort of put this place into a depression."

"Did you know him?"

"And the *newspaper* people and the *television* people. The town was full up already, it being March, the end of the tourist season, and some of them were even sleeping in their cars. Did I know him, did you say? Just casual, like he came in sometimes, always with a bunch of people. Hey, Mitch is making motions. I got to go earn my bread. Don't go away." She finished her drink, patted my hand, slid out, and ambled to her pink piano, swinging along in her silver pants, patting her silver hair, tapping her mike with a fingernail as she swung it close to her lips, saying in her oddly deep voice, "Well, here we are again, back into it, dears, don't all of you go away, because . . . recognize this? Of course you do. Made famous by a lot of people including me, your own Billy Jean Bailey. . . ."

Above her and beyond her I could see the night stars. Though the room was nearly empty, she didn't dog it. She worked her stint, making music, including one very showy arrangement of "Flight of the Bumblebee" based on the old Red Norvo arrangement, but without as much drive as the way Norvo did it because she did not have the power in her left hand to roll the heavy bass. She moved from that into her theme, at which point I went over and got another pair of drinks and got back to the table with them just as she arrived, delicately winded from the session, saying, "And that is all for this here Thursday night because it is ten past Cinderella. Saturday we go until two. Friday until one. Monday not at all, thank God."

"I enjoyed it."

"Good. It was kind of for you. I'm glad you happened along tonight. I don't know why, but I've been down. You know. All blah. What do you really do for a living anyway, McGee?"

"Free-lance salvage work."

"Like sunken treasure?"

"Sort of like that."

"But you're not working on this trip? You're just here with your friend whatzis."

"Meyer. I can help him out on . . ."

She beckoned to someone beyond and behind me. He

came over. He dragged a chair over from a table and plonked it down beside the shallow booth and sat down, saying, "Hi, B.J."

"How you, Nicky? I want you should meet my friend Harris McGee. McGee, this is Nicky Noyes. Nicky used to work for Mr. Lawless."

Noyes looked like an American Indian fullback who broke training five years ago. He had a lot of long black hair, a drooping pistolero mustache, rubbery brown jowls, flinty little eyes deep-set under thick black brows, buffalo shoulders, a lacy white guayabera stretched taut across chest and stomach, a lot of dangling gold trinkets on a thick gold chain nested in the black chest hair, and a sharp tang of some kind of insistent male perfume.

He looked me over with skeptical thoroughness. "So I used to work for Hub. Isn't that damn fascinating?"

"It makes me tingle all over," I said.

Chemistry was against us. We shared a simultaneous loathing for each other. No special reason. It was just there.

He turned toward the piano player, hunching his left shoulder forward to close me out. "You want to go over to Stel's?" he asked her.

"I don't know. I guess not tonight."

"You rather sit around and let somebody pick your brains about what you know about Lawless?"

"Come *on,* Nicky! McGee isn't in town about Lawless, honest."

He stared at me. "And you don't know the first thing about it, I bet."

I shrugged. "I heard some hick businessman and one of his business buddies took a couple of hookers out on a cabin cruiser and everybody got slopped and the hired captain passed out and the local big shot fell overboard and drowned, and everybody got all worked up about it.

But I guess there isn't much to get worked up about around here anyway."

It made his big neck bulge. It made his face darker. It turned big hands into fists and made his voice uneven. "Sure, you know a lot. All you know is that newspaper shit. I never see Hub Lawless liquored up in my life. Not once. And I happen to know the fellow ran the *Julie* for Hub, and old Van wouldn't take more than just one drink ever. As for what you call hookers, Hub didn't fool around. I wouldn't say not ever, but anyways not around here, where he was a director in the bank and a deacon in the church, with a good marriage and those two daughters. Who are you calling hookers anyway? 'Licia Ambar, she works in Top Forty Music over in the Baygate Plaza Mall, and she's a good kid. Michele Burns, she works waitress over to the Cove. She's no hooker."

"Nicky, she's about as close as you can get and not be. Jack had to tell Mishy not to come cruising this bar, remember? Come on, you guys. What's to get so edged up about?"

He gestured toward me. "People like McGoo here who know everything about everything, they gripe my ass, B.J."

"McGee," I said. "I think I know how *you* spell *your* last name."

"Hey, guys!" she said sharply. "You'll get me in trouble, dammit."

"Lawless didn't drown," he said to me, almost inaudibly.

"Nicky!" she said nervously.

"Shut up, B.J." He held up a big hand and ticked the items off on his fingers. "One. He sold off the trucks for cash, cheap. Two. He stopped paying all the accounts coming due, and at the very end he cleaned out the bank accounts. Three. That girl left town the next day."

"Girl?" I asked.

He hesitated and then sighed. "What am I doing? It isn't any business of yours anyway."

"Tell me one more thing, Noyes."

"What?"

"Do you believe in the tooth fairy too?"

That did it. He got up very nimbly for a man that size, leaned his perfume close to me, gold trinkets a-dangle, and said, "Outside, McGoo. Now!" And he left.

"I shouldn't have even noticed he was here," she said dolefully.

"It's okay," I said.

"You're not going out there!"

"Why not?"

"Because it's childish, and because he's really mad enough to really kill you. I've never seen Nicky so worked up."

"Do you know if he was ever a fighter?"

"I don't think so. He's never said anything. He was Mr. Lawless's superintendent, building those houses on that ranchland south of Baygate Plaza Mall. Please don't go out there, McGee."

"It's been too long since I've been childish, I guess. Want to come watch?"

She responded with a certain unwholesome anticipatory delight that she tried to conceal. Stripped down to essentials, it was a primitive situation. The two bull males and the nervous skittery female. He was in the parking area near the entrance to the lounge, standing near a blue Chevy pickup. It was a balmy night. He had shed his expensive guayabera, exposing an impressive mat of black hair. I told Billy Jean Bailey to stay where she was, under the palm trees, and I went on out to him, and he tried to finish it with one big looping right-hand lead. I got my left arm and shoulder up in time and moved a little bit inside it, but the inside of his wrist and forearm thumped the side of my head over the ear, enough so I knew he could hit. A lot of big men can't hit. A punch has to have snap in it, terminal whipping velocity; otherwise it is a big slow push.

I wanted him to be in a big hurry to finish it. I got my shoulders high and my arms high, and tucked my chin into my chest, bobbing under some of the roundhouse rights and lefts, taking others on my shoulders, elbows, forearms, moving in the direction of the punches to soften them as much I could. But they still hurt, laming my arms a little. He gave whistling grunts of effort with each swing. Canvas shoes squeaked and flapped on the asphalt. I wondered how the thumping and the thudding of the blows sounded to B. J. Bailey. When he began to tire, I encouraged him by backing away toward a pale car nearby. I encouraged him further by turning to my left and bending over so my back was toward him, my fists covering my ears, risking the chance he might know enough to take a really punishing shot at my right kidney.

"Had enough?" he gasped. "Had enough, you son of a bitch?"

It was not much of a risk—I had guessed from his style what he would probably do. He would put his left hand on my right shoulder, spin me around to face him, and pop me with that big right hand.

I felt the grasp of the left hand, resisted it for a moment, then spun with it, feet and heels braced just right, using all the momentum of the turn to drive my very best left hand deep into the sweaty meat just below the V of the floating ribs. I covered my jaw with my right arm as I swung, chin tucked into my elbow. To make a blow truly effective, you have to hit through the target. I tried to hit so far through it I would feel the knuckles of his spine against the knuckles of my left hand.

It burst the air out of him, drove him back, and dropped him. His right hand had hit me just over the left eye, lightly, as my punch landed. I felt the warmth run into my eye and down my cheek. Nicky rolled, groaning, onto his hands and knees and fell onto his side, hugging his middle. B.J. came running to me, gasped, and cried, "You're all bleeding!" Nicky rolled to his pickup and managed to climb up the side of it, hand over hand, until he was on his feet and could lean against it. I took the wad of tissue B.J. handed me, wiped my eye with one, and pressed the rest against my eyebrow. I walked over to the pickup.

Nicky had his right forearm pressed across his middle. "I think you bust something inside," he said huskily.

"What's my name?" I asked him. The ritual of the schoolyard, the necessary childishness.

"McGee," he said, with no hesitation and no resistance. "I can't hardly breathe at all."

I opened the truck door, turned him, helped him hoist himself up to sit behind the wheel. He dug into his pocket slowly and found the keys, sighed, sorted the right one out and sighed again, and put it into the switch.

"I'm hurt real bad," he said.

"Go home and get some rest," I told him. He started the truck, turned on the lights, and drove away.

"Do you have to call a doctor or anything?" she asked.

"I don't know."

"Jack isn't going to like it at all."

"Who's Jack?"

"The manager here. He doesn't like for there to be any kind of trouble."

"I don't think it's much. I think we could pull it together with some adhesive."

She had some in her cabaña beyond the pool. We kept to the shadows. She babbled nervously in a semiwhisper. I gathered that Jack wouldn't care for this sort of thing, either. She said these cabañas had been designed to look out toward the beach, but then they had to put up the tennis courts and the locker rooms, and so her windows looked at the back of the locker rooms and you couldn't see much of anything at all, but then again it went with the territory, and beggars couldn't be choosers, and there you are.

She unlocked the door and let us in, and pulled the heavy draperies across the windows before turning on the lights. She was, as she had explained, clean but not neat. Her three-quarter bed had not been made back into a couch. There was a bright spill of lady-clothes on the available furniture, sliding stacks of *Billboard* and *Variety* and sheet music. She had a little Sony music center and a tumbled cupboard of records and tapes. She had show-biz glossies of a lot of people I'd never seen before Scotch-taped to the walls.

She broke out some ice, and I wrapped some in a hand towel and got the bleeding slowed to where I could get a good look at the gash. It was an inch and a half long, quite shallow, close to the eyebrow, and slanting toward my left ear. The impact had evidently broken a little bleeder close to the surface. I had her cut a dozen very narrow strips of adhesive tape with her nail scissors. I sat on the closed lid of the toilet and held a hand mirror so I could instruct her in just how to pull the wound shut, lacing it with the narrow strips of tape in a series of X's. Then we placed a small gauze compress against it and taped that in place.

She said she knew how to get the dark dapplings of blood off the chest and shoulder of my pale blue shirt, and she took it into the tiny kitchen alcove and set it to soaking in something.

She told me she had thought he was giving me a terrible beating and it had made her start to cry. She told me it had been a funny time for her lately, kind of bored and listless and lonesome, like waiting for something to happen. She said if I was to happen to her, it would be okay, no matter what she said earlier. She said she knew what

45

she was doing. She wasn't any kid. In the right light she could pass for twenty-five because she'd had a real good Mexican lift, "but don't ask how old I really am because I always lie." She hung on me, and I took her to bed, but after a while she got up and put a yellow towel on a small lamp on the other side of the room and turned the other lights out and said she always slept with a night light on. She said she had some really good grass, and did I want to share a joint? I said I didn't, thanks, and she said she had some coke too, not very good because it was cut too far down, and maybe I'd like some. I said no thanks, and she said it really didn't mean anything to her one way or the other, except she didn't believe in the hard stuff, ever, but would I mind if she had just a little grass?—because then she could be sure of getting it off. I said I didn't mind, so she got a saved butt out of a little box in the nightstand drawer, good for five deep drags, well spaced, then pressed it out and came back down to me with that sad, sweet, oriental tang on her breath.

CHAPTER

4

I awoke a little after four in the morning. I could look across her to her improvised night light. It made yellow highlights on the sprawl of her small lean naked back and small mound of buttocks. She had her face pressed against my ribs, and I felt the long, slow heat of each exhalation from the depths of her sleep. She had one leg linked over mine, her right arm across my middle. A frizzle of that kinked platinum hair tickled me just under the armpit with each breath I took. The night bugs made small whirring sounds, and a wind made a sudden rain-sound in the palm fronds.

I sighed in a kind of habitual dismay at my own involvements. This one had a locker-room drabness about it. Hey, guys, the first night I stayed there, I screwed the piano player.

How was it, fella?

Well, to tell the truth, not bad. A lot of little extra frills and trills and improvisations, just like her piano playing, but not much real intensity, you know.

The why and when of the inadvertent affair is never

simply explained. I remembered a few years ago, Meyer pressing a book upon me by one L. Rust Hills, entitled *How to Be Good*. Mr. Hills was explaining to his peer group how one might retain a modicum of goodness in a sadly corrupt world. One chapter in particular seemed appropriate to the situation in which I now found myself. He described the awkward union which he terms "the charity fuck." This is when a person finds himself in a situation where he suddenly realizes that the other party is ready, willing, and eager to make love, and because the place is available and private, and the time is available, and both parties are reasonably healthy, the only possible reason for saying no thanks is because you find the other party physically unappealing. Any excuse at that time— not in the mood, have this little headache, and so on and so on—will be so feeble as to lead the spurned party to the inevitable conclusion that she is indeed sexually unappetizing. This is such an unthinkable blow to give to another person's ego and self-esteem, it is far more charitable to gird the old loins and hop to it.

So here she was in the sweet depths of her postcoital slumber, reassured once more of her sexuality and desirability. As I was wedged back against the wall, there was no hope of stealthy departure. I took hold of her shoulder and gave her a little shake.

"Whassawharra?" she said into my ribs.

"Got to leave, B.J."

She groaned and hoisted herself up onto her elbows and lifted a bleared face to stare at me. "Whachawannago?"

"Daylight soon. Don't want old Jack watching me creep out of here, do you?"

"Shidno, swee."

I clambered over her and got into my clothes.

"Shirdsonahanganashar."

"What? What?"

"When I got up before, I hung your shirt on a hanger in the shower, but it probally isn't dry."

"Oh."

It wasn't. Not quite. I pulled a sheet up to cover her. I kissed her lazy mouth and patted her rump, and she told me to make sure the door locked behind me. It did. I felt a dampness in the cool touch of the predawn air. My brow felt fine, but my arms were leaden and dulled by the deep ache of the bruises from Nicky Noyes's big fists. Hell of a night, all told. Too much travel, too much to drink, a stupid brawl, and finally some romping with a small wiry tanned lady who was lonely enough to be potential trouble. By diligent effort I seemed to be prolonging my adolescence to total absurdity.

On impulse I turned away from the walk and found my way by starlight down to the beach, and out of my east-coast habit looked for that touch of light along the horizon which would warn of the new day. Then I realized it would come up behind me, over the land. I walked to a chaise and stretched out on the damp canvas.

Between love and sleep, she had given drowsy answers to my elaborately casual questions.

—What did Nicky mean about a girl leaving town the next day?

—Huh? Oh, her. She left town the next day.

—Who?

—Who what?

—Who left town the next day?

—Well, they said she and Hub Lawless had something going. Then there were other people said there was always talk about a woman like that, like Kristin Petersen, whoever she was working for, and they said Hub and Julie Lawless had too good a marriage. Then her leaving town the very next day while the Coast Guard and everybody was hunting Hub's body . . .

Her voice had faded down into a muttering and then

into slow, heavy breathing. A little bit more for Meyer's notebook. One Kristin Petersen, who had worked for Hubbard Lawless in some capacity as yet unknown and who was a natural target for gossip. A veritable battalion of women were thronging the Timber Bay scene: B. J. Bailey, Felicia Ambar, Michele Burns, Julia Lawless, and now Kristin, who had departed.

There was beginning to be such a subtle additive of light that I could make out the ghostly shape of a marker off to my left, where North Pass entered Timber Bay, and beyond it some shadowy tree shapes on the outcroppings that sheltered the bay. The Gulf was quiet, with a gentle lap and slap of small waves on the packed wet sand. I heard a deep-throated diesel chugging through the wet noises of the sea and soon saw the outline of a shrimper heading out. There was a pale yellow rectangle in the amidships area, with a man standing against the glow, and I saw him lift his arm and realized that he was lifting a cup of coffee to his lips. It was so vivid I could smell the coffee.

And I had a sudden wrenching urge to shed my own identity and be somebody else. Somehow I had managed to lock myself into this unlikely and unsatisfying self, this Travis McGee, shabby knight errant, fighting for small, lost, unimportant causes, deluding himself with the belief that he is in some sense freer than your average fellow, and that it is a very good thing to have escaped the customary trap of regular hours, regular pay, home and kiddies, Christmas bonus, backyard bar-B-cue, hospitalization, and family burial plot.

All we have, I thought, is a trap of a slightly different size and shape. Just as the idea of an ancient hippie is gross and ludicrous, so is the idea of an elderly beach bum. I dreaded the shape of the gray years ahead and wished to hop out of myself, maybe into the skin of the coffee drinker now far out of sight in the just-brightening

morning. And he, the poor deluded bastard, would probably have changed places willingly.

I stood up and stretched my sore arms again and decided, What the hell, when in doubt turn to the obliga-
tions of the moment. Van Harder was a tough, humorless,
competent seaman, and I had given him my word, and he
deserved my best effort. If I questioned my own value,
then he was likely to get less than his money's worth. He
was the innocent bystander who'd been run down by
somebody else's fun machine, and all I had to do was re-
pair his reputation somehow. And stop moaning about
myself.

I went up to our second-floor suite, showered, changed,
and looked out at the early slant of sunshine, and at two
young men in warm-up suits volleying on the farthest tennis court, one strung so much tighter than the other that
the sounds were in different keys—*pink—punk—pink—
punk*. A shirt-sleeved, necktied man, thick around the
middle, came hurrying out. The boys looked up at the
windows of the hotel and shrugged and moved slowly and
disconsolately off the court, picking up the yellow balls
and putting them back in the cans. I guessed that the
necktie was Manager Jack, doing his managing. Beyond
the courts I could see the roof of the row of cabañas and
estimated the exact place where B.J. lay deep in sleep in
the yellow glow, surrounded by all the silent music, still
and dead in the grooves of the records, frozen into the
emulsion on the tapes, locked into the calligraphy of her
sheet music and the stilled cleverness of her piano hands.

"You up?" Meyer said, astonished. He had come out of
his bedroom into our shared sitting room. He plodded to
the corridor door, looked out to see if there was a morning paper there, and gave a grunt of annoyance on finding
that service not provided. He wore a robe in awning
stripes of pink, yellow, and black, and he looked and

acted like a cross performing bear which had escaped a small circus.

"You want some morning news?" I asked. When he stopped and glowered at me I said, "Mystery woman Kristin Petersen, employed by Hubbard Lawless, disappears the day after alleged drowning. Nicholas Noyes, onetime superintendent of Hula Construction, states that Lawless sold equipment for cash before disappearing. And cleaned out bank accounts. One of the two young ladies aboard the *Julie* the night of the accident was one Michele Burns, known as Mishy, who is a waitress at the Cove and is reputed to be a part-time hooker. The other, Felicia Ambar, known as 'Licia, works at Top Forty Music in the Baygate Plaza Mall."

The glower was unchanged. "So?" he said.

"Don't you want to write it down?"

"What happened to your face?"

"Nicky Noyes took an instant dislike to it."

Meyer nodded. "I can see his point." He went into the bath, and soon I heard the shower. Meyer is not a morning person. Neither am I. But he is one of the non-morning persons who set the standards for all the rest of us.

After his breakfast and after the morning paper, Meyer was ready for communication.

"Officially," I said, "I ran into that jungle-gym thing in the dark."

"Why?"

"Both combatants were last seen with one Billy Jean Bailey, who is the piano player here and has been for three years, and Jack the Manager does not like to have piano ladies causing fusses between bar patrons. Or guests of the house."

"Who fixed it?"

"Miss Bailey."

His nod was approving. "Neatly done."

"I've been wondering about the best way to use that great letter of yours."

He found the right page in his notebook. "The top man at the Coast National Bank and Trust is Devlin J. Boggs. And it is not a chain bank, a situation that gets more rare every day."

"Should I go along with you?"

He studied me, head tilted, and finally nodded. "I think so. We're going to be linked anyway. You'd better be working for me."

"As what?"

"Maybe . . . as knowledgeable in the area of groves and construction and marine holdings. And ranchland."

"I can handle that. I'll carry a pack of Marlboros and grunt a lot and look open-air sincere."

The Coast National Bank and Trust Company occupied most of the ground floor of a ten-story office building at the corner of Bay and Main. All the window glass had an orange-yellow tint, making a golden glow inside. The executive offices were glass cubicles along the left wall as you went in the main entrance on Bay. There were lines at the tellers, and people crisscrossing the broad expanse of carpeted floor. Friday is a busy banking day.

Boggs was talking to two men seated across his desk from him. Meyer gave the secretary his plainest and most impressive card after writing on the back of it, "Representing Emmett Allbritton." She started to put the card down, read what he had written, looked at us again, got up and tapped on the door and took the card in and placed it by Boggs's elbow, and came back out.

Within moments he was ushering the two men out. He came out with them and took us in and got us properly seated before he went around and sat in his judge's chair. Devlin Boggs was about fifty, a tall and very erect fellow with a long and lugubrious face, an iron-gray military haircut, a lantern jaw, and a dark and elegant suit.

After introductions, Meyer handed him the letter. Boggs read it and said, "I had the pleasure of meeting Mr. Allbritton about, I think, fifteen years ago. He spoke to the Association in Houston about future problems in energy supply. Prophetic indeed. It is quite . . . heartening to know that they have long-range plans for this area." He looked inquiringly at Meyer.

Meyer said, "I wouldn't, of course, be at liberty to discuss the little I know of those plans at this time."

"Of course. What sort of"—he looked at the letter again—"holdings large and small would he be interested in?"

"Anything available."

"Raw land, developed land, actual business operations?"

"He would expect me to make recommendations."

"But I assume you are coming to me because of the possible availability of some of Hubbard Lawless's holdings. We have all been terribly shocked by what has happened. We had great confidence in Hub's energy and judgment. He was one of our directors, you know. Things were slow this year. Everybody complained, Hub included. He had borrowed up to the statutory maximum percentage from the bank. Three million dollars. These loans were to four corporations he controlled, and also to himself as an individual. The loans were secured by the assets of the corporations. After . . . it happened, we were able to inventory, or try to inventory, the assets. The books were in . . . very untidy condition. It would seem that for many weeks he had been systematically selling off the assets of his companies for cash, out of town." He took out a snowy handkerchief and wiped his lips. "He had been ignoring his accounts payable, making a special effort on collections. During the week before he disappeared, he drained every single one of his corporate accounts down to minimum balance. He even took out the compensating balance against his personal loans, which he had agreed to leave untouched. Understand that the company accounts included tax reserves, FICA monies, retirement debits, money due for his upcoming payroll. He was down to about forty people from the hundred and twenty he employed at this same time last year."

"How much did he get away with?" I asked.

"There are too many ways to compute it, Mr. McGee, for me to make a valid estimate. My horseback guess would be between six and seven hundred thousand dollars. I would say that those assets remaining behind which can be converted into cash would result in a recovery of maybe one and a quarter million dollars, and most of that value would be in the appraised value of the ranch and grove lands."

"So the bank stands to take a bath of one and three quarters million dollars," Meyer said.

Boggs wiped his mouth again and said dolefully, "If it were only that simple. There are a lot of other claims and liens against those assets. We may have the senior debt instruments, but we might have to prove it in court. It is such a terrible tangle that it might drag on for years. Legal fees and court costs will eat up a great deal of the remaining equity. In the meanwhile, such a huge write-off against our loan-loss reserves might mean that we would have to . . . give favorable consideration to an acquisition offer we have been rejecting. I have always felt that a locally owned, locally managed bank is far more responsive to the needs of any community, and . . . excuse me. Our banking problems are of no interest to you."

Meyer gave a sympathetic sigh and said, "And I suppose that the state banking authorities and the examiners from the FDIC are stating that you didn't exercise prudence and good judgment in so setting up the loans to

Mr. Lawless that he was able to market the assets without your knowledge and able to withdraw his compensating balance."

"I see you know banking, sir."

"Everybody is always full of wisdom after the event."

"Hub was in and out of the bank a couple of times every day. He was a director. He was on the Loan Committee of the board. He was a very hardworking man. And very . . . personable. Anyway, I wish we were in a position to be able to offer to sell some of the remaining real-estate assets to Mr. Allbritton's corporation. But, with no legal decision as to whether Mr. Lawless is dead or alive, you can see the terrible legal tangle we are in here."

"Do you believe he is dead?"

Boggs hesitated a long time, choosing the right words. He said, "I did at first. Now I am not so sure. Neither, of course, is the insurance company. Julia Lawless is the owner of that two-million-dollar policy. It was taken out seven or eight years ago, for half a million, and as his affairs kept getting more involved, he kept adding to it. She owns the house free and clear. The land it's on was a gift from her father when they got married. I think she has some sort of very small income from her father's estate. Not enough, I wouldn't think, to run the house. I suppose . . . she is another of the victims of this disaster."

Meyer said, "I don't imagine you would have any objections if I set up a hypothetical situation. Suppose, just for instance, that Mr. Allbritton made a decision, based on our examination of the properties, to make an offer of one million dollars for Tract So-and-So. Could the various claimants be brought together to reach an understanding? Could title be passed somehow?"

For an instant a faint gleam of hope illuminated Devlin Boggs's long sad face, but it faded away. "I wouldn't think so. I don't know. It's a bureaucratic tangle as well as a legal tangle. Some kind of accommodation would have to be reached with the IRS . . . I suppose Harold Payne might be able to give you better answers than I can. He is the bank's attorney, and he handled Hub's affairs as well. Elfording, Payne and Morehouse. They're in this building. Seventh floor."

I awaited Meyer's next move. He was doing very, very well. One door had been wedged open. Duplicity was hard on Meyer. It frayed his nerves and upset his digestion.

"Mr. Boggs," he said, "it is quite evident from what we have heard so far that . . . people asking questions are not exactly welcome in Timber Bay lately. I can always show my letter of authority, but I would rather not do that except when dealing with a man of your position. Perhaps you might be able to give us . . . some sort of notes, possibly on the back of your business cards?"

Once he started, Meyer kept him going. Fifteen minutes later we were out on the broad sidewalk. Meyer leaned against the bank. I leafed through the little packet of cards. Devlin J. Boggs wrote in a very neat small black legible hand.

They were directed to Harold Payne, to Walter Olivera of the *Timber Bay Journal*, to Lou Latzov of Glennmore Realty, to Julia Lawless, and to Hack Ames, the Sheriff of Dixie County; and one read, "To Whom It May Concern."

In his tight little script he said that we had his confidence, and any help they could give us would be deeply and personally appreciated by Devlin J. Boggs.

Meyer was breathing deeply, eyes closed. "How was I?"

"You'll never be better. We start now from the top. A new sensation for Meyer and McGee. Tools of the power structure. Servants of the establishment."

He smiled modestly. "No, I was never better."

So we walked to where I'd parked, got into the car, and split up the cards. He took the lawyer and the real-estate broker. I took the Sheriff and the newspaperman. His were downtown, so I took the car.

CHAPTER

5

Haggermann "Hack" Ames maintained his headquarters in the East Wing of the County Court House. Once it had been determined I was not an emergency, I was told to sit and wait in a cramped and dingy little room. The tattered magazines on the table were all hunting, fishing, and firearms oriented, looking as if some very sweaty-handed people had tried to escape into them.

Florida elects its sheriffs on a party basis, a shockingly bad system. Elections come around too often. Unqualified men can slip in. People with political clout are seldom harassed by the Sheriff. Good politicians do lots of favors. Every time when, by a change in state law or by local option, they try to set the office up on an appointive basis with specific qualifications, thousands of loud right-wing nuts rise up out of the shrubbery and start screaming about being deprived of their democratic rights and their voting franchise. Law enforcement has become so complex, technical, and demanding, so dependent on the expert use of expert equipment, one might as well say it would make as much sense to elect brain surgeons from the public at large as sheriffs.

A surprising number of them are very good in spite of having to be political animals in order to survive. An unsurprising number of them are ninety-nine-point-nine percent worthless. Having heard from Van Harder of the attempt to kick him awake, I expected the second kind.

But as time passed, I began to revise my judgment. The people who hurried by the waiting-room door were slender and young and in smart uniforms, male and female. No fat-guts, pearl-handled, hat-tilted-over-the-eyes, good-old-boy deputies. I could almost make out the words of the woman handling communications, calling the codes for various types of alarms.

Finally I was sent in to the Sheriff's small office.

"Just a minute," he said. "Sit."

It was a tiny office with a steel desk, steel chairs, dark gray carpeting, off-white walls, and no window at all. A big steel floor lamp hurled so many watts against the white ceiling, it was bright enough in there to make a television series. Me and Hack. He was signing what appeared to be requisition forms. He was a medium man with dusty brown hair and an unhealthy pallor. He was carefully reviewing the list of items on each requisition.

When he had finished he pushed a button on the base of his fancy telephone, and a uniformed woman came briskly in and took the requisitions away.

"Between the damned state auditors and the goddamn nitpicking Washington desk jockeys, a man can spend his life doing the paperwork," he said. He stared at me carefully for the first time. His eyes were brown, and they looked as dry and dusty as his hair. "Didn't you get picked up here in Dixie County five–six years back?"

"No, Sheriff."

"I could have swore. Do me a favor. Stand up."

What can you do? I stood up. He came around his

desk and stood in front of me and looked up at my face. He backed off and bent and took a good look at my shoes.

He sat down again and said, "No lifts. The one I mean, the one that looked like you, he was about six foot even. Once a man gets his height, he don't grow any more than that. Sure looks like you in the face. What's your name again? McGee. From Lauderdale? What's that you got there?"

I reached across the desk and handed him Boggs's card. He read it, looked at me, read it again, and put it down in neat alignment with the corner of his desk. He reached his hand across to me and we shook hands.

"Nice to know you, Mr. McGee. Now just what is it that I can help you on? You just tell me and we'll give it a try." It was as if I had suddenly turned into a Dixie County voter.

"What's the current status of the investigation of the Hubbard Lawless disappearance?"

"My investigation isn't the only one in town."

"I didn't think it would be."

He shifted around in his chair. If he'd had a window, he'd have gotten up and stared out of it. "Our investigation so far tends to show that Hub Lawless is still alive."

"Where is he?"

He picked up Devlin Boggs's card again and asked me if I would mind stepping out of the office and closing the door. He said it wouldn't be more than a couple of minutes, and it wasn't. He called me back in and I sat down.

"You've got to keep this quiet, Mr. McGee."

"I intend to."

"I gave one of my deputies, a man name of Wright Fletcher, that speaks pretty good Mexican, leave of absence to go on down to Mexico with an investigator from the insurance company has the big policy on Hub's life.

Both those men thinks there's a pretty good chance of getting a line on him, and if they can locate him, there's enough federal heat involved, we should be able to get him extradited."

"So how did he get from the Gulf of Mexico to Mexico?"

"You know how he turned everything he could into cash, picked everything clean; that gave us the lead on premeditation."

"But wasn't there a hearing and a verdict that he was missing and presumed dead?"

"That was when the whole thing had just happened. Everybody liked Hub. What it looked like, he was just getting a bunch of cash together to put it into something good where he could turn it over fast and come out ahead. He'd done that kind of thing before. And nearly everybody knew he couldn't swim a stroke. It's like that with a lot of Florida native born. Me, I've lived all my life close enough to the Gulf to near spit in it, and I can't swim no more than Hub could. And the Gulf water is right cold in March. Once we get a line on Hub, we can open the whole thing up again. That insurance company sure-God doesn't want to presume him dead. And Julie Lawless wants to take them to court to get the money."

"What do you have to go on?"

"First there is kind of negative reasoning. We can show how he was turning stuff into cash. Hundred-dollar bills is all you can get hold of nowadays without attracting attention. You know how much space and weight is involved in six hundred thousand dollars? That is six thousand pieces of paper. It will weight right around twenty pounds. If it was all mint, which it wasn't, it would make a package six inches by seven and a half inches, and ten inches high. We've not found it or any part of it. And we have looked. We've looked good.

"The next part is negative reasoning too. When they

got around to inventorying the stuff on the books of those four corporations of his, there was a jeep missing he used a lot. An old yellow jeep with dune-buggy tires that he could run cross-country at the ranch and the grove. It has never turned up. His other two cars were here, but the jeep is gone."

"Do you have any positive reasoning, Sheriff?"

He looked at me, and in those dusty brown eyes I could read a very serious message. Though he looked like a mild man, I would not want to irritate him and not have a little card from Boggs to keep him in check. He exhaled and let his white knuckles relax.

"We got a lot of calls. After the whole thing went on the wire services, we got calls he was seen in Tacoma and on Maui and in Scranton, P-A. People called up and said that if there was a reward they'd tell us where to come pick him up. Key West, Detroit, Montreal. Everybody knew right where Hub Lawless was hiding. When a man has money and you can't find the body, these calls always come in."

"But that is—"

"Wait until I finish. We don't have the budget to check out all that nonsense. But we check out what looks possible. Just ten days ago in the Tuesday mail we got a letter from Orlando. There was a slide in it, in a cardboard mount. There was a typed note in with the slide. I've got a copy here of what the note said, and a print made from the slide."

He read me the note. " 'The man in this picture I took looks like the man in the newspaper pictures. I took this picture on Friday April eighth in Guadalajara. I can't give you my name or address because my boyfriend thinks I was in San Diego visiting my sister.' "

The print was a four-by-five, sharp and clear. It showed a sidewalk café, a sunny street, traffic, buses, buildings in the distance, nearby shops with signs in Spanish. There were several tables occupied. A man sat alone at one of them, off to the left. He was almost facing the camera. He was carefully pouring what was evidently beer into his glass.

Hack Ames came around the desk, leaned over my shoulder, and tapped that beer-pouring fellow with his finger. "Hub. No doubt of it. We projected that slide as big as we could with the best projector we could locate. Hell, it even shows the detail of his ring, the little scar at the corner of his mouth. The experts say it was taken on Ektachrome X with a good-quality lens that was a medium-wide angle, like maybe thirty-five millimeters. It was developed at one of the Kodak regional labs, and the date stamp in the cardboard of the mount says April. You can see that she wasn't trying to take a picture of Hub. I think she didn't even know what she had until she got the slides and used a viewer or a projector."

Hubbard Lawless was wearing an open khaki jacket with short sleeves over a yellow T-shirt. He had a blunt cheerful face, snub nose, bland brow, thinning blond hair combed and sprayed to hide the paucity of it. His hands were big, his forearms thick and muscular. He wore a small frown of concentration as he poured his beer.

"So it places him in Guadalajara a month and a half ago. That's where your deputy and the insurance investigator went?"

"With copies of this picture. Wright Fletcher is a very hard worker. He'll show that picture to ten thousand people if he has to. But they're going to concentrate on the clinics."

"Clinics?"

"That's the world center for cosmetic surgery. Lifts, nose jobs, hair plants. There are dozens of very qualified surgeons working down there."

"Makes sense."

"If he's been and gone, there'll be before-and-after pictures in the files. That and this picture and the date of the operation would prove he didn't drown when he allegedly fell off the *Julie*."

"What about Kristin Petersen?"

"You mean is she with Hub? It looks that way. Funny thing. A man gets to be forty and he gets itchy, and it's usually a woman sets him off, trying for a different kind of life. It happens every day. But most men, when they go off the deep end, they don't influence the lives of so many other people. They don't raise such hell with a community. This has upset a lot of applecarts."

"We're staying at the North Bay Resort. Maybe you could let me know if your deputy finds out anything."

"I don't exactly see where you fit into this."

"We fit where Mr. Boggs said we fit."

"Sure," said the Sheriff. "Great."

"Can I keep the picture?"

"If you want it. We had a lot made."

"Are the city police in on this in any way?"

"There aren't any. There was a referendum and the county took over law enforcement for everything inside the county. They get more service for less money this way. We absorbed their staff and equipment and gave up their office space two years ago."

"Where is the *Julie*, Sheriff?"

"Over to Cedar Pass Marina. The fellow that was mate, DeeGee Walloway, he's living aboard and keeping an eye on it."

"Can I tell him it's okay with you if I take a look at it?"

"Now why would you want to do that?"

"It can't hurt anything, can it?"

"I guess not. But there's been enough people trying to be some kind of Shylock Holmes around here."

"Was Harder really drunk?"

"He looked drunk, smelled drunk, talked drunk,

walked drunk, and all-around acted drunk. So, like it said in the paper, I didn't get him tested for drunk. So I can't swear he was passed-out drunk. Besides, he'd done a lot of jail time for D and D."

"Before he was born again."

"Those born-again ones fall off too, McGee. And hate to admit it. One drink, Van said. Like the ones we pick up wavering all over the road. Two little beers, they say. John Tuckerman and those girls swore Hub took Van up just that one drink. But he could have had a pint bottle in his coat, sucked it dry, and heaved it over the side. He comes from here, you know. And a lot of people remember the hell he raised when he was young. He finally left here and moved on down to Everglades City, did some guiding and gator poaching, got in trouble down there, found Jesus, moved to Lauderdale, and finally wound up back here again. The ones that swear off, most of them they go back onto it sooner or later, get pig drunk and locked up."

"Something special you've got against drunks, Sheriff?"

"Married to one for a long time. Too long. She finally drove into a tree one night."

"Nice of you to give me so much time, Sheriff."

"What happened there, over your eye?"

"I cut across the grounds last night, heading toward the beach, and ran into some of that playground stuff in the dark. Nothing important. Appreciate your help."

When I stood up, he tilted his chair back and looked up at me. "There have been some people coming into Timber Bay, nosing around here and there, thinking to come up with the kind of leverage that might would get them a piece of the money Hub is supposed to taken."

"I can well imagine."

"It would hurt me to find out that you people had conned Devlin Boggs and you're after the same thing as those other sharpshooters."

"You mean they think the money is here?" I asked, trying to look as though I were stupid enough to ask such a question.

With patient exasperation he said, "They hope to get a line *here* on where he went *from* here. And then they hope to go to wherever they think he is and take the money away from him."

"Oh."

"Hub Lawless could be a real surprise to anybody who found him and had ideas."

"How do you mean?"

"One time some red-hots up from Tampa tried to take the payroll money at Hula Marina—that was before he sold out to Associated Foods. There were three of them and Hub shot one in the stomach, threw one of them into a wall, and broke the wrist on the third. He moves fast. I've hunted with him. He's got real good reflexes, and he stays in shape. Jogging and so on. Weights."

I thanked him again and left. This was one complicated man, this Sheriff Ames. He had a mild look. But those dusty brown eyes kept asking more questions than were spoken. He made me wonder if I had actually come to Timber Bay to get a line on all that money. He made me feel guilty for things I'd never done. He made me conscious of that capacity for blackhearted evil which every one of us shares with everyone else—and never speaks about.

CHAPTER

6

I was the first to arrive at the Captain's Galley for lunch, having set up the date by phone with Walter Olivera, phoned Dave Bellamy for the reservation, and left word at the desk at the North Bay Resort for Meyer to join us. I had a one-drink wait at the bar, and then Bellamy brought Walter Olivera over.

At first glance I thought he was a high-school kid. Tall, skinny, with long dank blond hair, a goatee, embroidered jeans, two strands of heishi, and little Ben Franklin glasses. But each time I got a better look at him, I added five years, and I finally guessed him at thirty.

Meyer arrived right after him, and Bellamy gave us the same booth as on our first visit. Olivera sat on the inside, and I sat across from them. The place was full of locals from the marts of trade—secretaries, brokers, salesmen, and city-hall types, along with lawyers, dentists, and contractors. It made a cheerful midday din of voices, ice, silverware, and laughter.

Olivera said, "Sure, my by-line was on almost all the Hub Lawless stories, and on almost everything else too.

What it is, we don't have the horses to put out the *Bay Journal* seven mornings a week, and we don't have the budget. It is an ABC figure of fifteen thousand, and we were picked up two years ago by Southern Communications, Incorporated, which has maybe twenty smallish papers and a dozen FM rock radio stations. They sit up there in Atlanta with their computer printouts, looking at the gross and the net, and they write ugly letters to Harry Dister—he runs the paper and has ulcers on his ulcers—asking how come he paid fourteen cents more a ream for copy paper this year than last year. They don't give a shit what our editorial position is or our politics. They make us buy the cheapest syndicated crud on the market, and they make poor Harry hustle his ass off for advertising linage." He picked up his glass of white wine. "No point in telling you *all* my problems, gentlemen. Yes, I covered the Lawless mess, and I didn't do any digging because I can't spend or spare the time."

Meyer said, "I hope you understand our position, Mr. Olivera. If Lawless is alive and well, we have to go after the available property in one way, and if he is indeed drowned, then we go after it another way."

"I can see that, sure."

"So I guess what we are looking for—with Devlin Boggs's help—is an educated guess on what to expect," I said.

Walter Olivera took his time. "I see it this way," he said finally. "Mr. Lawless was a proud man. He was born right here in Timber Bay. When he was in his second year at the University of Florida at Gainesville, his mother, father, and older brother were killed in a light-plane accident. His brother had rented the plane. Hit power lines trying to set it down in a field when the motor quit. After everything was settled, there was just enough left to see Hub through school. He took business courses. He came back here and married Julia Herron. Her father was D.

Jake Herron, who was a state legislator from this area for thirty years, right up to when he died.

"Hub borrowed some money from his father-in-law to get started in the construction and land-development business, and paid it all back with interest. He worked hard. He worked all hours. Every time he got a little bit ahead, he'd branch out. He started Hula Marine Enterprises, Double L Ranches, and Lawless Groves and nursed them through the early years and turned them into profitable businesses. It was a process of constant expansion. I think he was a millionaire, on paper at least, by the time he was thirty-five. He *liked* making things work out. But luck always enters in. He had no way of knowing everything would start to go sour at about the same time."

"Everything?" Meyer asked.

"Just about. He took the money he got from selling Hula Marine to Associated Foods, and he put it into two big tracts of land, one about two miles east of the city line on State Road Three fifty-nine, and the other way out beyond the south end of Bay, down on a little road that winds on down toward Pepperfish Key. Good waterfront land, and a lot of it. The land on Three fifty-nine was to be a shopping center, a big one. You can drive out and take a look at it. He got the land prepared, roads paved, foundations set. The waterfront land was going to be a big condominium development. Six high-rise buildings, fifteen hundred units. He'd borrowed right up to the hilt, and he was counting on the cash flow he could generate from his other interests to keep the new ventures going."

Meyer nodded and said, "Hard freeze?"

"You bet it was. A little freeze is okay. It even helps make the crop juicier. They say Hub was up all night long, roaring around in that yellow jeep. They burned smudge pots and tires and ran big fans off generators. They tried everything. But when there is absolutely no wind and the temperature stays below eighteen degrees for almost five hours, there isn't anything anybody can do. It froze and split some of his older trees. He didn't even end up with cattle feed. And you know what has happened to the price of beef and beef cattle in Florida. They say he could have squeaked through, by getting the shopping center up as fast as he could. The center was going to be anchored by a big store, one of the big chains. He had a good lease, all signed. And a lot of little people were beginning to flock around on account of the traffic that would be generated by the chain store. And all of a sudden they went the way of Grant's. Bankrupt. Finished. And his lease was worthless. He wanted to make the condominium project first priority, but all of a sudden the state came into the act and said that the project was going to damage valuable wetlands. They wanted a setback from the beach that would have made it impossible for him to put the buildings up in the area left, and they asked for an environmental-impact study, which would have delayed it at least eighteen months even if the answer had been favorable to him.

"He was a very up-front guy. He admitted everything wasn't going too great. But he smiled a lot and he was confident, and everybody figured Hub Lawless would work his way out of it the same as other times when he had been caught in a narrow place. I heard rumors he was sleeping on a cot out at his ranch office, and that his marriage had gone bad and he had something going with a woman named Petersen. She was an architect, and she was supposed to be helping with the designs of the shopping center and condominium project. If he had something going, then maybe he wasn't thinking too clearly. As I said, he was proud. If he hung around, he was certainly going to go steadily and inevitably down the tube. He was going to have to see those corporations go into bankruptcy, and he was going to have to go into personal bankruptcy, resign from the board of the bank, resign from a lot of civic activities and church things. It was certainly going to spoil his image with his daughters, Tracy and Lynn. Sixteen and fourteen are tough years to suddenly go broke. So he decided to milk every dime he could out of every account, every source of funds, fake his own death, and go on the run, realizing that nobody could step in and grab the proceeds of the big insurance coverage on his life away from Julia Lawless. I want the lentil soup, please, a big bowl, and an order of the whole wheat toast, no butter."

After we had all ordered, Olivera made his little summary. "He had no really good choices. He had no way of knowing that it would look so suspicious that the insurance company would refuse to pay the claim. He did so many things so well, it's funny he didn't manage his own disappearance better."

"Would you guess he's in Mexico?" I asked.

"That seems to be the current rumor. I wouldn't fault it. He went down there quite a few times. He liked the country. He and John Tuckerman used to go down and hunt a lot. Hub spoke enough bad Spanish to get by. Apparently he started squirreling away cash about the first of the year. It would give him a lot of time, almost three months, to establish a new identity."

"With the lady architect?"

"And lots and lots of pesos," Olivera said cheerfully.

"Apparently Tuckerman was in on the deception," Meyer said.

"Had to be. And I think it was very, very rough on John Tuckerman. He thought Hub Lawless was the finest man who ever walked. Hub had a way of generating a lot of loyalty. If Hub had asked John to set himself on fire, he'd have run after the gasoline and the matches. Unquestioning. Okay, John helped him, and did exactly as he was told. And after it happened, John crawled into the bottle and he's been there ever since."

"What was his position anyway?"

"He was supposed to be a vice-president of each of the four corporations. What he did was make sure the cars were gassed and maintained, and he made reservations and carried luggage and told jokes. He has no family except a sister. Hub Lawless was his family, and the Lawless enterprises were his home."

"What's he doing now?"

"Drinking. He has a beach shack down there on the land Hub bought for the condominium project. The ownership of that land is in limbo. He's a squatter, technically, but I don't think he'll be rousted out of there right soon. If I had to make a guess, I would say that Hub probably gave John enough cash to keep him going."

"*If* you had to make a guess," Meyer said.

Olivera turned and stared at Meyer and then over at me. "Look, you guys. This is a favor, okay? Boggs, the big man, asked me to cooperate."

Meyer looked wounded. "Please don't misunderstand, Walter. Did I sound disapproving? I wasn't. We're here to make guesses. Good newspaper people make guesses based on hunch and experience and then check them out to find the facts, right?"

Olivera relaxed again. "What I'm working on is not exactly the *Washington Post*."

"Does the paper do any crusading?" I asked.

"If it doesn't cost anything."

"Here's one that might not cost much. If we assume Hub Lawless had the whole thing planned ahead, and if we assume John Tuckerman was in on it and helped out, then it follows that Van Harder, running the boat, was given a funny drink. So he lost his license to skipper a boat carrying passengers for hire. So he got labeled a drunk who passed out while the owner fell overboard."

Olivera thought it over, frowning, turning it this way and that. "I suppose we could have an editorial. But to get his case reconsidered, there would have to be some hard facts."

I decided to run a little test. "Hard facts. For example, a reliable eyewitness who'd swear to having seen Lawless in Mexico in April?"

"That might do it," he said. "That would be great, sure."

So either he was a great actor or he didn't know about the photograph. I resisted the temptation to be a nine-cent hero and take the picture out and explain it to him.

"What's all this about Harder anyway?" he asked.

"He's just a sample of all the people who get hurt when somebody pulls something off, when somebody sets up a conspiracy to defraud," I said.

While we ate, quite a few people who passed our booth on their way out spoke to Walter Olivera. He kept grinning and nodding and flapping his hand at them. And it seemed obvious that every one of them was wondering who we were. Small cities have a very compact power structure, and it is always more evident when the tourist season is over.

"It was really a hell of a blow to this town," Olivera said, when his lentil soup was gone. "High hopes. You know. Two big projects. More jobs. The best thing that could happen would be if some organization could come in and pick up right where Hub left off, iron out the bugs, and get those projects moving again. I would think most of the creditors would listen to reason."

"If we knew who to buy the rights from," Meyer said.

"I know. The official result was: Missing, presumed dead by misadventure. Now the general feeling is: Missing, presumed alive. If seven years pass with no trace of him, I think they can declare him dead. And that is too damned long to wait."

74

He had to get back to the paper. He shook hands around, thanked us for the lunch, told us he would be glad to help in any way he could. And he said that everybody he could think of would be glad to help us too.

After he was gone we ordered more coffee. I told Meyer the Haggermann Ames story and gave him a stealthy look at the picture of Hub Lawless in Guadalajara. He was enchanted, but agreed with me that it was the kind of evidence that would not stand up in any court of law. It would have to be backed up by direct examination of the person who had taken the photograph.

He had spent all his time with Harold Payne and said, "One very cool and cautious fellow. Very reluctant to violate any client-attorney relationship, even after I hinted that, if Mr. Allbritton's firm came in here, I would recommend they use his services for local legal matters. That didn't thaw him. He said he had been Mr. Lawless's personal attorney for many years and that he had set up the corporations Mr. Lawless had controlled and had advised him on tax and estate matters. He said he had blocked an attempt by the IRS to proceed with a computation of estate tax and had contested a writ to have his client's personal safety-deposit box opened. He had not filed a copy of the will and would not do so until there was positive proof that Hubbard Lawless was deceased."

"Did he have any opinions about what happened?"

"He didn't express any direct opinion. He said it was entirely possible that, had his client not met with an accident on the night of March twenty-second last, he would have been able to explain his very good reasons for having enhanced his cash position."

" 'Enhanced his cash position'?" I said.

"A direct quote," Meyer said. "Payne is okay. The firm represents the bank, too. It puts him in a curious position, a sort of ex post facto conflict of interest. So he is doing the smart thing, following the letter of the law, keeping his head down, keeping everything in stasis until more information comes to light."

"Are we getting anywhere?" I asked. "Are we doing Van Harder any good? That's what this is all about. Remember?"

"To replace the fledgling in the nest, one must first climb to the top of the tall tree."

"Oh, boy."

"About five or six o'clock back at the Resort—forgive the expression?"

"Have a nice afternoon."

CHAPTER

7

The vast expanses of the parking areas at Baygate Plaza were less than half filled, and I wondered at the wisdom of Hub Lawless's decision to build another big shopping center in Timber Bay.

Once I found my way into the Mall, I located an orientation map, one of those YOU ARE HERE! things, and found where I was in relation to Top 40 Music. I plodded along the tile-finished concrete under the perpetual fluorescence, past all the jewelry stores, shoe stores, cut-rate blue-jeans stores, gift marts, caramel-corn outlets, and health-food hustles. I plodded along in the din of canned music, in the perpetual carnival atmosphere of everyday, past the custom T-shirts, the pregnant ladies eating ice cream cones, and the lines of children on school holiday waiting to get into another revival of *Star Wars*, shrieking and jabbing at one another and pretending to die of serious wounds.

When I came to Top 40 Music, I turned out of the slow parade and went in, feeling as if I were leaning into the blare of somebody electronically amplified, yelling, "Babybabybabybaby . . ."

There was an extraordinarily beautiful young woman in there, in white slacks and a pink top, with flawless figure and flawless complexion. She had one disconcerting flaw, though—she had such a mouthful of big white projecting teeth that she couldn't quite close her lips. She had a smoky drift of dark hair, dark eyes, and a fine way of holding herself, of walking. I could almost read her lips and knew she was asking me if she could do anything for me.

I leaned toward her and yelled into her ear, "Miss Ambar?"

"Yes?"

"Can we go somewhere and talk?"

"What about?"

"Hub Lawless."

"No way!"

I handed her the To Whom It May Concern card signed by Devlin Boggs. She looked at it and shrugged, then handed it back.

"Please?" I shouted.

She looked me over more carefully. I tried to look responsible and respectable. I could almost hear her sigh. She hurried into the back and came out with a small white-haired lady with a smudge of dust on her cheek. Then Miss Ambar walked by me and out into the pedestrian traffic. She turned back and looked at me. "So come on!" her lips said, inaudible in all that *babybabybaby* din.

We sat at a counter fifty yards from the music store. I had coffee and she ordered a tall Red Zinger tea with honey. She had the ghost of an accent. We kept our voices down.

"What she did, what Mishy did, she call me up like I

guess it was two o'clock that day, and she said, Hey, 'Li-cia, you wan we go on a boat tonight down to Clear-water? I said I din wan to do nothing like that at all, I had a date and so on, but she begged and begged and said how it was such a nice boat and all, real fast, real lovely, and where she works, the Cove, she had heard Mister Tuckerman, he was saying they were going down in the boat, and she asked maybe a fren of hers and her could come along, and he said, Hell, why not? So she wouldn't go without me and she said she had a girlfren there in Clearwater, we could stay in her place, and then her girlfren's boyfren, he could drive us back up here next day. Chee, I tole this seven tousand times, I think. Over and over and over."

"Are you originally from Mexico?"

"From Honduras. When I was a little kid. I got no accent now at all. How you can tell?"

"I just guessed."

"Okay, so I got to the Cove about eight thirty all set to go, and pretty soon Mr. Tuckerman, he picks us up, and then he picks up Mr. Lawless from downtown, and we go down to the marine place and get on, and it was beautiful, it really was. I didn't know they were so nice inside. Just like in some kind of high-price trailer, television and hi-fi and everything, and ice and booze. I thought that what it was, it was some kind of pass. You know, like we were going to put out on account of we were so grateful to be on that boat. What Mishy does is her business, but I wasn't going to, no matter what. But it was no problem on account of they acted like maybe we weren't there at all. They were in the other end of that living-room-type place, having a drink, talking in low voices, talking business. After we had been gone from the dock about twenty minutes, maybe less, Mr. Lawless made a drink and took it up and gave it to that Captain Harder. I din know his name then. I found out his name later on. Okay, so they were talking again, Lawless and Tuckerman, and the boat was going up and down, kind of, and I began to feel kind of sick. I said I was feeling sick, and Mr. Tuckerman said I should go up topside and the cold air would make me feel better. I went on up there and it really was cold and the wind was blowing something scary. Then I saw that Captain Harder on the floor up there, like he was dead. I ran back down there screaming and the men went running up, and then Mr. Tuckerman came back down and said they had decided to go back to Timber Bay, which was just fine with me, because by then I was sorry I'd ever said I'd come along for the ride, and Mishy was sorry too because she wasn't feeling real great either. It was more bouncy on the way back, and it seemed to take longer, which I found out later it did, on account of Mr. Lawless was driving it by hand. What Mishy and I were doing, we were running in and out of that funny little bathroom, throwing up, taking turns. Then finally the wind wasn't so strong, but we were bouncing up and down terrible, and there was one awful jolt that threw me right on the floor—I mean deck. Then Mishy thought she heard somebody yelling for us and then I heard it too, and neither of us would go up alone, so we both went. We were inside the pass by then, I think. Mr. Tuckerman yelled to us that Mr. Lawless had fallen overboard and we were to help look. The Captain was still on the deck passed out. It was a real nightmare. You couldn't see nothing. Nobody could run the radio they have on boats like that. So we had to go in. Mr. Tuckerman banged the boat something terrible against the dock and there was some man there who came running to help with the lines, and pretty soon the police and everybody was there, and by then, I can tell you, I didn't give a damn what anybody did with me, I was so glad to have my feet back on ground again. I was so glad I could hardly stand it. I thought it had to be about three in the morning, but you know what? It was only about an hour and a half, just a little more than an hour and a half from the time we'd left. It was a terrible experience, I can tell you. We had to make statements and wait and sign them after they were typed up for us, and later we had to testify at the hearing. I'd never done that before. It isn't as bad as I thought it would be. It was the worst night of my life. I din wan to go in the first place. That damn Mishy. She gets me into bad things. I doan wan to do anything with her again. But you know how it is when somebody keeps calling up. What the hell. She's some crazy person, that Mishy. She likes a lot of stuff happening, and it sure happens aroun her. I tole all this nine tousand times. It's been in the papers, every word of it."

"Weren't you going to get into Clearwater pretty late?"

"Like four in the morning. Something like that. It was a crazy thing to do, but that's how Mishy is."

"Why were Mr. Tuckerman and Mr. Lawless going down there by water? Did you get any clue to that?"

"Some kind of business thing. Nobody really said."

"And the Captain was really out?"

"Man, I thought he was dead!"

"Were they drinking?"

"Little bit. Not much."

I smiled at her. "Somebody said last night over at the North Bay Resort lounge that you're a nice person."

She lighted up. "Hey! Who says that?"

"Nicky Noyes."

She lost the sparkle. "Oh, *that* one. I see him around. I doan go out with him. He used to work for Mr. Lawless, you know? Some kind of good job, he says. I couldn't say. Lunchtime some guy I know was in buying tapes and he said Nicky was in the hospital from being in some kind of fight someplace."

"Does he get in fights a lot?"

"Not often on account of he's so big. But he comes on

evil—bigmout', you know. He was over to North Bay last night. Huh! What happen over your eye anyhow?"

"I ran into something in the dark."

"Something like Nicky?"

Her very dark eyes were merry. So take a chance, McGee. "What if it was?"

"Good for *you!* That sumbitch likes hurting. He busted Mishy's finger once. He walk into a room, she walks out, you bet." She looked at me more carefully. "No more marks? Just one? Maybe you had a stick?"

"Footwork."

"That bank card says help you out. From the president yet. And you go around hitting. That doesn't sound like a bank."

"Did the fellow say how Nicky is?"

"Oh, he is okay. He said they were letting him out. He was just in, you know, for overnight. He goes to Emergency a lot. Nicky is always worried about his bod. If he feels hot, right away he wants to find out his temperature, and he thinks maybe he's dying. He was some kind of big person around here in high school, and then he went to play football in Tallahassee, but he got sent home for some kind of gambling. He had a good job with Mr. Lawless. I doan know what now. For a little bit, he drove beer. Now he seems to be okay for money, but they say he's a dealer, nothing real real heavy, just grass and coke and hash. Mishy is into that sometimes when she feels real down, but not me. Never. It's too scary. I got to know where I am and where I'm coming from."

"Is Mishy a special friend of John Tuckerman?"

"Huh? Oh, you wanna know if it's all that special? Maybe. It wouldn't mean all that much to Michele. I mean he's kinda nice and funny. But she never mentioned it especially."

"Is it okay to tell her I talked to you?"

"Sure. But why bother anyway, with me or her?"

"I'm working for people who want to buy Mr. Lawless's land. So we need to find out if he's dead."

"Chee, we can't help. I'm telling you, there was a hell of a lot of black water out there, all bouncing up and down, and me knocked on the fl—deck. They say he couldn't swim at all. They say he's in Mexico. What that means is he didn't have to swim. Mishy and I talked about that. So if he comes ashore, he's in Timber Bay, where all around the bay it's built up. A wet man walking around? They say the tide was going out strong. What was there? A boat? I doan know, mister. You said your name is what? McGee? I just doan know. I theenk that sumbitch is dead. Hey, I got to get back or Carol'll kill me dead. Sure. Talk to Mishy. But for what?"

The Cove was about two hundred yards south of the North Bay Resort, a rambling frame sun-bleached structure which extended out over the bay, supported by thick pilings. The dining area was the farthest from the shore, beyond a large bar area hung with nets, glass floats, mounted fish, and funny sayings. They were having their midafternoon lull. A salesman was playing pinball, hammering the corners of the machine with the heels of his hands. A chubby white-haired couple wearing identical horn-rimmed glasses sat at a corner table drinking draft beer and playing gin. A tall hollow-chested bartender with a gay-nineties mustache and hairstyle was polishing stemware and inserting it upside down into the overhead racks.

I slid onto a padded bar stool and said, "Mishy Burns around?"

"She comes on at four," he said.

"Draft beer, please."

He served it with a nice head. He said, "When she does come on, she's working. She has to set up the tables. When she comes on, she's not on her own time."

"Are you trying to be unpleasant?"

"I'm just telling you the way it is, friend. What she does on her own time is her business."

"You own this place?"

"I'm one of the owners."

I was getting very tired of contentious attitudes. I smiled at him. I said, "I've always wondered about places like this."

"Wondered what?"

"Suppose, just for the hell of it, you took a list of all the regulatory agencies that have any kind of authority over the way you do business here. County, city, state, federal. You know, the food-handling ordinances, and the tax people and the liquor people. Then suppose you went through this place and made a list of every single violation of every law, ordinance, and regulation."

"We run a good clean place here. We don't violate anything!"

"Nonsense, good buddy. There is no way to avoid being in violation of something. The rules are contradictory. You know it and I know it. Right now you are subject to fines, suspension of licenses, civil suits. That's the way the establishment keeps you in line. If you get feisty, they come and look you over and tell you you have to build a whole new kitchen, or replace all your wiring, or put in ten more parking spaces."

"Who the hell *are* you?"

"I am the fellow who came in here a little while ago, very quietly, and sat right here and asked you if Mishy Burns was around, and got a big discussion of her working hours and who pays her. We can start over again. Okay? Mishy Burns around?"

"She comes on at four," he said.

"Draft beer, please," I said, and he took the empty and refilled it and moved down the bar and left me alone, which was exactly what I wanted.

Michele came in ten minutes later. I had been building a mental picture of her, and so I was totally unprepared for a twenty-two-year-old Doris Day. She came a-dancing and bubbling in, full of warmth and life and high spirits. She brightened the place up. The salesman knew her and the gin players knew her. The bartender motioned to me and she came over and put her hand out and said, beaming, "Hello! I'm Mishy Burns."

"Travis McGee. The man says you're on his time and you can't talk to me."

"About what, love?"

"I've been talking to 'Licia about your cruise."

She made a face. "Oh, God. That again!"

She was in constant motion, constant changes of expression, posture, tossing her hair back, rocking from heel to toe, so much so that one wanted to clamp firm hands on her shoulders and settle her down, position her, quiet her. I realized that all the animation gave the impression of prettiness, and that perhaps in repose her face would look quite plain.

"Harley gets itchy, don't you, Harley? Look, love, let me go put on the house garments and brush up the dining room a little and then we can talk, because things will be dead as a snake until five past five and all the car doors start chunking shut out there in the lot."

I saw her in a little while, trotting back and forth in the dining room, wearing a crotch-length tennis dress with a sailor collar and a little white yachtsman's cap. Another waitress had joined her. A couple of construction workers—off at four—came in for beers. Somebody started the juke. I watched Michele. She had absolutely great legs. I felt guilty at the way I was going to try to booby-trap my question. Not very guilty. Anticipatory guilt, the kind that Meyer calls chessboard guilt, when you realize that the weaker player is making a frail response to a standard opening, and you are about to ram your bishops down his throat.

When she beckoned to me, I went into the dining room and followed her over to a service bar where she had coffee waiting. She said, "Coffee? Black? Okay. Look, I have talked myself out on that boat ride. Believe me, it was a long, long time ago. To me, two months is long. Lots and lots of things happen in two months. I have told about it so much that what I remember now is not the boat ride but all the times I talked about it."

"It can happen. Felicia is just as tired of it, I guess."

"You would never believe how sick we got. Maybe I would have been okay, but as soon as she lost it, I was gone too."

"There was just one thing I wanted to get straight, Michele."

"Such as?"

"Exactly how did John Tuckerman word it when he asked you to come along for the ride and bring a friend?"

"You got it wrong. I asked him if we could go along."

" 'Licia says that's what Tuckerman told you to say."

"Why, God *damn* her! She agreed never to tell anybody—"

And suddenly she stopped all motion. She was a subdued, plain-faced blonde with deeply bitten fingernails, staring at me from way inside herself, like an animal looking out of the brush.

"You rotten bastard," she said in a low voice. "You faked me out, didn't you?"

"Look at it this way. If Lawless is still alive somewhere, the whole thing was a conspiracy to defraud. He needed bodies to dress up the conspiracy."

"That shows how much you know, you bastard."

"I know this. You lied under oath. Right? So far, that's between the two of us. And Felicia. But you keep on with the garbage mouth, I see no reason to keep your little secret."

We stood facing each other, each with an elbow on the service bar. For a few more moments the wary creature stared through her eyes at me, out of the thickets at the back of her mind, and then dropped out of sight, and she was Miss Cheerleader again, all bounce and joy, all twinkle and grin.

With breathy laugh and salacious wink, she said, "What it was, and I'll trust you, I really will, John Tuckerman has this thing about Felicia. You wouldn't believe how horny he is for her, right from the first look he got at her. He said he would give me a nice present if I could get 'Licia to come along. What it was, it was a way of getting maybe a good chance to set her up. She didn't know what was coming down. She's a funny kid. She's not much for sex. She lived with some cat for a while but she'll never talk about it, and I think it was some kind of bad start for her, so now it's all yeck to her. What happened was we got seasick, and then Harder passed out and we had to come back and you know what happened. Right in the beginning John Tuckerman had told me to say it was me asked him if we could come along. Later on he said it was even more important I should say that, because if it got out he asked us, it would look bad. Mr. Lawless wasn't real turned on by having us come along. He hardly spoke to us at all. The way Felicia found out was, after the testimony and all, I got a little high and I started kidding Felicia about Tuckerman giving me a hundred dollars to talk her into that terrible boat ride. She was really pissed off at me. She wouldn't talk to me for a week, but then she began to see how funny it was and she forgave me. She said even if it had been the best boat ride the world ever saw, Tuckerman wasted a hundred dollars. I don't see why she's like that. He's sort of old for her. He's thirty-eight, he says, but probably forty. I told her he's not kinky or anything like that, and very sweet and generous, and he lives on that great beach, but she doesn't want anything to do with him. It isn't as if she thinks she's the world's best. She has this idea she's ugly. Somebody told her once that with those teeth she could eat a Big Mac through a venetian blind. She doesn't see why anybody would want her."

"Which finger did Nicky Noyes break?"

Her face got red. "She's got all those big white teeth and she's got a great big mouth too."

"Here come customers."

"Oh, God, with four kids yet. We close the kitchen at ten and I'm off by ten thirty."

"If I'm not at the bar there by ten thirty, give up on me."

"But you'll be around?"

"Sure. For a while."

CHAPTER

I went right from the Cove to 215 South Oak Lane, to the long white house with the three-car garage. I arrived at about quarter to five. There were two cars in the drive, a weatherbeaten old Cadillac convertible, rusting out under the white paint, and a new little gray Honda Accord. The front door was open. Through the screen I heard women laughing—not social laughter, but contagious yelps of delight.

I had to ring the bell a couple of times. A woman came hurrying to the door and looked out at me, brows raised in query. She was small and lean and sun-brown in yellow shorts and a T-shirt. The black-gray bangs of her Prince Valiant hairstyle came almost to her black brows. Her face was sun-weathered, hollow-cheeked, with deep squint lines, deep brackets around her mouth. Her eyes were dark blue.

"Mrs. Lawless?" I said.

"Yes, but I don't want a thing, thanks."

"I represent a group trying to purchase Double L

Ranches and Lawless Groves, and I would appreciate a little of your time."

I sorted out the calling card which said on the back "Dear Julia" and was signed "Dev." She opened the door a whole quarter inch to receive the card and then latched it again.

After she read it slowly and carefully, she frowned at me and said, "I can't sell that land. You certainly know that much."

"If your husband is alive, the problem is more complicated."

"Hub is dead."

"Perhaps you could help us ascertain that fact."

"I'm through talking to people about my husband."

"Because they wouldn't listen?"

"Something like that."

"I listen pretty good. Not as good as D. Jake Herron used to. But pretty good."

Her face softened slightly. "You knew my father?"

"Just slightly. A friend of mine and I helped D. Jake nail a game warden some years back who was in the alligator-hide business as a sideline. The warden took a couple of shots at us."

"I *remember* hearing about that!"

"I remember him saying that night that nobody ever wasted their time listening."

"Well . . . come on in. Maybe you'll buy something."

"I don't understand."

"We're tagging stuff for the biggest garage sale ever presented on South Oak Lane. Maybe the only garage sale."

I went through the house with her and out to the area in the rear. There was a big screened cage, a swimming pool, a flagstone terrace beyond the cage, and a barbecue area beyond the terrace. Two women were working with Julia Lawless. There was a beefy cheerful redhead named

Doris Jennings and a sallow and mocking blonde named Freddy Ellis. One Lawless daughter was there, introduced as Lynn. She looked familiar, and I suddenly remembered where I had seen her.

"Nice going, tiger," I said to her.

"For what?" she said, looking at me with that apathy they reserve for ancient male strangers.

"For whipping Miss Languid in the salmon dress over at the North Bay Resort courts. She wouldn't shake hands on it, I noticed."

She gave me a quick, warning wink. "Thanks. That was Sandra Ellis. I never beat her before."

Freddy Ellis said, "Hey. You mean my snitty little daughter lost ungraciously?"

"I didn't mind, honest," Lynn said.

"*I* mind," Freddy said ominously.

Doris Jennings asked me if I would be willing to look at the prices they had put on Hub's possessions and see if they were out of line. She said she had gotten advice from the sporting-goods stores which had sold him a lot of the things. They were arranged on display in the nearest stall of the garage.

I moved slowly and carefully past Hubbard Lawless's golf clubs, golf cart, tennis equipment, bowling ball and bowling shoes, shotguns, rifles, target pistol, fly rods, spinning rods, surf rods, tuna rods, reels and reel cases, boxes of lures, boxes of flies, weights, punching bag, Nikon cameras, lenses, lens cases, strobe lights, tripods, slide boxes, slide projectors, movie cameras, movie projectors, light stands, ten-speed tour bike, binoculars, sheath knives . . .

The man liked nice things, and he kept them in good shape. He didn't buy things and put them away. They showed signs of wear and signs of care.

A splendid custom shotgun caught my eye. It was in a fitted pigskin case, with an extra set of side-by-side barrels. Spanish walnut stock. Initials inlaid in gold. H.R.L. Beavertail forearm. Single nonselective trigger. Ventilated rib. English scroll engraving on white steel. It was Orvis Custom, built to Hub Lawless's physical dimensions, and I knew it had to represent a minimum three-thousand-dollar investment. A dandy toy for a grown-up boy. It was priced to move at five hundred. I assembled it and tried it. The drop at the comb and the heel was wrong, trigger distance wrong. And the initials were wrong. A man the same size as Hub Lawless could find a great bargain here.

I moved along and then went back to the billfish tackle, and fended off a lust to buy some of it. The man had good taste in equipment.

"Well?" Julia asked.

"You got good advice. The prices of the things I know about are in line. Fair for the buyer and the seller."

"He never stinted himself," she said flatly. "Good old Hub. The best was just barely good enough."

"Mother!" Lynn said, defending the beloved daddy.

"Sorry, chick," Julia said, reaching to ruffle the girl's hair. "Thanks for easing my mind about the prices. They seemed kind of low. I know what he paid for some of those things."

"I know nothing about golf equipment or bicycles."

"Oh, those prices are okay. I didn't know about the outdoor jock stuff."

The next stall of the garage was filled with standard garage-sale household items, Julia's and also items brought over by Doris Jennings and Freddy Ellis, for a joint effort. It was a predictable array: Cribs and high chairs. Ornate beer steins and souvenir plates. Bonus books from book clubs. Floor lamps and suitcases. Rotisseries and bulletin boards. Tricycles and feather headdresses. End tables and tablecloths. On being pressed, I said it looked as if they had a lot of good stuff there.

Finally, as a reward for my patience and help, and for

having known her father, she took me back into the living room for the obligatory conversation.

She sat curled in a corner of a large couch. I sat across from her, with a glass coffee table between us.

"It's so damned depressing," she said. "I've still not tackled his dressing room. I've got to get rid of all that stuff. Goodwill, I guess. Or the Salvation Army or somebody."

"A lot of people seem to think he's in Mexico."

"Say the rest of it too, Mr. McGee."

"Such as?"

"He stole the money and ran. He took off with his Norwegian piece of ass to live happily ever after."

"He was having an affair with her. An architect, wasn't she?"

"Okay. So he was having an affair. His very first. Believe me, it was his first. It started last year. In the summer. She was recommended to him. She was supposed to be some kind of an expert in the design of shopping centers. She did a big one in Atlanta and one in Jacksonville. When everything went to hell with the one he was supposed to build here, she should have taken off, right? But she stayed on, drawing pay from the big shot who was going broke. Oh, I am so goddamn sick of these little Scandinavian broads with their little breathy accents and no makeup, maybe a trace of lipstick, and their pale green eyes and their big boobs and no more morals than rabbits. I don't mind telling you I was really really hurt. I couldn't believe it at first. Then when we had a nose-to-nose battle, he wouldn't deny it. Finally he confessed and promised he would break up with her, but he didn't. He claimed he tried, but he didn't try hard enough. I asked him if he gave a damn about Tracy and Lynn. It marks a child terribly when there is family trouble when they're in their mid-teens, just sixteen and fourteen. We had more rotten fights and then he started sleeping out at the ranch, in a room back of the ranch office out there. That was in late January. I've had a chance to think lately. And I can . . . almost begin to understand this Kristin business. Hub had a dream. He admired my daddy so much. What he wanted to do was build a base. Money and power. And then one day he was going to run for governor and become somebody in Florida. But last year, when times were hard and things began to go bad, he could see his dream fading. He had been too confident. He'd made a bad judgment of the situation. It was going to spoil his track record to be brought down after forty. And there wouldn't be enough time to build it all up again. He was really seriously upset. He always had such great drive and spirit, and he couldn't find a way out of the spot he was in. Some men would go a little crazy. Some would take to the bottle or go onto Valium. Hub took up with that architect person, proving his manhood, I guess. Maybe she kept telling him he was a great man. Maybe I should have done that so she wouldn't have to. Maybe I nagged him some. And maybe it was Hub's way of going a little bit crazy. Am I making any sense?"

"I think you are."

"You *really* listen, don't you?"

"I'm interested."

"You have been sitting there, looking right at me, and nodding and making little sounds in your throat. You are so damned earnest about listening to me, you made me rattle on and on and on."

"You wanted to talk about it. That's all."

"So I open up to you and I don't even know you."

"That's the easiest way of all, when you don't know the other person."

"Maybe."

"What makes you so sure he's dead?"

"We were always very close. Very close, until the last eight months of his life. We were in touch with each other

94

on some kind of level most people don't have. Once I had a feeling of blackness, of terrible fear. He'd gone hunting with John Tuckerman. I wrote down the exact time it happened. I couldn't get in touch with him. I was beside myself with worry. Finally he phoned me from Waycross, Georgia, and said he'd been bitten on the wrist by a big cottonmouth, but he'd been treated and it was going to be okay and he would be home in two days. When we compared my note with the time he had been bitten, it was correct to the very minute. He knew the time because it had bitten him on the left wrist, near where his wristwatch was. Once when the girls were both in school, in the first and third grades, he came charging home in the middle of the afternoon, convinced something was wrong. I'd fallen from the shed roof and wrenched my back so badly I couldn't stand up. I couldn't even crawl to the phone or to the neighbors, it hurt so badly. I'd ruptured a disc. I knew that if I waited he'd come. I knew that he knew I was in trouble, and he came. There were lots of little things like that that happened between us. Those are just two of the biggest ones. When they told me that night that Hub was lost off the *Julie* and believed drowned, I didn't believe it. I kind of reached into that private world where he and I were always in contact, and I knew he was still there, so he couldn't be dead."

"I don't understand."

"It was a distasteful situation—with those two young girls going with two middle-aged men out on that lovely boat named for me—but not some kind of disaster, really. I didn't know what was going on. I got to sleep quite late. The girls were terribly upset, Tracy and Lynn, and I had to get them settled down. They loved their father so much. They couldn't understand what was happening to their world. I am very concerned about them, about Tracy particularly, she's getting so strange and secretive. Anyway, I took a sleeping pill and I didn't wake up until after ten the next morning, March twenty-third. Everything came rushing back into my mind and I reached out, or over, or down, in some direction I can't describe, to find the same reassurance I'd felt the night before, and there was nothing. Absolutely nothing. It was a cold, dead, abandoned place in my mind. I knew he was gone. There is no doubt at all in my mind. My husband is dead."

"Forgive me, but that is not exactly the sort of evidence that will mean much to the insurance company."

"I found that out. They want any excuse not to pay, because it is a very big policy. I wouldn't be at all surprised if they hadn't started all these rumors about Hub being in Mexico. He loved Mexico, granted. *If* he were alive, it would be a reasonable place for him to run to, if he wanted to hide."

"Cleaning out those bank accounts makes it look as if he had running and hiding on his mind."

"Maybe he did. I don't know. We weren't communicating. I suppose it would have eased his conscience about me and the girls if he could fake his own death and leave that insurance for me."

"What if he tried to fake it, and something went wrong and he died?"

"That would fit the way he acted before he disappeared, and it would fit the way I feel about his being so definitely dead."

"Hypothetical question. Suppose somebody showed you a picture of Hubbard Lawless taken at a sidewalk café in Guadalajara on the eighth day of April, sitting and pouring dark beer into a glass?"

"I would have to say the picture is a fake."

"Who would bother to fake it?"

"The insurance company, of course. To muddy the waters and hang onto their two million dollars. The insurance is mine. I am the owner of that policy. It's all in the records of the trust department at Coast National Bank and Trust. You can ask Rob Gaylor all about it. He's the Senior Trust Officer. He handles what my daddy left in trust for me. It isn't enough to maintain this house and raise two girls. Thus the garage sale, and also, I am going to list the house and look for something smaller and less expensive to maintain."

"It's a beautiful house, Mrs. Lawless."

"Julie, please. I know. But houses can go sour on you, all of a sudden. You remember too many birthdays and Christmases. What do people call you?"

"Travis. Trav. I wonder if you could tell me who could give me the most information on Kristin Petersen, Julie."

"She wasn't the sort of person who goes around making dozens of new friends. She subleased a condo apartment at North Pass Vista. That's just north of the North Bay Resort, where you saw Lynn beat Sandra Ellis—"

"And where I'm staying with my associate, Meyer."

"North Pass Vista is a kind of town-house arrangement. They have a rental office there where you could ask."

"If I think of more questions I want to ask you, may I come back again?"

"Of course. But you are not really interested in buying land, are you?"

"My associate is."

She looked at me steadily, with care. "I think he probably is, but not to the extent you'd have me believe. You're here for something entirely different. To find out something. To help someone."

"You know, you could make me pretty uncomfortable with all that."

"I don't want to. I'm not a witch. I just can read some people sometimes. Whatever you do, Travis, you are very damn good at it."

"Thank you. I'm not sure you're correct."

"I've got to get back out there to the old-table-lamp department and start pricing. Will you tell me some day why you're here?"

"If you're interested."

"I wouldn't ask if I weren't."

I got back to the North Bay Yacht and Tennis Resort at quarter past six, feeling grainy, listless, and depressed. There was no Meyer and no note from Meyer. I peeled off the little compress and then, with great care, pulled off the thin strips of adhesive. The skin held together nicely, so I dabbed some disinfectant on it, purchased from a drugstore near the bank, and covered it with a flesh-colored waterproof Band-Aid from the same source. I stared into my own pale and skeptical eyes. An unenamored lady had once termed them "spit-colored." Deep-water tan, a few little white scars here and there, a nose but slightly bent, a scuffle of sun-baked hair, responding to no known discipline and seldom subjected to any.

Out on that ketch, the *Antsie*, beating our interminable way up from the Grenadines to the Virgins to Keasler's Peninsula, I had wanted the night lights and the gentle ladies and the best of booze, with enough music to make them mix properly. And here I was, up to my hocks in all such ingredients and wishing I was back aboard the *Antsie*, being yanked and hammered and pounded by the ever-insisting sea. Life is a perverse art indeed.

I left a note to Meyer that he could find me in the lounge. Feeling somewhat better after the shower and the change of clothes, I went on down and walked in on a very busy bar, plus Billy Jean Bailey tinkling away on background music as opposed to the performance numbers she did later at night. When she saw me, her smile lighted her up from inside, like candles in a pumpkin, and my heart sank. She had on a silver-blue cowboy shirt and tight white jeans. She switched the music to tell me that I had come along from out of nowhere, and then she had me walking out of a dream, and then the music said she was in love, in love, in love, with a wonderful guy.

"No, no, no," I yelled, in the back of my brain, and beat on the cell bars. "No way. Please."

When she took a break, she came around to the far end of the bar and wormed her way in to stand close beside me, with maximum contact. She put her hand on my neck and pulled my ear down to where she could talk into it. "I've had the most goddamn delicious day of my whole life, thinking about you, bun."

"Uh."

"I've never turned on like that before. Couldn't you tell?"

"Uh."

"We're so fantastic, I can almost get it off just thinking about how it was. I can get right to the edge, bun."

"Bun?"

"Bun rabbit. My dear darling bun rabbit baby. Oh, God, time is going so slow, it will *never* be midnight."

"Don't you go Friday until one?"

"Oh, Christ! It *is* Friday."

"Yes. It sure is."

She kissed me on the ear and went switching back to her piano. I was conscious of considerable amusement among the bystanders. She had not exactly concealed the relationship. My ears felt hot. Visitor makes immediate dear friend of the piano player.

I wrote her a very short note, paid for my drink, took the note over to the piano, and put it where she could read it. She did so and made a kiss shape with her small mouth and then a big happy smile, and I went lumbering out and met Meyer just as I got outside the door.

"Where are *you* going?" he asked.

"It's very close in there."

"With that ceiling?"

"Take my word. Close. Very close. Let's . . . uh . . . have a drink at the Cove. Very close by. Walking distance."

"I know. I saw it. Are you all right? You act strange."

"Tell me about your afternoon, Meyer."

"Mr. Glenn and Mr. Latzov drove me all over this county and showed me fantastic bargains in ranchland, grove land, raw land, development opportunities, waterfront land, and swamplands. They told me this area is right on the threshold of fantastic, unbelievable growth, and every dollar put into land values here would be like investing in St. Petersburg Beach in nineteen fifty. Every time I tried to bring up the Lawless holdings, they would whip me out into the scrub country and show me something much better, available right now."

Once we were wedged into a corner of the long bar at the Cove, I asked him what Mr. Glenn and Mr. Latzov thought about the Lawless affair.

"A terrible tragedy. A legal tangle. A sorry affair. You never know what a man will do when he's pushed too far. They said that considering how smart Hub Lawless is, the odds are very small that anybody will ever find him. And they estimated his getaway money at closer to a million."

It was payday in Timber Bay. The noise level at the Cove was overwhelming. Waitresses worked at a dead run. Harley had two helpers behind the bar. Suddenly I noticed Nicky Noyes over in a corner of the bar area, at a bare table beyond the row of pinball machines. He sat behind a round table, and the two couples with him looked as if they had just climbed down off their big road cycles. They looked quaint. They are fading into history, like Pancho Villa's irregulars. All the macho whiskers and the leather clothes and the dead eyes and their feral, abused little women. Hundreds of them roar up and down the highway in formation, making formal protest about the law forcing them to wear a helmet. It is a violation of their freedom and liberty, they say. Very macho. But when they don't wear helmets, they abuse the taxpayers, taking a couple of weeks to die in intensive care, their primitive brains jellied by hard impact with the concrete highway. Somebody has to pick them up when they go down and deliver them to Emergency, regrettably.

I saw Noyes gesture toward the bar, and moments later all five of them were looking directly at me, a stare of speculation and obscure challenge.

I said to Meyer, "Beyond the pinball machines at the round table, the fellow with his back to the wall, facing us directly, is Nicky Noyes."

"With the headband and all the gold trinkets?"

"Himself."

"Wholesome company he keeps."

"Isn't it, though? I keep getting the feeling that Nicky isn't very tightly wrapped. He could be working himself up to jump me."

"Right here?"

"Or wait outside for me."

"For us."

"Thank you, Meyer. Very nice instinct. Here he comes, incidentally."

Nicky came plodding toward me. He walked oddly, putting his feet down with care. His strong cologne arrived three steps before he did. I shifted carefully, coiling all my springs without appearing to do so. Nicky came inside my normal space and stopped, broad belly almost touching me. His gaze moved rapidly side to side, up and down, back and forth.

"You are part of the trial," he said, chanting it in such a way he sounded like a Sunday television preacher.

"Trial?"

"Certain things are going to happen, and you are part of them, and when it is all over, we'll all be back at the beginning, every one of us but you."

"Have you been sampling your own merchandise, Noyes?"

"Soon you'll see the shape of everything yet to come and the part you're going to play, but it will be too late by then. It is up to me to turn it on and turn it off. It mustn't go too fast. You understand? Everything is part of it now."

And he turned away from me and walked to the door and on out, still walking with that strange care, as if he might step too heavily, break through the floor of the world, and fall forever. One worn-out-looking woman at the table where Noyes had been sitting caught my eye, smiled wearily, and circled a forefinger near her temple.

A big young man was standing near us at the bar. He turned his red whiskers toward me and said, "Don't you mind ol' Nicky, hear? He's okay. I drove a truck for Hula Construction for nearly three years, and Nicky was the foreman part of the time, and superintendent the last year I was there."

"I hope he used to make more sense."

"He did. He didn't used to be at all like the way he is now. He's weird now. You know about Hub Lawless taking off with all the money?"

"Yes. I've heard about it."

"Well, Nick thought Lawless was the finest man ever walked the earth. He worked all kind of hours for Hub. He sprained a gut for Hub. And the hell of it was, Hub took off owing Nicky two months' pay. I tell you, it soured Nicky. It turned him kind of mean. He used to laugh a lot, and he used to fight for fun, and not very often. Now it's like he's against the world. I don't even speak to him any more because I don't want to get into some kind of argument with him. He always treated me fine."

"Could you hear what he was saying to me?"

"Sure could. Didn't make any sense. I guess from what

you said to him, you know he's a dealer now. It's a small-potatoes thing with him from what I hear. He lives okay on it, maybe even pretty good. A couple of times he give me and my wife Betty free samples, but we flushed them down. I don't make enough driving for the county to want to pick up any habit where I got to buy it from Nicky. They say he is using his own stuff, and they say he's messing up his head."

"Sometimes he's better than other times?"

"That's right, but I'd say that each time he gets weird he seems to get a little weirder than the time before, and I never heard him so far out over the edge as he was tonight." He put a big hand out. "My name is Ron Shermerhorn."

"McGee. And this is Meyer. Ron Shermerhorn."

"Pleased to meet you. I don't want to talk about Nicky too much, you know. He was always okay to me. I just didn't want you to think he was just another one of your ordinary crazies, is all."

"He jumped me last night," I said. "In the parking lot outside the North Bay Resort lounge. I don't really know why. I walked out with the piano player, Billy Jean Bailey, and there he was, ready and waiting, shirt off, spitting on his hands."

Ron was looking me over for signs of damage. "Talk him out of it?"

"No, we went around a little, and then I helped him climb into his truck."

"You've got to be pretty good."

"I faked him out."

He was still staring dubiously at me when a man on the other side of Meyer spun around so violently he knocked Meyer back against me. The man then went charging toward the men's room, back of his hand pressed to his mouth, and disappeared.

"What's all that?" Meyer demanded indignantly.

"Oh," Ron said, "that's just Fritz Plous. Works for the paper. He's in here a lot. Throws up a lot. It takes him sudden. It's what they call auto–auto—"

"Autointoxication?" Meyer suggested.

"That's it! The doctor has told him not to think about throwing up. But he sort of gets it on his mind and he can't get his mind off it and all of a sudden he has to make a run for it."

"You have your share of unusual people here in Timber Bay," I said.

"No more than anywhere," Ron said with a trace of indignation. He drained his glass and put it down. "See you guys," he said, and went on out into the evening.

Meyer and I stood silently side by side. The man named Plous came back to the bar, gray and sweaty. We stood in a blur of ambient noise, of Muzak and laughter, tinkle and clatter, rumble and chatter, and *tink* of ice.

Ever since Noyes had delivered his cryptic speech I had felt even more depressed than had been my usual quota lately. I was aware that Meyer was studying me thoughtfully, carefully.

"What's with you?" I said in irritation.

"Where has gone all that lazy mocking charm of yesteryear?" he asked. "Where is the beach wanderer, the amiable oaf I used to know?"

"Knock it off. Okay?"

"What the hell is making you so edgy!"

I had to use a surprising amount of control to quell the impulse to yap at him again, like a cross dog. I forced the deep breath and said, "I don't know. Maybe I'm coming down with something. I'd like a bowl of hot chicken soup and a feather bed. An empty feather bed. I can't relate to this paragon, this splendid fellow who left with the money. I can't get used to all the leverage we have, Meyer. Everybody wants to be nice to us because we might represent new money in town. The Sheriff makes me very nervous. I met a lovely girl who hates her own teeth. All the way up from the Grenadines to the Virgins I had no one to talk to but Duke Davis, and you know how he is. Two words a day does it. Then one hell of a three-day party at St. Croix, and more weeks of silence. I think I got used to it, Meyer. I am getting edgy talking to these people. I hate the sound of my own voice. And not too far from here, not far enough, there is a hundred-pound piano player fixing to fasten onto me the way a King's Crown attaches itself to a clam, and I have to shake her off somehow."

"I think you *are* coming down with something."

"Julia Lawless is bitter and angry at the world. She's selling Hub's toyland. At a garage sale, for God's sake. You should see the Orvis rods and shotguns. Is there a name for what I'm coming down with?"

"Some kind of culture shock. It manifests itself in an inability to see a reality untainted by temporary hang-ups."

"And yesterday when I was waiting to cross the street near the bank, I could look into all the cars roaring by, and the people in them had kind of a dead look. As if they were hurrying so as not to be late for their own funerals. Is there any cure for my disease?"

"When Harder comes waddling into the marina with the *Flush*, you'll perk up. Hermit crabs get very nervous when they have to scrounge around without their shell."

"I can't wait that long. I feel as if some absolutely unimaginable catastrophe was getting itself ready to happen. And I feel as if, for no reason in the world, I was going to suddenly—for God's sake—start *crying!*"

He looked at me then with a startled compassion, intently, somberly. "Hey," he said softly. "Hey, Travis."

"Sorry."

"I thought it was just a little everyday weltschmerz. We're not here on some great big thing, you know."

"It's as big a thing as Harder can possibly think of."

"Did you and Duke Davis stand watches all the way up?"

"Yes, why? We decided it was best because the automatic pilot wasn't reliable in any kind of chop, and we were in shipping lanes most of the way. Besides, we didn't get any really long reaches on the way up. We fought wind all the way."

"What did you think about all that time?"

"Come *on!* I played all the games of What if. I counted the ladies I have known. I replayed the hard shots—given and taken. Remembered grief, remembered pleasure. I thought of all the choices made, the doors I've slammed shut, the seasons which have closed down on me, games called on account of pain. All that shit, Meyer. You know. A man's head goes round and about. Filth and glory. The whole schmear."

"But mostly . . . Who am I? Where am I going?"

"I guess."

"And the answer?"

I shrugged. "Answer shmanser. In the immortal words of Popeye, I yam what I yam. I know my patterns and limitations, needs and hang-ups. So I go on. Right? I endure. I enjoy what I can. There aren't any more forks in the road to take. Keep walking."

"You have felt that horrid rotten exhalation, Travis, that breath from the grave, that terminal sigh. You've been singing laments for yourself. Laments, regrets, remorses."

"Light the pyre. Float me out on my boat. Come on, Meyer. I've always been perfectly willing to accept the risks as they come along. If I make it, I make it. And if I don't, I had one hell of a time trying."

"And what you *do*, the services you render, are important."

"Are they?"

"Aren't they?" he asked.

"If you get somebody out of one bad screw-up, haul them out, brush them off, and send them on their way, they will head right back into some other kind of screw-up."

"Ah-hah!"

"What's with this Ah-hah?"

"You question the validity of the mission. Thus you question the validity of the missionary. A loss of faith. That is corrosive. At that point you question existence itself, the meaning of it. A common human condition. Those with no imagination never really feel despair. Congratulations!"

"Good God, Meyer!"

"I'll phone my new friend, and we shall have Boodles and beef at the Captain's Galley."

"Everybody has to be somewhere, I guess."

Meyer learned that there would be a table. We walked back to the lot and got the rental and drove on out to the Galley.

Meyer was turning something around and around in his mind. He had that look. One does not make conversation when Meyer has that look. At the table he finally sighed and smiled and gave it a try.

"Travis, I've mentioned to you the second law of thermodynamics."

"Which is?"

"That all organized systems tend to slide slowly into chaos and disorder. Energy tends to run down. The universe itself heads inevitably toward darkness and stasis."

"Cheering thought."

"Prigogine altered this concept with his idea of dissipative structures."

"Who?"

"Ilya Prigogine, the Belgian mathematician."

"Oh."

"He used the analogy of a walled city and an open city. The walled city, isolated from its surroundings, will run down, decay, and die. The open city will have an exchange of material and energy with its surroundings and will become larger and more complex, capable of dissipating energy even as it grows. I have been thinking that it would not warp the analogy too badly to extend it to a single individual."

"The walled person versus the open person?"

"The walled person would decline, fade, decay."

"Meyer, dammit, I have a lot more interchange of material and energy with my environment than most."

"In a physical sense, but you are not decaying in any physical sense. Great Scott, look at you. You look as if you could get up and run right through that wall."

"The decay is emotional?"

"And you are walled, in an emotional sense. There is no genuine give-and-take. There is no real involvement, lately. You are going through the motions. As with the piano player. As with Nick Noyes. You are vaguely predatory lately. And irritable. And listless. You are getting no emotional feedback."

"Where do I go looking for some?"

"That's the catch. You can't. It isn't that mechanical. You merely have to be receptive and hope it comes along."

"Meanwhile, I am being ground down by the second law of thermodynamics?"

"In a sense, yes."

"Thank you so much. I never would have known."

"Like I said. Irritable."

CHAPTER

At ten o'clock on Saturday morning, I took a chance on some strong black coffee. My throat clenched and my stomach worked and leaped, but settled down slowly. I felt of my face carefully.

"What's the matter?" Meyer asked.

"My face feels as if it had been sliced off, Cuisinarted, chilled, and slapped back on. If I turn my head too fast, it will slide off. Is there a pile driver working nearby?"

"That's tennis you hear."

"How was I?"

"I would say you weren't listless. And you were audible. Lord, yes! You were audible."

"I thought I had long since outgrown that kind of thing."

"You had enough screwdrivers to empty your average orange tree. I lost count."

"What happened to me?"

"You had a large wish to stop thinking, to turn your head off. You were not happy with yourself, so you decided to dim your lights. And you did. You became some-one else. Completely."

"Anybody we know?"

"McGee, you were loud, amiable, patriotic, and on key. You let me drive. We seemed to accumulate quite a group of new friends. We stopped at the Cove and picked up one blond Mishy Burns and we brought the whole pack here to the Cove. B. J. Bailey did not approve of you at all. Jack the Manager did not approve of the group. We were deprived of the chance of a midnight swim in the pool, but there was no way he could close the beach. You passed out on one of those canvas chaises. The piano player came after you at about quarter past one. There was some serious contention between the piano player and Miss Burns over your recumbent body, though I must say you seemed of very little value to anyone. There were some brisk face-slappings, some pungent dialogue, and then some yanking of hair, at which point they fell to the sand and went rolling over and over down the slope of the beach, yelping and biting. I chose that opportunity to yank you to your feet and walk you away. You began singing again, but not loudly. It was another rendition of 'Ragged but Right.' You had favored us with an estimated twenty renditions."

"What did I do to deserve all this? No, don't tell me. The question was rhetorical. God, Meyer, my hair aches and my skin doesn't fit and all my teeth feel loose."

"Last night we agreed the next thing we should do is go see John Tuckerman. I know how to find his place. It's about nine miles down the coast. Feel well enough to leave?"

"I am going to feel absolutely rotten wherever I happen to be, so I might as well be in the car as out of it. You drive."

I sat lumpily beside him, feeling squalid and faintly nauseated as he headed south, making the big half circle around the bay front, past the marinas and commercial docks and fish houses. Two blocks before we came to the end of Bay Street, Meyer turned right. We went through a couple of blocks of waterfront enterprise, ship's chandlers, old rooming houses, saloons, and sundries stores, and soon the street had turned into two-lane rough country asphalt, past trailer parks and junkyards, running between shallow ditches where coarse weeds and grasses grew high. By the time we were in empty country, the road was much worse. The potholes were deep. In places the wind had drifted sand across the road. The occasional hawk sat atop a phone pole, watching the clumps of marsh grass.

An armadillo trundled across the road, delicate little head upraised, full of false security, trusting too much in its body armor.

To keep my attention off wondering how soon I was going to be sick, I said, briskly conversational, "In Texas they scoop those out and make baskets out of them and sell them in roadside stands."

After a few moments of silence, Meyer said, "It is to be hoped that on some planet far beyond our galaxy a race of sentient armadillos is busy scooping out Texans and selling them at roadside stands, possibly as Lister bags."

That did it. "Whoa," I said in a small chastened voice. He whoaed and I sprang out and made it to the ditch, there paying one of the more ordinary penalties of abuse. I went back to the car and looked in at him. "How much farther?"

"I'd say three miles."

"Please drive straight ahead two miles, park, and wait for me."

The road curved. Two miles took him out of sight. The May sun was hot on my shoulders. I swung along, taking big strides but feeling clammy. And unwell. With a monstrous effort I kicked myself into a trot. For a little while I thought I would pass out, but suddenly I began to sweat properly. I stopped gasping and began to breathe properly. I stopped landing on my heels, jarring myself, and got up onto the balls of my feet. At the end of an estimated mile I began to get that good feeling of having all the parts of the machine working, thighs lifting properly, lungs filling deeply, arms swinging in cadence, lots of muscles flexing and relaxing.

"You'll live," Meyer said when I got to the car.

"I'm beginning to feel as if I might want to."

"We have to look for a sand road that turns off to the right at a shallow angle. With a yellow mailbox at the corner."

The yellow mailbox had an aluminum sign on top of it, the kind of sign where you buy the letters and slide them into a groove. The letters said TUCKERM.

The sand road wound between big bushes, angling toward the beach. We came upon a large faded sign which announced to nobody in particular, "Future Site of Pepperfish Village. A Planned Condominium Community. 1500 Units. Complete Recreation Facilities. Private Beach. Yacht Club. Golf Course. Shopping Plaza. A Hub-Law Development. Planning and Design by Kristin Petersen, AIA. Construction by Hula Construction, Inc. Occupation of first phase by   " Somebody had obliterated the rest of it with a big broad slap of red paint.

"So ends the dream," Meyer said.

"They could have built a better mousetrap."

"The world is beating a path down to this improbable peninsula, mousetraps or no. But it does seem to be a strange location."

Soon we came upon Tuckerman's place, off to the right of the road. It was atop spindly pilings ten feet high. The house was about thirty feet square. A veranda deck extended ten feet beyond it all the way around. The peaked roof was of galvanized sheet metal, weathered to a powdery white. The house and deck were of native pine, slapped up green and now weathered to gray, warped and twisted, with long-ago paint scoured off by the wind-driven sand. There was an old Fiat parked under the deck, square and green, sagging in the off right haunch with some kind of sprained underpinning.

Out behind the house, between the house and the long row of sand dunes, a woman stopped poking into a 55-gallon drum with a long stick and turned to look at us through the thicket of pilings supporting the house. She'd spent a lot of weeks in hot sun. She wore the bottom half of a string bikini, in red-orange Day Glo. Without haste or emphasis, she turned and located the bikini top, slipped it on, hammocked herself into it, and tied it in back. She then peered into the drum and began prodding again with the stick.

We walked around to where she was. There were two clotheslines hung with damp clothing. The drum was up on concrete blocks. There was a driftwood fire under it, flames almost too pale to see in the bright sunlight. Steam came off the soapy water in the drum. Bright clothing came into view and sank again as she prodded away.

"If you are the guys from Maytag," she said, "it is about time. This thing don't cycle worth a hoot."

"How is it on spin dry?" Meyer asked.

"Beyond belief." As she spoke, water began to spill over the top of a second drum a dozen feet away. She sprinted to a small plywood shack and turned something off. A pump gasped and died. She came back and took the hose out of the newly filled drum. She was sweaty from working so near the fire. She was a big woman, middle twenties, tall, with solid bone structure, slender waist, great shoulders. Muscle rolled in her back as she dug into the drum with her thick piece of driftwood. She levered a sopping wad of clothing up and looked at it.

"I can say," she said, "without fear or favor, that all

this stuff is cleaner than it was. Beyond that I will not go."

With a grunt of effort she levered the mass out of the drum and carried it to the other drum and dropped it in, and the displaced water sloshed out.

"Have you come to take him away?" she asked.

"No," I said.

"Which leaves me with mixed emotions."

The next wad of wet clothing was too heavy for her. I stepped in and carried it over to the rinse-water drum. She had brown hair, coarse with sun and salt, looking as if she had cropped it herself. She had a solid jaw, a broad mouth, dark brown eyes, and a jutting, high-bridged, no-nonsense nose.

"But you're looking for him?"

"For a talk," Meyer said.

She fished the final garment out of the hot water and put it in the other drum, turned and stared at us, seemed to see something that reassured her, smiled, and put her hand out. "I'm Gretel Howard."

After introductions, Meyer explained that we were trying to get the title cleared up somehow on some of Hubbard Lawless's holdings so that an offer could be made.

She looked at him and then at me. "Real-estate people? Not really."

"Not really," I said. "He's doing a favor for a friend. I'm with him."

"You look like the sort of man who can fix an antique Kohler five-thousand-watt generator, McGee."

"I can look at it and make reassuring noises."

"Follow me."

We went to the plywood shed. It was a big brute. The gas was in a drum on a scaffolding arrangement behind the shed. Plenty of gas. I couldn't check the condition of the batteries. It was rigged to start up at power demand. Turn on a hundred watts anywhere in the circuit and it would or should begin. A thin little metal leaf, like a spring, was supposed to be activated by the demand and bend over and touch a terminal. I pushed it over against the terminal, and with a great popping stuttering roar, the generator came to life.

Gretel sprang backward and hit the back of her head against the frame of the low doorway into the shed. Meyer backed into the little gasoline water pump and burned the back of his ankle on the still-hot housing. They each made appropriately fevered statements in the silence after I had released the little contact leaf. I examined it carefully. The vibration of the generator had caused the setscrew to work loose. I tightened it with the edge of a dime until the leaf was a sixteenth of an inch from the contact. There was a light in the shed, a hanging bulb. I turned it on, and the generator roared into life. I turned it off, smiling, smug and happy.

"My undying gratitude," she said. "We'll go find John. But first I have to churn my rinse a little."

As she churned, Meyer said, "You *have* heard of Laundromats?"

"I know. You're being ironic. Yes, love, and I could have bundled all this scrungy stuff into Brenda—that is little green Brenda over there, my dear lopsided auto— and gone Laundromating with a lot of gratitude for the benefits of civilization and so on. But I have this pioneer hang-up. I love doing things the hard way."

Making it evident we weren't going to be given the reason.

"I didn't mean to pry," Meyer said.

"Of *course* you didn't. I can wring this stuff out and hang it later, gentlemen. Let's go up on the deck and see if we can spot John pursuing lunch."

We climbed the warped and weathered stairway to the deck, climbed from one world into another. From the deck one could see across the top of the dunes, out to the blue Gulf dotted with infrequent whitecaps in the morning breeze. To the south was a curve of beach and the continuing line of dunes. To the north, far away, were a few white towers of Timber Bay rising up out of the city smudge. To the east was the north-south wavery line of the old asphalt road, heat shimmering from it.

She went into the house and came out with binoculars, and located him far up the beach. They were big old Navy ten-power, hard to hand-hold. She gave them to me, stood beside me. I was very conscious of her there, of a radiation of her body heat as we stood in the shade of the overhang, of the way the top of her brown head came higher than my eyes. Few women stand that tall in bare brown feet. I guessed her at a fraction of an inch over six feet.

I focused on John Tuckerman. He was a mile away, standing to mid-thigh in the waves, casting out beyond where they were beginning to lift and break.

"You can walk up there and talk to him," she said. "But don't . . . expect too much. He's quite confused."

"How so?"

"I thought when I got every last trace of alcohol out of his system, he would be like he used to be. Poor John. It's a wonder I haven't killed him, running him up and down that beach. I asked Dr. Sam Stuart about it and he said it was due to alcoholic spasm destroying brain tissue. He changed during the month after Hub disappeared. He was drinking so very heavily, I understand. He was . . . the way he is by the time I got here, by the time I *could* get here."

"Should we both go?" I asked her.

"It might make him anxious to see two of you coming. Just you alone would be better, I think."

He noticed me when I was a hundred yards from him. He saw me when he had drawn back his arm to cast. He stayed frozen in that position for a few moments and then lowered the rod and stood waiting. He looked like a Clark Gable gone seriously to seed. His dark hair was tangled and long. His black mustache had grown down over his lip. He had a four-day stubble of beard. But the cheekbones were high and hard, the brow jutting, the eyes dark, deepset, and merry. He was bigger than I had expected, almost as tall as I am, and wider, but soft. Tan helped hide the softness, the sagging belly, the varicosities on the husky legs. He wore ragged shorts. There was a tackle box on the sand and a stringer staked close by, with the line leading into the wave wash.

"Any luck?" I asked.

"Not good today. Just some of those little suckers that taste like iodine. And a little shark I let go."

"What are you using, John?"

"I got these tired pieces of cut bait. They're beginning to smell. Say, how'd you know my name?"

"Gretel pointed you out up the beach here and told me you're fishing for lunch. She seems like a nice person."

"Oh, she's a wonderful girl. Just wonderful. She's taking real good care of me. I can't remember the last time I had a drink. What's your name?"

"McGee. Travis McGee. I came out here with a friend of mine. His name is Meyer. He's back at the house with Gretel. We came to Timber Bay a few days ago to find out about buying Hub's ranch and grove land. We wondered if you could help us."

"No, I couldn't help you with anything like that. I was just a friend. That's all. We grew up together and went to school together and stayed friends. Hub was the smart one."

"I thought you were a vice-president of those companies he had."

"Oh, I was, sure. I guess I still am, come to think of it. But it didn't mean anything, not anything at all. He said it was so I could be expensed. I don't know why what I got paid couldn't have come out of just one of the businesses. I wasn't getting a free ride, though. I did a lot of things for Hub. And for Julie and the kids too. Pretty important things, sometimes. Like making sure something would get delivered on time to the right person."

Finally I was able to put a name to what was so strange about him: it was his childlike quality. The amiable open manner, the pleasant eagerness were those of a manly child, eager for approval.

"Deliveries can be *very* important," I said.

"You just bet they can!"

I saw some action out beyond the waves and wondered if I could find him some better bait. I took off shoes and socks, rolled my pant legs up, went down to the edge of the water, and began digging in the soft wet sand. After a little while I dug up a sand flea, oyster-white, multilegged, and snatched him before he could burrow back into the wet sand. He was as big around as my thumb and half as long. I took him and impaled him on John Tuckerman's hook.

"That's an *ugly* thing!" he said. "Where did you find it?"

"There should be a lot of them along this beach. Cast out over in that direction and reel in fast."

"Fast? Okay."

In the first ten feet of retrieve he got a hard strike. He yelled with excitement and pleasure. He worked the fish expertly, but when we got a look at it, his shoulders sagged. "Oh, nuts. Another kind of trash fish. A darn jackfish."

He had a fish knife in his tackle box. I pulled the four-pound jack farther up the beach, slit its throat, and pulled it back into the water, holding it captive by the leader. It pumped strings and strands of dark blood into the water until it weakened and died. The sea had washed away all the pink blush of blood.

"What did you do that for?" he demanded. He looked upset and disapproving.

"Because it is second cousin to a pompano, and now the meat won't be dark and heavy, and it makes a good panfish."

As the knife was sharp enough, I filleted the fish on the spot, washed the two slabs of meat in the sea, and threw the rest out beyond the surf, where the crabs would clean it up quickly.

"You sure did that fast," John Tuckerman said.

"Lots of practice."

"Say, were you ever a guide? Did you do guiding out of Marathon, ever? You look like a fellow me and Hub hired down there a long time ago. No, you couldn't be. That was maybe fifteen years ago. He'd be a lot older by now than you are."

"I've found fish for a lot of people, but not for hire."

"What did you say your name is?"

"Travis McGee."

"Trav?"

"Sure."

"I used to remember names real good. It is sort of a trick. You know. You find some way to match up the name to the way the people look. Like if there is a woman named Fowler with a big mouth and a real loud voice, you say to yourself, She is Fowler the Howler, and then you never forget. But I have stopped remembering somehow. I used to be able to tell ten thousand jokes. I was known for telling jokes. The other day I was fishing and I tried to remember one. Just one. And I couldn't."

"If this fish is lunch, we ought to get it back to the house."

"Hey, you're right!"

We picked up our stuff and walked back along the

beach toward the cottage. The roof gleamed white in the sunlight on the far side of the dune. I could see the dark shade on the veranda and a sudden glint, and knew she was taking a look at us through the binoculars.

Trite and repetitive thoughts march endlessly through every mind. I cannot use or even think of binoculars without my memory banks making a printout of the overly familiar fact that in World War II the Israeli hero Dayan, serving with the British, lost his eye when a sniper slug hit the binoculars he was using. I do not need to know this all my life. I do not need my memory dredging it up. We have no way of turning these things off. Every brain, including those of Kissinger breadth and force, is cluttered with these bits and snippets, these everlasting echoes.

"House been there long?" I asked him.

"A long time. I don't know how long. It was there when Hub bought the whole tract. That damn Kristin talked him into buying it. It was unique, she said. It sure is unique. It is too far from anything. Hub said I could use it as a beach house. I fixed it up a little. Got a new well dug. Put the generator in and did some wiring. But the generator won't work now."

"I fixed it."

"You did? So quick!"

"A setscrew had worked loose. It wasn't much."

"Gee, Gretel and I are sure glad it's fixed."

"And now you live out here?"

"With no money coming in at all, I couldn't keep the nice apartment I had at North Pass Vista. It was more like a whole house than an apartment."

"Kristin lived there too?"

"She lived in Melody unit. I was over in Symphony, nearer the beach. They're named after music things. Concerto, Harmony, Opera, and so on. The wife of the guy that put them up was a harp player. There are four town houses in each unit. Like Symphony One, Symphony Two, and so on. Mine was Symphony Four. I put my stuff in storage. I didn't want to bring it down here to the beach to this place. I don't think I can keep up the payments on the storage. I'll probably lose that too."

"Too?"

"Like I lost the car. They say I ran it into a tree, but I don't remember. I shouldn't have been driving anyway because my license was suspended. The car was totaled and the insurance company wouldn't pay a dime because I wasn't a licensed driver any more. How do you like that? I was with them sixteen years! It was right about then that Gretel got here, thank God. Now that she's here, everything will be okay."

"When we got here she was doing the laundry in those big drums. Are you two so hard up you can't spare quarters for a coin laundry? We passed one back at the edge of town."

"Oh, we could afford that, but Gretel is stubborn. And she gets these ideas about things. She wants to see just how independent of everything we can be. No telephones or power companies. She's trying to grow stuff in a garden she planted way the other side of the hard road, on the edge of the marsh, but the birds and rabbits are giving her a hard time. And the mosquitoes eat her when she goes over to work on it. But she won't give up. Not on anything. Ever."

We came to the path that wound up to the crest of the dune and down the other side. Gretel and Meyer were on the deck. John Tuckerman held up the fillets of jack, and Gretel applauded him.

She came down and got the fish. Once she had hefted it, she asked us to stay to lunch. Meyer sidestepped the question and left it up to me. I said we'd be delighted, and thanks very much for asking us.

We tipped the soapy-water drum downslope, and she grilled the fish over the embers from the driftwood fire.

While I had been with John Tuckerman, Gretel and Meyer had wrung out and hung up the clothes. We had lunch off chipped blue willowware plates at a table by the windows in the small bare living room of the beach cottage. We had the grilled fish, canned peas, and black coffee. The biggest object in the room was the fireplace. There was seashells on the windowsills and the mantel. Gretel put on a blue work shirt over her bikini before coming to the table. She glowed with strength and health and vitality. I envied John Tuckerman. There were golden flecks in the deep brown pigment of her eyes, near the pupils. The whites of her eyes were the blue-white of peak physical condition. Through the meal we talked fishing, and over coffee I said, "Where were you before you came here, Gretel?"

"I came out of the nowhere into the here."

"We don't answer questions," John said earnestly. "That's one of the rules. She says I could get into real—"

"Hey!" she said. "We don't have to explain why we don't answer questions."

"Okay," he said grumpily. "But you sure are bossy."

"There are reasons," she said. She smiled at Meyer. "We've had other visitors."

"Like Fletcher. Like that damned Fletcher."

"Hush, dear," she said.

"A deputy sheriff?" I asked. "Now in Mexico with the insurance investigator?"

"He said they were going there," John said.

She glared at me, her face darkening in anger. She said, "I think it is pretty damned low to keep digging and digging away at somebody who . . . who . . ." She didn't know how to say it in front of him.

"You're cute," I said. "Both of you. You make a cute couple. Speaking about low. Sure, John Tuckerman. Keep your mouth shut. And deprive a very decent hard-luck man named Van Harder from making a living at his trade. There is a smell of money in the wind, lady, and you seem to turn toward it like some kind of weathervane. You came out of the nowhere into the here to brush up an old affair and get closer to the money."

She stared at me, aghast. "You think I'm his old lady?"

"She's his sister," Meyer said. And as soon as it was said, I could see it. Bone structures, coloring.

She thumped the table with her fist, making coffee dance in the cups. "I came here to help John any way I can, because there isn't anybody else left in the world who will help him."

"In spite of all your marvelous motives and family spirit and so on, Gretel, it still leaves Van Harder on the beach."

"He ran the *Julie*," John said. "Hub put half of one of those horse capsules in—"

"John! Shut up, shut up, shut up! Jesus God! They can nail you for conspiracy to defraud, or whatever the right words for it are. Now tell me, John, what really happened to Van Harder?"

"I guess he must have had that big drink Hub gave him on an empty stomach. Or else he brought some liquor aboard with him and drank it too. He passed out when we were on automatic pilot, and one of the girls got sick and went up there and saw him and came down and told us. We decided we'd better go back to Timber Bay. When we found the pass and started in, Hub went up on the bow and—"

I interrupted him. He had been reciting it. He had learned it by rote. "Okay, okay," I said. "Van got half a horse tranquilizer. I know the other story by heart too."

John looked at Gretel for guidance. She said to me, "I guess you can understand why we can't help your friend. Why John can't help your friend. The establishment took such a beating, they would be glad to stuff anybody in jail."

John Tuckerman made a muffled sound. We all looked at him. His eyes had filled and one tear broke and ran down his cheek. "He could have taken me with him," he said. "Everything would have been all right. If he had to go, he could have taken me. Instead of that bitch architect. That dirty rotten bitch architect." His voice broke.

Meyer said in his jolliest tone, "John and I are going to clean up here, while you and Travis take a walk on the beach, Gretel."

She looked at him and then she looked at me, a steady, suspicious, interrogatory look, trying to see through my eyes and into my skull. There was a sudden impact, almost tangible. I wanted to be more than I was, for her. I wanted to stop being tiresome and listless and predictable. I wanted to be thrice life-size, witty and urbane, bright and reliable, sincere and impressive—all for her. She merited better than the pedestrian person she stared at.

The hostility and suspicion faded into a look of doubt, a lip-biting tension. "So come on," she said, and I had to hurry to catch her halfway up the dune.

We stopped at the crest, the early afternoon sun speckling the sea with silver mirrors, aiming arrows of light at us. To the south, birds worked a moiled area of bait.

"We have to trust somebody," she said. She looked sidelong at me. "I've had terrible luck in the trusting department."

Before I could respond she was off down the slope, leggy and swift, heading south down the beach.

CHAPTER

10

"You can't really appreciate the change in John unless you'd known him before. So quick and funny and exasperating. If he'd just had the motivation, he could have been a successful person. Well, maybe he was a successful person. At least he had sense enough not to try marriage. He would have made a terrible husband. As bad, I guess, as the one I married too young, Billy Howard. I think John has always been more than half in love with Julie Lawless anyway."

We were two miles down the beach from the cottage. A driftwood weatherworn section of wooden dock projected from the shallow slope of the dune—a shelf for sitting. She poked at the sand with a stick as she talked, making small avalanches.

"He tied his life to Hub Lawless's life. And when everything went sour for Hub and he decided to run, he shucked John off. John has been an intensely loyal person. He drank for oblivion, and I think he found some . . . permanent kind. He is . . . a simplified personality now. At the time of the hearing and the investigation, he was himself. I couldn't be here then, but I could tell from the newspaper stories. He could handle it. He couldn't get through that sort of thing now. He can be tricked, like a child."

"The way I was tricking him."

"Yes. It made me angry."

"You didn't hide it."

"Short fuse, friend."

"Short fuse and long talk. You talk around and around it, and you keep on wondering if you should tell me anything, or if you should keep on waffling."

"I just met you a few hours ago."

"I came here at Van Harder's request, to clear his name."

"You're a private detective, then?"

"Me? No. Those people have to have licenses and be bonded and carry insurance and report to the law people wherever they go. They charge fees and have office phones and all that. I just do favors for friends. Sort of salvage work."

"But Van Harder is paying you?"

"No. He offered me ten thousand dollars in time payments if I could do it. He thinks his good name is worth twenty thousand. When I find things for people, I keep half. But I won't take that kind of money from him. I'll have to find some way of saving his pride, *if* I can get his situation reconsidered. He's spent his life on the water. It isn't fair that he should be victimized by some sharp operator rigging his own disappearance with other people's money."

"And leaving his best friend, as he always called John, flat broke in the bargain."

"Self-preservation. A strong instinct."

She poked away at the sand, bent so far forward I could not see her face. I looked at the smooth brown legs, the flow of the complex curves, one into the next, lovely as music. She had shed the work shirt. It lay on the weathered wood between us. The bikini string bit into the skin of her warm brown back, and I followed the way her back narrowed down to her waist, then flared to the hips. I read the calligraphy of the round knuckles of the bent spine, and of the twinned dimples farther down.

She turned sharply and caught me staring at her. She said, "I suppose your hairy pal is worming it all out of John anyway."

"I could say yes in hopes it would open you up. Actually, I don't know. He may be leaving it up to you to decide."

She laughed. "When we were alone he gave me a little lecture on how people have washed their garments, down through the ages. He's really a nice person."

"Maybe we both are."

"I have a track record that tells me not to trust my instincts. I have been undone by scoundrels, sir."

"And probably scoundrels have been undone by you."

"Sometimes. Thanks for the confidence. Anyway . . ." She told me what she had learned from her brother, little by little.

When things had begun to go bad, Hub had begun joking about escape. He and John had made up wild plans, as a sort of running fantasy. But as things got worse, the jokes became strained, and the planning became more serious. John had not learned until very far along in the planning process that it had been Hub's wish, all along, to take Kristin Petersen with him, or to meet her there. John had thought this ironic, as the architect was really the person who had encouraged Hub to make the land purchases which had finally foundered him. Apparently, according to John's observations, the affair between Hub and Kristin was intensely physical, the kind of obsessive infatuation which seemed to blind him to all consequences.

The most delicate and intricate chore had been the conversion, over three months, of assets into cash, with frequent trips to Tampa, Clearwater, and Orlando. They had taken a four-day trip to Mexico in late February, ostensibly to hunt cat in the mountains, actually to arrange for surgery in Guadalajara at a later date, and to set up a hideaway for Hub and Kristin after the operations.

When I asked where, she said that John didn't know, that he had remained in Guadalajara while Hub flew off somewhere, but John had the impression Hub went to Yucatan.

They had done a lot of the planning right there in the cottage, arguing, picking flaws, finding solutions.

The cash had been hidden at the ranch. On March twenty-second, Hub Lawless had put the cash in the yellow jeep and driven out to the cottage. John Tuckerman had driven out there and picked him up and taken him back into Timber Bay. John had arranged for the two girls to come along on the *Julie* so that there would be innocent witnesses to the accident. Hub had made certain neither girl saw the powerful tranquilizer in powder form being dumped into Harder's token drink.

Just when it was about time for one of them, John or Hub, to go topside and "discover" Harder, one of the girls became seasick and went up and saved them the trouble. After she came down, they went up to see, then turned the cruiser around to go back. Hub went below and told the girls what they were doing, and also told them that now they were going into the wind, and it was very cold and ugly up above.

Hub went back up. John had taken the *Julie* as close inshore as he dared. When they came opposite the harsh gleam of the Coleman lantern John had left lighted on the deck railing of the beach cottage, Hub clapped John on the back, thanked him, shook his hand, and went overboard. When he was in the sea, he quickly yanked the cord that inflated the life belt he was wearing. They had tested it several times in rough water off John Tuckerman's beach. Hub was confident using it and could make good time through the water.

John piloted the *Julie* to Timber Bay, went in the pass, thumped the bow onto the sandbar, began yelling for the girls, and threw the life ring over. He stayed and answered all questions, over and over and over. It was very late when he got back to his apartment. In the early morning he drove out to the cottage and to his consternation, saw that the yellow jeep was still there. He found Hub Lawless on the cot in the corner of the living room, gray, sweaty, and short of breath. Hub had the feeling, he said, that some round heavy weight was pushing down on his chest. It was more of a feeling of pressure than of pain. He had been much farther from shore than he had realized when he went overboard. He had struggled for a long time and had finally come to shore, exhausted, a long way south of the lantern light. The cold wind chilled him as he walked up the beach, and he had a nagging pain in his left arm and shoulder. It was not until he had climbed the dune that he had fainted. He did not know how long he was out, but he did not think it was very long. He got himself up the stairs and into the cottage, stripped off his sodden clothes, and dressed in the fresh dry clothing. The nausea had started then, and the weakness. He did not feel equal to driving the jeep to Tampa, as planned, and anyway he had already missed his early flight from Tampa to Houston and thus also his Houston-Guadalajara connection. The tickets and the tourist card were in the false name he had selected, Steven Pickering, the name he had used with the clinic in Guadalajara.

He told John Tuckerman to drive back to Timber Bay, contact Kristin Petersen, and tell her what had happened and to come to the cottage. In the original plan she had been supposed to hang around for a week, mourning Hub, and then go back to Atlanta, where she had lived when they met. Later—originally—she was to fly to Mexico and join him at some unknown place in Yucatan. But now, Hub gave John a sealed note to give her. He told John to conceal the jeep nearby in the brush before he left and to stay away from the cottage for a few days.

When John went back to the cottage, there was no one there. Hub was gone. The jeep was gone. There was no note and no money. John had understood that Hub was going to leave him some of the money, which he was to tuck away in a very safe place and not dip into for as long as possible.

"So they went off together in the jeep? With the woman driving, if he couldn't."

"That's what it looks like."

"What was going to happen to the jeep if they'd followed the original plan?"

"Hub was going to leave the claim check for the jeep and the jeep keys in an envelope at the National Airlines desk, and John was going to get down there somehow and claim the jeep and bring it back and take the back roads to get onto the ranch property, and then just park it somewhere on the ranch, as though Hub had left it there."

"Why a jeep, not a car?"

"This road and the hard road become almost impassable five miles south of here. A storm tore it all up. A car couldn't make it, but the jeep could. He was going to come ashore and change, drive the jeep south, and be in Tampa before dawn."

"Carrying money, lots of money? Oh, sure. No baggage check leaving this country, and no baggage check disembarking in Mexico."

"Especially for the first-class passengers. And he had been in and out enough times to know the routines."

"Having the woman leave Timber Bay on the twenty-third, with its being pretty much common knowledge there was something between them—that made it look more like an arranged disappearance."

"Yes, it did. My brother worried about that. He says that Hub worked so hard and carefully to make sure Julia would get the insurance money, it's a shame that all these rumors started. I suppose it was unavoidable. If he couldn't manage the running all by himself, the woman had to help him."

"It seems Hub made it to Guadalajara. Deputy Fletcher and the insurance investigator are down there now."

"Who told them about Guadalajara?"

"When a case like this breaks in the papers, the police get a flood of crank mail and phone calls. They sort them out. Some young woman in Orlando sent an anonymous letter with a color slide to the Sheriff. She had taken the pictures on a Friday, April eighth, at a sidewalk café, of a street scene. She recognized the man in the left of the picture later as being the man whose picture was in all the area newspapers. She said she couldn't come forward because her boyfriend thought she was visiting a friend in California. Sheriff Hack Ames made the connection with the big face-lift and cosmetic-surgery business there."

She stabbed the stick viciously into the sand. "I could spit," she said. "He sits down there fat and happy, and he left all this ruin behind him. Will they find him?"

"I don't know. Bringing him back would be something else. We have an extradition agreement. But he didn't hold anything up with a gun. Right now there isn't any warrant out for him that I know of. And if he has any political friends down there, it could take a long, long time."

"Was that woman in the picture too?"

"No."

"She must be a real charmer. A dandy person."

"Hub Lawless must have been vulnerable."

"Like my dear little husband, Billy Howard, was vulnerable. Vulnerable and full of big schemes. God! I was eighteen when I married him. We got a job managing a ski resort forty miles from the end of the earth, and I learned to ski well enough to teach beginners. I cooked and kept the books and waited table and cleaned the rooms and drove the bus and sold the gear too. We crapped out. Too much snow. They couldn't keep the roads clear. The customers couldn't get in. We operated a tennis camp for an old pro who gave the lessons and kept trying to hustle me into the bushes. I cooked and kept the books and waited table and cleaned the rooms and drove the bus and sold the gear, and got to play pretty good tennis. Until the old pro dropped dead on the court and his sister fired us. Shall I go on? Why am I telling you all this?"

"Because I want to know all this."

"Sure. We ran a summer camp for little rich kids. I taught archery, riding, swimming, diving, woodcraft, judo, finger painting, and track. I cooked and kept the books and waited table and drove the bus and pitched softball. Billy made a pass at one of the young mothers who came up to visit, and she told the owners, and we got hurled out in the middle of August. More?"

"Can there be more?"

"You can believe it. So we got a job running a fat farm for California ladies. A dietician cooked. Local high-school girls waited table and cleaned the rooms. All I had to do was run all the exercise classes, keep the books, keep the weight charts, organize their day to keep them all busy, drive the bus, and so on and so on. So I was taking them on a little jog, and I looked back, still jogging, to see how the stragglers were coming along, and one of them ahead of me fell down, and I tripped over her and broke my wrist. See, it wasn't set exactly right. It's a little bit lumpy."

I examined her right wrist. The bone seemed to jut out a little. Her forearm was baked to a warm golden brown, with the fine hairs, scorched white by the sun, lying against the brown with a tender, infinite neatness. I said it didn't look lumpy.

"We're coming to the best part," she said. "I couldn't keep the books and records. The owners had to hire a bookkeeper. They cut my pay. The bookkeeper was cute. Dear darling Billy ran off with her. She couldn't even keep the books right. She was one of those helpless ones with the big melting eyes. She sighed a lot. I don't think she bathed as much as her mother might have wished. And the reason I couldn't come here sooner, after I had seen the whole mess in the papers and called John, was because I was not supposed to leave the state until I got the final papers of divorce. The lawyer said it might gum things up. He said I could go if I wanted, and it would probably be all right. But I wanted to be very damned sure that my seven years of marriage were over. Aren't we supposed to change completely every seven years, all the cells or something? I was ready. Wow, was I ever ready! I put in seven years of sixteen-hour days. Seven years of hard, hard labor."

"What are you going to do afterward? After all this?"

"When the time comes, I'll think about it."

Our eyes caught and held for a few moments. When she looked away, I had a very strange feeling. I felt as if I had shucked some kind of drab outer skin. It was old and brittle, and as I stretched and moved, it shattered and fell off. I could breathe more deeply. The Gulf was a sharper blue. There was wine in the air. I saw every grain of sand, every fragment of seashell, every movement of the beach grasses in the May breeze. It was an awakening. I was full of juices and thirsts, energies and hungers, and I wanted to laugh for no reason at all.

I reached and caught the lumpy wrist, and she looked at me with surprise and faint irritation, gave one tug to get away, and then did not resist. I did not have to worry about her reaction. I could make her understand anything.

"Gretel, thanks for telling me all you know. Thanks for trusting me. I'm going to help you with this. Meyer and I will help you, and we'll get it all sorted out."

"For half of what?"

"For half of the way you look right now."

"Come *on!* You've been in the sun too long."

She snatched her work shirt and we headed back. She seemed to have been infected by some of my exuberance. At one point she sprinted away from me, running on the packed sand where the tide had receded. She ran well, and it took a determined effort to overtake her. She stopped when I clapped my right hand on her left shoulder. She was breathing hard, and she inspected me and discovered I wasn't.

"Good shape, huh?" she gasped.

"Better than my usual. I helped a friend bring a big ketch up from the Grenadines to Lauderdale. Lots of wind, all from the wrong direction. A person could get in the same kind of good shape by spending a month working with weights while rolling downhill."

"Are you a freak about condition?" She was recovering her wind quickly.

"I guess to a certain extent. I get into situations where it is nice to be quick, and healthy to be persuasive. I get into them oftener than most. If I get bloated and slow, somebody is going to put me out of business. So when I get the slow bloats, I get the guilts, and when I'm in shape I feel righteous and smug—but what I do is keep going from one extreme to the other, and getting it back gets rougher every year. How about you? Freaky?"

"Not really. But I'm sort of a jock. You know, born with good coordination and good muscle memory. I learn physical things quickly. I like competition. I don't have to tell you I am one big girl. Six foot one-half inch. One hundred and forty-eight pounds of meat. Solid meat. You are one man who doesn't make me feel all that huge, though. I guess I like to stay in shape because you can do things better, and you feel so much better. It's kind of a . . . a hummy feeling. You know your motor is running."

We went back to the cottage. Meyer was on the veranda deck reading a copy of the *Reader's Digest* for July 1936. He said it had a lot of uplift in it. He said he had heard that the ideal article for the *Reader's Digest* would have a rather long title: "I Dropped My Crutches, Abandoned My Electronic Submarine, Climbed the Undersea Mountain and Found God." He said John Tuckerman was napping. He had felt very tired.

John came yawning out as we talked. He sat in an old rocker and nodded from time to time as Gretel told him that she had told me all about the plan he had cooked up with Hub for the disappearance. He did not seem especially concerned.

He smiled at me and said, "I tried to talk Hub out of it. I really did. I told him he was letting all his friends down. He was letting down the people who were still working for him, who were still loyal. He wouldn't listen. He said everything had gone to hell and there was no way to salvage any of it, except to leave and take what he could with him. All he could really think about was getting into the Petersen woman's pants. Excuse me, Gretel."

"Was she all that great?" Gretel asked.

"Depends on what you like," John said. "She's kind of pale and round-faced. but with hollows in her cheeks, pale green eyes, soft quiet little voice, silver-blond hair that she braids a lot, and a slender body, but with real big tits. She's quiet but she's used to giving orders, and when she tells somebody to do something she has a way of making them jump and do it. She walks into a room and you know she is . . . somebody. Somebody important."

"How did she act when you gave her the message?" I asked him.

"Oh, she was upset. She paced around her place, nibbling her thumb knuckle, telling me to shut up whenever I tried to say I was leaving."

"She had opened the note?"

"Yes, but she didn't tell me what it said."

"But the verbal message," Meyer asked, "as I think you told me before your nap, was to tell her to come out to the cottage, was it not?"

"Yes. To tell her he'd had some kind of mild heart attack, and to come out. He told me to stay away from the cottage for a few days and to hide the jeep in the brush before I left."

"Then," said Meyer, "the written message had to be some kind of instruction to her, to do something *before* coming out, because if he was going to see her out there, he would be able to tell her any other instruction. And it had to be something he didn't want to tell you."

"I don't know what that would be. He knew he could trust me."

"We have one problem to solve first," Meyer said. We looked at him. He looked very pleased with himself. "It's so obvious," he said. "Certainly she didn't *walk* out here from the town!"

In the silence, Gretel said, "It's like that game of logic where you have to get everybody across the river in one boat in so many trips. What kind of car did she have, Johnny?"

"A small rental car. A red Mazda five-door hatchback. Hub rented it for her from Garner Wedley, owns the Texaco station out on Dixie Boulevard and has the franchise for Bonus Rental. I know because I had to take it to be gassed and serviced a few times. It drove nice."

"Oh, John, did you have to do things like that for him? Putting gas in his girl friend's car?"

He shook his head as if in irritation at her denseness. "Honey, you just don't understand. Anything that Hub asked me to do, I was *glad* to do. It didn't matter what. I worked for him, and I was his friend too. And I still am, no matter what."

"Did the Texaco station man get his car back?" I asked. I saw Meyer nod his approval out of the corner of my eye.

John Tuckerman frowned. "My memory has gone so rotten. It seems I remember Garn chewing at me about something or other, about that car. But a lot of people were chewing at me about a lot of things back then, that last little bitty part of March. My feeling is he got it back but there was something wrong with it, wrong with the deal somehow."

We asked some more questions. What sort of container was the money in? It was in a fake gas can chained and padlocked to the rack on the back of the jeep. How much money? Hub never said. But it was a lot. A real lot. Hub said he was sorry he'd never see his daughters again, and never see John again. But a man had to do what he had to do.

Where had the money been hidden out at the ranch? As they had collected more and more of it, turning pieces of paper and equipment and supplies into cash, Hub had kept it in various places, moving it every time he got nervous about it. And the more it got to be, the more often he got nervous.

What did you mean by a fake gas can? It was one of those heavy-duty GI gas cans, tall and narrow and painted yellow like the jeep. There were two of them, and they fitted in brackets in the back, on either side of the spare-tire bracket. Hub had hacksawed a can in half and soldered a flange on the inside of the lower half, so the top half could be fitted back on. He packed all the money in there, put the can in the bracket, ran the heavy-duty rubberized chain through the heavy handle that was part of the top of the can, pulled the chain tight, and padlocked it. From then on he felt easy about the money. He could park it right down near the bank. Whenever he left the jeep, he took the distributor rotor along with him. He made jokes with John Tuckerman about the kind of gas in the gas can. He told John some of it was his and would be left behind.

I said to John, "I suppose you've hunted for the money, for what he was supposed to leave here for you."

John looked at me. He wore the somewhat defiant expression of a sly child. "I won't say."

"We looked for it," Gretel said wearily.

"We never did!" John yelled. "Never!"

And from the subtle gesture she made, I knew it was time for us to go.

It was almost four fifteen on Saturday afternoon when we headed back toward Timber Bay.

Meyer said, "I haven't heard that infuriatingly tuneless whistling of yours for a long, long time. Congratulations."

"On what?"

"On coming back to the land of the living."

"It shows? I was that bad?"

"You were that bad, and for a long time. You were, in fact, committing the eighth deadly sin."

"I was? What is that?"

"You were boring, Travis. Very boring."

"Oh?"

"Self-involved people are always boring. Nobody can ever be as interested in them as they are in themselves."

"Sorry about that."

"You probably couldn't help it. It's been coming on since before we went up to Bayside that time."

"If I've been so depressing, why didn't you just bug off?"

"There was always the chance you'd come out of it."

"I feel as if I had."

"She seems to be an exceptional person."

"Gretel? Yes. Yes, she is. I like these dunes. They give it a nice wild unspoiled look. We'll have to cruise this coast sometime. Maybe head north from here."

"What are you smiling at?"

"Me? Was I smiling?"

CHAPTER

11

The light breeze was out of the southwest. The sky was cloudless. The late afternoon sun was hot. Shopping centers were jammed. So were the beaches and tennis courts. Meyer took the Dodge to go find out about the rental Mazda. I walked north along the uplands above the beach until I came to North Pass Vista.

I walked around the place for a few minutes and located Symphony, where John Tuckerman had lived, and Melody. Each was a cluster of four small two-story town houses. Melody Three was where Kristin Petersen had lived. Someone else was in there. A slight baldheaded man was in the narrow carport, painting a small chest of drawers, biting his lip as he made each careful stroke.

The office was in a unit farthest from the water. There was a sign stuck into the lawn and another over the doorbell. A man opened the door and looked out at me. He had half glasses and a boot-camp haircut. He looked to be about forty.

"Yes?" he said, managing to inject hostility and disbelief into that single syllable.

"I want to ask some questions about Kristin Petersen, please."

"I have no interest in answering them."

As he started to close the door I put my palm against it and gave a hearty shove. It drove him back and banged the door open.

"Hey!" he said. "You can't force your way in here!"

The foyer was a shallow office, with a secretarial desk, two chairs, and a gray file cabinet. He picked up the phone and dialed the operator. I took my time finding the To Whom It May Concern card from Devlin Boggs. He asked the operator for the police. I held the card up in front of him. He told the police it was a mistake and he was sorry. He took the card, turned it over and read the message, and handed it back.

"What's your interest in Miss Petersen?"

"My interest is enough to drop subpoenas on you if I think you are holding back."

"Oh. You're an attorney?"

"What is your name?"

"Stanley Moran."

"Mr. Stanley Moran, I don't want you to keep asking me questions. I am not here to answer questions. I am here to ask them. Maybe you would like to phone Mr. Boggs and get his opinion on whether or not you should ask me a lot of questions."

"But how do I know you—"

"Or I can come back with Hack Ames, or Deputy Fletcher, or anybody you might think of who can reassure you."

"Why are you smiling like that?"

"Because the angrier I get, the more I smile. It's a form of nervous anxiety. When I break out laughing, I usually hit people."

He sat down behind the desk, picked a pencil up and

put it down, and moved a stapler a few inches to the left to line it up with the edge of the small desk.

"There's nothing I've said or done to get angry at."

"When did she leave here?"

"Do you know how many times I've had to answer—"

"Stanley, I'm smiling again."

"Oh. She left here on the twenty-third. The precise time cannot be established. She had a visitor at ten thirty that morning. The police were very interested in that, and they finally were able to identify the visitor as Mr. Tuckerman, who was then living in Symphony Four. After he left, she drove out and was gone the rest of the day. People were interested in her movements because of her—cough—relationship with Mr. Lawless, who at that time was believed drowned out in the bay. They were searching for the body. Her car was seen back in her carport at about eleven on the night of the twenty-third; however, it was gone when I walked around the area at six the following morning. I rise early. So the assumption is that she departed during the night of the twenty-third, or very very early on the morning of the twenty-fourth."

"She took everything with her?"

"Well . . . *practically* everything. All her personal things, of course. But she left a few things she had bought for the unit. Let me see now. Two very primitive-looking pottery bowls. Ugly things, actually. One small table, of blond wood with the top inset with blue and green tiles. One framed print that I can't make head or tail of—you can hardly tell which way up to hang it. Our storage space here is very limited. There's a limit to how long I can hold these items. I might say that Miss Petersen was not exactly my favorite tenant here at Vista. She made *very* disparaging remarks about the decor and the architecture. My wife and I have worked very hard to make these units attractive and livable. She had no reason to call them vulgar. We do not set ourselves up as moral arbitrators or—"

"Arbiters."

"What?"

"I have been listening to a man named Meyer too long. Go ahead. You were saying?"

"People's morals are their own affair. But she did, time and again, 'entertain' Mr. Lawless here overnight. His car would be parked in her drive and I would sometimes see him leave in the early morning."

"Shameless!" I said.

"What else do you want to know?"

"Did mail keep coming for her?"

"Yes, until I filled out a permanent change-of-address card and signed her name to it. I had it sent to the Atlanta address she gave me when she rented Melody Three. Of course, I have told all of this so many times that—"

"Did she have any particular friends among the other renters?"

"Not one that I know of."

"And you would know."

"I like to think so. After the projects for which Mr. Lawless had hired her were indefinitely delayed, we thought she would probably go right back to Atlanta, but she stayed on. She would go over onto our beach for a little while every day, and she would swim in the pool. I know that quite a few men tried to strike up a conversation with her. She was quite . . . noticeable in her swimming attire. But she never responded at all."

"What do you think happened to her, Mr. Moran?"

"Why do you want to know what I *think?*"

"Why do you always answer a question with a question?"

"Do I? Excuse me. My wife and I think she ran away

with Mr. Lawless. We think they are living in Mexico under new names."

"Why would she leave her profession?"

"Because of being in love with Mr. Lawless, I would guess. Anyway, I don't know that she was really good at being an architect. They say that the other things she has designed were really not great successes. They say she wasn't in great demand, actually."

"Did she leave owing you money?"

"Heavens, no! We ask for the first and the last two months in advance. Technically you could say she was paid up through this month, through May."

"Did she pay by check on an Atlanta bank?"

"Yes. I can tell you which bank. Just a moment. I noted it on my copy of the lease."

He got it out of the file. "The first check was for fifteen hundred and sixty dollars, including tax, on Atlanta Southern Bank and Trust, check number eight-twenty, account number four-four-eight, four-four-one."

I wrote it down and said, "You keep good records."

"Thank you, mister—"

"McGee," I said, moving toward the door. "And thank you for everything."

"No trouble at all," he said. "Any time."

The world is full of contention and contentious people. They will not tell you the time of day or day of the month without their little display of hostility. I have argued with Meyer about it. It is more than a reflex, I think. It is an affirmation of importance. Each one is saying, "I can afford to be nasty to you because I don't need any favors from you, buster." It is also, perhaps, a warped application of today's necessity to be cool. Stan Moran in his half glasses and brush cut and improvised office, managing the Vista in order to save rent, was all too conscious of being nobody, and it had curdled him. I guessed he would have some sort of disability pension from somewhere. Or

144

maybe he was a retired enlisted man who had been company clerk for too many abusive officers. If I were King of the World I would roam my kingdom in rags, incognito, dropping fortunes onto the people who are nice with no special reason to be nice, and having my troops lop off the heads of the mean, small, embittered little bastards who try to inflate their self-esteem by stomping on yours. I would start the lopping among post-office employees, bank tellers, bus drivers, and pharmacists. I would go on to checkout clerks, bellboys, prowl-car cops, telephone operators, and U.S. Embassy clerks. By God, there would be so many heads rolling here and there, the world would look like a berserk bowling alley. Meyer says this shows a tad of hostility.

As Meyer was not yet back, I decided to walk all the way around to the Cedar Pass Marina and take a look at the *Julie* and have a couple of words with DeeGee Walloway, resident aboard. It was a fine time of day for walking, and there was lots to look at around that great curve of Bay Street. I whistled one of my tuneless tunes, strode my loose-jointed, ambling, ground-covering way, squinted when the sun shone between the buildings on the bay shore. I smiled at a brown cocky city dog and nodded at a fish-house cat nested into a windowsill. Gulls tipped and dipped, yelling derision and dirty gull-words. Steel tools made music when dropped on concrete floors. Cars and trucks belched blue, gunning at the lights. A paste-white lady with sulfur curls, wearing bullfighter pants and a leopard top, slouched in a doorway and gave me a kissy-looking smile. Spillane had shot her in the stomach a generation ago, and she was still working the streets. I told her it was a lovely evening and kept going. Even the wind-sped half sheet of newsprint that wrapped itself around my ankle had some magic meaning, just beyond the edge of comprehension. I picked it off and read that firebombs had crisped four more West German children, that 30 percent of Florida high-school graduates couldn't make change, and 50 percent couldn't comprehend a traffic citation. I read that unemployment was stabilized, UFOs had been seen over Elmira, the latest oil spill was as yet unidentified, and, to make a room look larger, use cool colors on the walls, such as blues and greens and grays.

I wadded it to walnut size and threw it some fifteen feet at a trash container. The swing lid of the trash container was open about an inch and a half. If it went in, I would live forever. It didn't even touch the edges as it disappeared inside. I wished it was all a sound stage, that the orchestra was out of sight. I wished I was Gene Kelly. I wished I could dance.

I went into the marina office. It was shipshape, clean, efficient-looking. The man in white behind the desk looked like a Lufthansa pilot. "Sir?" he said with measured smile.

"My name is McGee. I phoned from Lauderdale earlier in the week, about dock space for a houseboat."

He flipped through his cards. "Yes. The arrival date was indefinite. I have it here you will arrive between the twenty-fifth, next Wednesday, and the twenty-ninth. Let me see. Marjory took the call. I assume she told you it is no problem this time of year. Fifty-three feet. *The Busted Flush?*"

"As in poker, not as in plumbing."

"Length of stay indefinite?"

"That's correct. I'll let you people know as soon as I know." I hesitated, and decided to try it out. "Captain Van Harder is bringing her around for me."

It did startle him. The eyes of eagles clouded for a moment. The muscles of the square jaw worked. "I probably should not say anything to you. Van is as good as there is around here. I don't think he should have lost his license. Did you know he had?"

"Yes."

"This is something a lot of people do not know—if you hire a man to operate your boat and he doesn't have a license, if there is any trouble, you might have difficulty with your insurance company."

"I knew him years ago when he fished charter out of Bahia Mar at Lauderdale, before he went into shrimp and had his bad luck. He's bringing it around as a favor to me. No hiring involved and no passengers aboard. So I think it's okay."

He nodded. "I would think it's okay too."

"What is the status of the *Julie?*"

"The legal status? Clouded. The bank has put a lien on her. So she just sits, God knows how long. I know that nobody is going to move her until we get our dock rental. The mate is living aboard."

"Is he there now?"

He started to say he didn't know, but a smallish, dark, and pretty woman came in from the room behind the office. He introduced us. She remembered my call. He asked Marjory if she'd seen Walloway leave the marina and she said she thought he was still aboard.

I remembered the *Julie* from having seen her at Pier 66. She looked even better in the dying day. She sparkled from one end to the other. The brightwork was like mirrors. Varnish gleamed. Lines were smartly coiled, all the fenders perfectly placed. The boat basin had two main docks at right angles to the shoreline, with finger piers extending out on either side of the main docks. Small stuff was moored at the finger piers between the two docks, where there was less maneuvering room. The *Julie* was on the outside of the left-hand dock, moored to one of the middle finger piers, stern toward the dock, starboard against the finger pier.

A hinged section of rail was turned back amidships to make space for the little boarding ramp. Its wheels moved very slightly as the breeze moved the hull of the vessel.

DeeGee Walloway came toward the ramp, stuffing his keys into the pocket of his tight whipcord cowboy pants. He wore boots, a silver-gray shirt with lots of piping and pearl buttons, a blue neckerchief, and a Saturday-night cowboy hat. He looked like Billy Carter, except he was half again as tall and twice as broad.

I knew at once why that name had rung a small bell in the back of my head. He stopped and stared at me. He snapped his fingers, rubbed his mouth, shoved his hat back, and said, "McGee!"

"How you, Deej?"

"Son of a bitch! Hey, is Van bringing your houseboat around from the other side?"

"Word sure gets around."

"What happened, he phoned Eleanor Ann the other day, and she said he sounded a little more up than he has lately, and he told her everything would be working out for him, but I don't see how the hell it can. He told her he was bringing a houseboat around—and it would take maybe seven or eight days—for a fellow name of McGee he used to know in Lauderdale. So I figured it might just be the same one. I only knew you that one time, but I never forgot it."

Somebody had brought him to Meyer's annual birthday chili bash one year. After enough drinks he had decided to whip people. He told me later that it usually came out that way. Not ugly, not loud, not mean. Just an urge to whip people for the fun of it. If I had gotten him fresh, I don't think I could have handled it. But he had whipped Jack Case and Howie Villetti before Chookie looked me up and told me some jerk named Walloway was spoiling the party. Jack and Howie had put quite a strain on Deej. He had a little sprain in his neck that made him hold his head funny, and he wasn't going to be able to see out of his left eye much longer. We had the party that year on a sandspit called Instant Island. He was grinning and chuckling. He was a happy man, doing what he liked best. I spent a disheartening fifteen minutes before he finally stayed down. He came at me the next day and, because I had learned his tricks, it took about ten minutes. He came at me the third day, and that was the day I saw one coming at me so late that all I could do was duck my head into it. It broke his hand and left me with double vision for two weeks.

"I just *know,*" he said, "that I should have been able to whip you."

"No, DeeGee. No. Get your mind off it."

"It still bothers me. But what the hell. I'm not in no kind of shape like I was then. Look at the gut on me. And I hardly got any wind at all. You, you look like you're in training for something. You get yourself lean and mean to come over see old DeeGee Walloway?"

"Get your mind off it."

"The only way I could take you now is sucker-punch you first. And that isn't my style. There's no fun in that."

"Can you whip everybody in Timber Bay?"

"Pretty much most of them."

"Nicky Noyes?"

"Oh, *hell,* yes! He hits like he was throwing rocks, but he don't aim. What you doing right now? Want to walk around to a couple of places and check the action? We can find us some ass and bring it back here to the boat. It isn't widespread like you got it in Lauderdale, but it's around if you look. That's what I was planning on, it being Saturday night."

"Can I take a look at the *Julie?* Don't mean to trouble you."

"Hell, no trouble."

He gave me the tour. I looked it all over. In spite of

my protests, I had to look at the engines. He lifted the hatch and shone a light on the big GM diesels. The daylight was almost gone.

"A man could *eat* off that block there," he said proudly. "That's one thing ol' Van always yapped about. And I ain't slacked off an inch since he got busted."

"What's going to happen to her?"

"God only knows. The bank is giving me walk-around money for staying aboard her and keeping her up. I expect they'll get the title cleared and sell her."

"I understand you were out of town when the trouble happened."

"That's right. I was up to Waycross, where I come from. My daddy was bad off. It had been coming on a long time, but he was a stubborn old coot. He got hoarse and it hurt him to swaller. And his neck started getting bigger. My mom noticed that and she nagged him and nagged him until he went to the doctor. Soon as the doctor told him he wasn't a-going to make it, my daddy started going fast. He was nearly gone when I got there, but he could smile and nod at me, and write words on a pad. You know, I never made that man happy with me. Not one time. I damn almost did when I got into the University of Georgia on a football scholarship, but then I got throwed out of the first two games I got into. I was a right tackle, and then I got throwed out of the school itself, signed on in the Navy, and got throwed out of that for discipline problems. He wanted so bad for me to be somebody. But, shit, I'm all I want to be. I think my daddy lasted two days and a half or so after I heard Mr. Lawless got lost overboard. I was holding his hand there at the end. His hand gave this little quiver and then lay slack. Felt weird."

I went forward to the spot where Lawless was supposed to have fallen overboard. There was a bow rail, braided cable threaded through stanchions, ending abruptly about eight feet from the bow, where the cable was angled down from the final stanchion and made fast to a fitting in the deck. So, if he was on the starboard side, say about seven feet back from the bow and pointed out to the right, bracing himself for the vessel to turn sharp left, and it had instead turned sharp right, then the angled cable would have hit him in the shins and he would have tripped over into the chop and into the night's blackness. They had worked the story out nicely.

"Seen enough?" he asked. "Let's go get a drink, McGee."

As we walked by the lighted office, the little dark-haired lady waved. "Don't futz with that one there," DeeGee said. "Marjory is Coop's old lady. He's the one right there, in the white, runs the place. She acts like she'd fool around, but she doesn't."

"What do you think about the Hub Lawless situation?"

"I wouldn't tell you this if you weren't my friend. Anybody whips me like you did, they're my friend. I think they decided there was no way they could buy Van off. He's straight. So they give him a mickey. Hell, I know the routine. Whenever we got rolling, whenever we settled into cruising speed, Mr. Lawless would bring a couple of drinks topside, one for me and one for Van. He'd check the dials and the course and look around at the weather and either stay with us and have his drink up topside with us, or go on back below with whoever he had aboard."

"Women passengers?"

"No way. Not even that Norway ass he got mixed up with. Jumpin' B. Jesus, but I would have liked me a chop at that one. She was steamy, I'm telling you. She had a fire burned all the time. A tilty little swivel-ass like to break your heart, and she knew it and she waved it. And really great wheels. Mr. Lawless got into that and stopped giving a damn for much of anything else, and no man would blame him too much. But he never brought her aboard. I couldn't hardly believe that he and John Tuckerman had Mishy and that Mexican friend of hers aboard. Mishy is okay. I'd guess offhand that Tuckerman chopped her once in a while. She isn't exactly a pro, but she likes to work you, you know? She needs room rent, or some damn thing, or something to send her poor old mother for her birthday. The way I see it, it was easy to give Van a mickey because of the way Mr. Lawless always gave him a drink. The two girls were below, and I think they were just to dress up the act a little. I think there was somebody in a boat waiting for him to jump, and they took him to an airplane somewhere, maybe a seaplane. They say he took off with a million dollars. You can buy a lot of help for a small piece of that kind of money."

"And he's in Mexico?"

"Sure. He went there a lot. Him and John Tuckerman, hunting, fishing, horsing around. They were best friends of each other. John has been way into the sauce ever since. Bombed out of his mind. What did he ever have besides being Hub's best friend?"

"You liked Lawless?"

"Hell, yes. *Everybody* that worked for him liked him. It really hurt him bad when he had to start laying people off from the businesses he ran. And I know for a fact he was trying to sell the *Julie*. Some people came aboard and looked her over. But it's hard to move a boat like that. She won't suit people with really big money, and she's too much for the average boat fella. I guess if he'd sold her, he'd have had to disappear some other way that would look like he died, so the insurance would go to Mrs. Lawless and the girls."

"Did they come out on the boat much?"

"His family? Oh, sure. But a lot oftener before than after things started to get tight for him. I mean you can run a lot of dollars through those diesels just to move that thing out for an afternoon picnic. She's way overdue for bottom work right now, too. Like the man said, if you have to ask, you can't afford it."

He stopped and motioned me ahead of him, and we went into a place called Lucille's. It was long and dark, with a mahogany bar, a brass rail, sawdust, spittoons, Victorian nudes in gilt frames, bowls of salted peanuts, and a game show on the television perched over the far end of the bar. Lucille squeezed past one of her bartenders to come down toward the entrance and take care of us herself. She was roughly the same size as Walloway, and of only slightly different dimensions. She wore what looked at first glance like a blue bathrobe. She had curly shiny black hair, like a poodle. Her face was white and stiff as wallboard, and she wore lots of eye makeup and lots of burgundy lipstick. I guessed her at about sixty.

"No thumping anybody tonight, Deej!" she ordered in a whiskey contralto.

"Meet my friend name of McGee. He whipped me three times."

She looked me over. "Looks as if he could do it again if he had a mind to. Welcome to my place. Deej, you start anything, you can bet your bucket I'm calling the law early."

"I was only funnin', honey."

"What would you done to him was you serious?"

"I've never been serious in my whole life. Double Bellows and a Millers chaser." I settled for the chaser. He was almost offended, but I explained I had other places to go and I didn't want to start more than I could arrange to finish. I said the previous night was still too fresh in my memory, what I remembered of it.

He told Lucille we had been talking about Lawless and Tuckerman. "If I had a shiny dime for every time I've heard those names in the last two months, I could quit and live ladylike," she said.

"Seen John Tuckerman lately?" he asked her.

"No. He's down to that shack on that land nine miles south Hub bought for his girl friend to design apartments on, and they say his sister is there and she has got him dried out and she's keeping him dry, but his brains are still mush. I don't never want to see him back in here. He was flat-out pitiful. I don't want to see people that make me sorry I sell the stuff. I don't need that kind of guilts. I got more than enough other kinds to go around."

"Did you know Hubbard Lawless?"

"*Everybody* knew Hub. The business people in this town, of which I am one, aren't never going to find it easy to forgive him for what he done to the town. He left us in a depression here. Everything is tied into everything else, and when something quits, other things get hard up on account of it. They say we got fourteen percent unemployment here, and I can feel it in my gross, believe me. But at the same time, everybody knows Hub worked hard to make things work, and he did things for the good of the place too. He contributed to everything when he was doing well. Community Chest, Boys' Club, Cedar Pass Park, bandstand, the Pirate Pageant. He didn't keep regular hours. He was out at that ranch by dawn. He'd work at getting stuff shipped in the middle of the night. Nobody ever knew when that man slept. He always had a smile and a little joke. The way it looks to me, when he got the money for Hula Marine, he should have used it to shore up the other businesses instead of buying the wrong land at the wrong time for the shopping center and that condominium thing."

"What you forget, Lucille," DeeGee said, "he wasn't thinking straight. He had a bad case of nooky disease."

"I don't allow dirty talk in here, and you know it."

"I would have said it nice if I knowed how, Lucille, dammit. You know as well as I do that architect woman had him going in circles."

"Well," she said, "nobody is perfect, and I hope that

wherever he is, Mexico or wherever, he's found some kind of peace, because he sure got awful jumpy before he took off. The town will make out. People will keep coming down from the north. Things will keep going. They always have."

"You have a kind heart, Lucille," DeeGee said.

"Not kind enough to set you up a freebie."

"Okay. Hit me again anyway. Same thing. You, McGee?"

I excused myself and left. He seemed disappointed to have me go. I imagine he got over it in about forty seconds. It would take him about that long to get a good look at the two young women who were going in as I was leaving.

CHAPTER

12

I found Meyer in a booth in the lounge. Business was better than usual. Billy Jean Bailey was tinkling away at her compulsory background-music stint, with no one listening. She looked at me and through me, with no change of expression, and looked away, smiling and nodding at someone else.

After I brought a drink back to the booth, Meyer reported on the rental Mazda.

"I had to wait quite a while for Mr. Wedley. He was out with the tow truck on a pickup. Shorthanded. The boy pumping gas did not know anything about anything. When Wedley came back he was busy on the phone for ten minutes. Finally he was able to tell me about the Mazda. Five days after Lawless disappeared, he got a collect call from airport administration at Orlando. The car had been left in rental car return with the keys behind the sun visor. No one knew when it had been left. Airport administration got into it when Hertz complained that it was their space and they needed it. Garner Wedley's Texaco station address and phone was on the key tag, so they had phoned him and he had arranged to get it picked up. He said that Bonus Rental was a small operation and he had an area franchise, and it said on the rental contract that the car had to be returned to him, but it wasn't. It made him angry to talk about. He said that Hub had rented it for that Scandihoovian female of his, and it worked out to ninety-five seventy-five Hub owed him that he would never see. He told the Sheriff about it, and after an investigation the Sheriff said that it was reasonable to assume that Miss Petersen had driven the car to Orlando, arriving during the morning of the twenty-fourth. He had obtained a picture of her, from the files of the *Bay Journal*, taken when Lawless had given a press party to announce the plans for the new shopping plaza, and had carried the picture over to Orlando and questioned the airline personnel, but found no one who remembered her. He questioned the rental-car people as well, because it has apparently become a popular device to abandon an automobile in an airport parking area and immediately rent another and drive away. Did you know that?"

"Not until this minute."

"If there is any point in it, I suppose we could get one of those pictures from Walter Olivera. But we seem to be getting far afield from Van Harder's problem."

"We are and we aren't. I don't think anybody in authority would take anything Tuckerman might say seriously enough to get Harder some kind of reconsideration. One thing we might do is ask that doctor if Harder's symptoms were consistent with the brand of horse tranquilizer Lawless used at the ranch."

Meyer looked into his notebook, thumbing the pages over. "Here it is. Dr. Sam Stuart. Tuckerman's doctor too, apparently. Shall I make a note of that for Monday? And do it myself?"

"Who else have you got written down there, that we should see?"

"There's Van Harder's wife. Eleanor Ann Harder. She's a nurse at Bay General. And the insurance investigator. I found out his name, by the way. Frederic Tannoy. The company is Planters Mutual General. Tannoy is a troubleshooter for a consortium of middle-sized insurance companies, working on a fee-and-percentage basis. The local agent who sold the policies is a general agent named Ralph Stennenmacher, in the Coast National building."

"Tannoy is with that deputy in Mexico," I said. "Meanwhile, I'll see Stennenmacher on Monday."

B. J. Bailey walked past our booth, giving me one brilliantly venomous glance as she went by. It depressed me. I often wonder what basic insecurity I must have to make me so anxious for approval. I touched the tape over my eye. It had not been entrapment, or even pursuit. No promises made. It had been a happening, not important, happening only because of the time and the place and the shared, nagging sense of depression. There in the yellow-glowing darkness she had been small, limber, greedy, slightly sweaty, her hair stiff from sprayings, humming with her pleasures and making them last. I knew the reason for the hate. No matter how she thought of herself, she was a severely conventional little person and could not accept pleasure for the sake of pleasure, but had to cloak it in romantic rationalization. Like one of her lyrics—it must be love because it feels so good.

I found it ironic that I shared her disease, that puritanical necessity to put acceptable labels on things. The quick jump had always made me feel uneasy. Life cannot become a candy box without some kind of retribution from the watchful gods. I had shared her bed with such a familiar anticipation of the uneasiness that would follow that I had been unable to enjoy her completely. This is the penalty paid by the demipagans, always to have the pleasures diluted by the apprehensions, unless all the labels are in order.

She had found the only label which permitted her all the customary fictions. She was woman betrayed by a scoundrel, a low fellow who had won her with promises, promises, and then turned his back on all her bounty. I leaned out of the booth and looked for her, saw her in the center of a small group of men, laughing with them, drinking with them, eyes a-sparkle. I decided that, when the chance occurred, I would give her a further fiction to apply like a fresh dressing to her pride. Maybe I was in danger and sought to avoid endangering her. Or I was an alcoholic, or dying of something, or had a wife and six kiddies—anything, in fact, which would fit into your average morning soap opera as something worth dramatic dialogue. Meanwhile I would have to accept being an object of hatred, one of your good old boys, one of your male-chauvinist-pig types that went around thinking of women as being something you used when you felt the need, receptacles rather than persons.

"As I was saying," Meyer said.

"Sorry about that."

"Now that I have your attention, let's go over the actual movements of the vehicles and people, as we understand it at the moment. Let this matchbook be the beach cottage. And this one be the Vista. And this one way over here is Orlando. This match is the jeep. This match is the car Tuckerman no longer has. This match is the Petersen Mazda. Here is Tuckerman driving down to the cottage on the morning of the twenty-third to find that Lawless is still there, and sick. Here he goes back to the Vista. He stays there. Kristin goes down to the cottage in the Mazda, let us say in the late morning of the twenty-third. Tuckerman stays away, as Lawless asked, and goes back on the twenty-fifth or -sixth, and finds nothing. The Mazda had been driven to Orlando, where it was discovered on the twenty-seventh. Now let's see how many assumptions we can make about the vanished jeep."

"How many? Lawless recovered enough to drive it on south, over that bad portion of the road, down to Horseshoe Beach, and then he cut over to the main road, and went on down to an airport somewhere, and flew to Mexico."

"And if he didn't recover enough to drive?"

"Let me see. Kristin drove to the cottage on the afternoon of the twenty-third. She finds he is too sick to drive. If he wasn't, they could have stayed with the original plan, for her to hang around mourning her drowned boyfriend for a week or so before following him to Mexico. But with him too sick, she goes back to the Vista after dark, packs, loads the stuff into the Mazda, and comes down and gets him. She could have had him in the back with the luggage, covered with a blanket or something, when they went back through town. They abandoned the Mazda in Orlando, took a flight to Miami, let's say, traveling separately, and flew Mexicana from there over to Cancun, Yucatan."

"You've developed an interesting point, Travis. About their adhering to the original plan if he was well enough to drive the jeep. But what happened to the jeep, if we follow your scenario?"

I shrugged. "Ran it into the swamps or into a deep pond."

"If he wasn't well enough to drive, he wasn't well enough to hide a jeep."

"I see her as an intelligent woman, and physically competent. It wouldn't be anything she couldn't handle."

"Let me change your scenario in one respect. Rather than make two trips out to the cottage in a conspicuous red car, she could have brought Lawless back in with her when she packed up her belongings and left her apartment."

"I'll buy that. It was dark when she drove back. It's a better guess than two trips."

We sat at the booth, staring at the matchbook covers and the matches. "Whichever," I said, "he got to Mexico."

"Whichever," Meyer said, nodding.

There was a deep-throated din of male voices in the big room. Piano tinkle had begun again. I did not want the half drink left in my glass. My stomach felt close to rebellion. This room was not real. It seemed misted and murky, like the contrived visuals in French movies of the second class. Nine miles south reality began, in the long flowing line, that most gentle curve, of the top of a caramel thigh. It began in flecks of gold set close to the black pupil. It began with that elegant balance of the upper body on the pelvic structure, moving in grace to a long long stride.

"Who *was* Gretel?" I asked Meyer.

"She was pretty shrewd. She held an old chicken bone out of the cage for the witch to feel, to hide the fact she was getting plump enough to cook and eat."

"How about a nice beach picnic tomorrow?"

"Nine miles from here?"

He looked at his notebook again. "Eleanor Ann, Stennenmacher, Dr. Stuart."

"Monday we see them. Okay? Monday."

When we walked out of the place, Noyes lurched into me. It seemed half intentional, half inadvertent. He was sweating heavily. His pistolero mustache looked dank and defeated. He had a pale blue guayabera on, so wet the matted chest hair showed through it. The flinty little Neanderthal eyes stared at me, hostile and slightly unfocused.

"B.J. told me the whole thing, you son of a bitch."

"Hey. Take it easy."

"Don't tell me how to take anything, nark."

"Nark?"

"And it's supposed to look like I resisted arrest, right? You don't like people out on bail, right?"

"You must be drunk."

"Check with Mitch. I haven't had drink one."

"Get out of the way, please."

"You think I'm going to let you kill me?"

"You are boring us, Nicky. You are boring me and you are boring my friend Meyer. And you were boring the people at your table at the Cove last night. You are making a new career out of boring people."

"You want to come outside?"

"Walloway says you can hit, but you can't aim. Save yourself a short walk."

He stepped sideways to catch his balance, putting a hand out to grab at the edge of the bar. He muttered something I could not quite hear.

We left. Meyer said we were in a rut, but we might as well try the Captain's Galley again. We were in no special hurry. I looked back and was surprised to see Nicky Noyes, burly in the shadows, following us toward the lot. I stopped and he stopped. Meyer missed me and turned and saw him.

"What's he going to do?" Meyer asked.

"Nothing at all. Trying to bug me a little, I guess."

We went on and he followed. When I looked back again, he was angling over toward his pickup truck. As we neared the gray rental Dodge, I heard the pickup door chunk shut. We reached the Dodge. Meyer reached for the door handle on the passenger side as I took a stride to walk around the front. I heard a very small squeak of tennis shoe rubber on asphalt. I heard a dual *snick-snick*, oily and metallic and horridly efficient. There is some good elemental machinery in my skull, left over from the million years of hunting, of eating and being eaten. I am delighted to have that machinery. If I didn't have it, I would long since have been forcibly retired from my line of work. Primitive computers worked out the direction of the sound, the distance, the probable angle of fire. I spun and dived in a flat trajectory at right angles to the line of fire. My shoulder hit the partially open door and slammed it shut again, a microsecond before I hit Meyer at mid-thigh and tumbled him and myself all the way back to a point six feet behind the right rear wheel. There was a bright-throated *blam-blam,* two great sounds not quite simultaneous, deafeningly close to us, and as I rolled up to one knee I saw Nicky Noyes stagger back and fall heavily.

He broke the gun open, fumbled something out of his pocket, snapped the old shotgun shut again just as I ran through the powder stink, caught the warm double barrels, and ripped it out of his hands.

"Kill you!" he yelled in a raw high voice as he was struggling up. "Kill you!" He turned and ran. For a fellow so unsteady on his feet, he was running pretty good. He was barreling right along. He ran right toward the long curve of Bay Street. Traffic was heavy and fairly fast.

"Oh, no," Meyer said softly, beside me.

Nicky tripped slightly just before he reached the curbing. He went out into traffic in that head-down, forward-tilting manner of the fullback when it's third and one. He ran his head, shoulders, and chest across the hood of a big pale Cadillac, and the front right post of the windshield hit him at waist level. It was slanted enough to hurl him into the air, and more slanted after it had done so. It was almost horizontal, with the white roof buckled into big lumps. His momentum and the impact threw him farther out into traffic, with one sodden bounce and then a floppy roll. Tires of a half-dozen vehicles screamed torment. There were two heavy metallic chunking noises of rear-end collisions, also some thinner sounds as grilles gnashed at fenders. The pale Cadillac had swerved violently to the right to miss running over what remained of Noyes. It came across the curbing and wedged itself between a pair of young banyan trees. People began the yelling and the screaming. People ran out of the North Bay Resort. A car horn began a seemingly endless braying.

I put the shotgun on the front seat of the pickup. I trotted after Meyer. A trucker was lighting some highway flares and setting them out. Meyer hurried toward Noyes, then swerved and galloped to the pale Cadillac. It hadn't wedged itself between the trees as far as the doors. In the reflected brightness of headlights and the red glow of the flares, I saw a white-haired man slumped against the horn ring and, beyond him, crouched low under the bent post and car roof, a plump blond lady. When Meyer eased the man back off the ring, the huge horn-noise ceased.

"He ran right in front of us!" the woman shrilled. "Right in front of the car!"

Meyer stuck his fingers into the side of the driver's throat. He looked at me and shook his head. And so, ignoring the woman, we tugged that old gentleman out of his Cadillac and stretched him out supine on the nearest flat ground. Meyer knelt on the left side near the shoulders and put his left hand under the nape of the man's neck, his right palm on the man's forehead. He pulled up on the neck and pushed down on the forehead to give the head a pronounced backward tilt and clear the airway. He put his ear close to the man's mouth and looked along the chest as he did so, to detect any movement. I knelt at the man's right side and found the place to brace the heel of my right hand, two finger widths above the sternum, left hand atop right hand, elbows straight and locked. Meyer checked the pulse again and gave three quick exhalations into the man's mouth, holding the nose clamped shut with the thumb and finger of his right hand.

After the third exhalation, I began my chore, pushing down hard and releasing, saying my cadence out loud. "One—and—two—and—three—and—four—and—five—and—one—and—two—" I pushed down on the number, released on the "and." The cadence was ninety pushes a minute. When the heart stops, irreversible brain damage starts after four minutes. I guess he'd been about forty seconds to a minute from the time of cardiac arrest until we went to work on him. The air we breathe in is about 21 percent oxygen. The air we exhale is about 15 percent oxygen. Meyer was oxygenating the lungs. I was pumping the heart by compressing it between the sternum and the spine. Done properly, this can establish a blood pressure and an oxygenation of the brain adequate to sustain the brain undamaged.

The woman was not making things any easier. She had crawled out of the car and was dancing around us, yelling, "Get a doctor! Get an ambulance! Stop that! Stop that this minute!"

She tugged at me and then at Meyer, and between breaths he yelled at her, "I am a doctor, madam!"

"Is he dead?" she yelled. "Is he? Is he?"

We had attracted a part of the crowd. The crowd was fragmented, watching different parts of the show, as at a carnival midway. A couple of women in our crowd grabbed the wife and hauled her away.

I kept counting, and at one point I felt a gentle crackling sound under my hands and knew it was some ribs going. When it is properly done, you will almost always break some ribs. The choice is clear—a dead person with nice whole ribs, or a potentially alive person with some rib fractures. I checked the position of my hands and kept going. I wondered where the hell the official medics were. Suddenly the unconscious man vomited. Meyer, leaning toward him, caught quite a bit of it. Meyer did what everyone does in such circumstances. He turned aside and threw up too. A husky kid about sixteen dropped to his knees beside Meyer and swabbed the man's mouth with tissue, rolled his head to the side and then back. Meyer tried to give the next breath and couldn't manage it. The kid muscled him aside and took over, doing the job with perfect timing. It is essential not to break the rhythm, because it can set the person way back. Meyer got up slowly, gagging and coughing. I heard the sirens coming. We kept going. Though it seemed longer, I imagine we gave that man cardiopulmonary resuscitation for about twelve to fourteen minutes before the medics moved in with their specialized equipment and their direct electronic links to hospital Emergency.

Ambulances were soon leaving. Tow trucks were untangling the torn metal. The flares were extinguished, traffic resumed, and the spectators began drifting away.

The kid said, "That's the first time I used it for real. You done it often, mister?"

"Second time for me. The first was a drowning. Didn't make it."

"You take the CPR course?" he asked.

"Nobody should ever try cardiopulmonary resuscitation without taking the course. You could do more harm than good."

"That's what they told us too. You think that old guy will make it?"

"I hope so," I said. I saw B. J. Bailey heading back toward the main building of the Resort, and I hurried and stopped her by clamping a hand on her shoulder.

She turned and said, "And what the hell do you want?"

"I want to know how you got Nicky so charged up about me. What the hell did you tell him?"

"I didn't tell him anything."

"Listen to me, Billy Jean. Whatever you told him, it made him come after us with a shotgun. He shot to kill. Believe me. He missed. He tried to reload. I took the gun away from him. He ran out into traffic and got hit and killed."

"Killed!" she said, aghast. "You're joking. You got to be joking."

"You killed him, Billy Jean."

We stood near a driveway lamp, and it shone pale yellow across her small face. Her mouth broke and she hunched her shoulders high. "No, I didn't! I didn't! I told him you came here after him. He gets kind of weird about maybe there are people after him. He's on crystal. It makes people like that. I thought he would fight again, is all. I thought maybe he'd beat you up this time. I didn't think he would . . . oh, no. Oh, no."

She stood hunched and sobbing.

I gave her some clumsy pats on the back and said, "Look, I didn't mean to hurt your feelings last night."

"You came back here with . . ."

"I know, I know. That was dumb. I do some very dumb things like that. Frequently. Forget you ever knew me."

"I can't stop thinking about Nicky. I just can't. I can't work tonight. Oh, Jesus. Look. One thing. You get the hell away from me. Okay? Get away and stay away. Okay?" She glared up at me out of her grief-swollen face. I stood and watched her walk away.

Meyer came up behind me and said, "More diplomacy?"

"Are you all right?"

"I'm going up to the room for a few minutes. Where will you be?"

"Right here, waiting for the Sheriff."

"You called?" Sheriff Ames said, at my elbow. He said

we could both come with him—sit in his car and chat a while. I explained Meyer's problem, and he pointed to where he was parked and let Meyer go to freshen up.

CHAPTER

13

I told him the story while we sat in his car waiting for Meyer to return. When Meyer returned, he had Meyer tell it again. He got the shotgun out of the pickup and found the right barrel loaded with a fresh shell of number 12. We went over and studied the rental Dodge. The first barrel had blown a hunk the size of a cantaloupe out of the right front tire at seven o'clock. For a time we couldn't find where the second one had gone, and it was Meyer who spotted the tiny streaks of ricochet atop the mound of the trunk cover. So he had been swinging it when he fired, and the first one had slain the tire and kicked the muzzle up, so that only the bottom few pellets of the pattern touched the trunk when the rest of them sailed off toward the tennis courts. I could estimate that the second pattern had been directly over us as we tumbled past the rear of the car. I had one skinned elbow and the knee was gone out of my slacks. Meyer had taken a crack on the back of the head and slid through grease on his behind.

Ames drove us to the hospital, and we went in through Emergency. Meyer and I sat in wicker chairs in a small waiting room while Ames went wandering off after information. The clock ticked. Nurses rustled by. A child was crying. The available magazines were devoted to health, diet, maintaining the right attitude toward life, and how to manage a hospital. Two young, thin black girls came in and sat on the couch, hugging each other and sniffling. A nurse came and got them, and a little while later I heard a terrible grieving desolate scream, and wondered if it had come from one of them.

Ames sauntered back in, pale, worn, and dusty-looking, a drab man of no particular emphasis or importance. He sat and said, "They're still working on Noyes, still operating on him, but I get the feeling they're giving up. Now they're doing what's called the practice of medicine, with Dr. Ted Scudder running the show. He'll come on down here shortly, I'd say."

"What about that old man?"

"That was a Mr. and Mrs. Whittaker Davis, from Watertown, New York, looking for a place to retire. Safe to say it won't be here."

"Was?" Meyer asked. "Or is?"

"Oh. Sorry. Is. At least for now. They're breathing for him, but they've got heart action. He's in cardiac intensive care, all wired up to the machinery." He turned so as to look directly at Meyer, frowning. "His wife says a man who looks like you, who worked on him, and who would be you, wouldn't it?—she said he said he was a doctor. There's a law I'd have to look up about impersonating a licensed profession."

"I'm a doctor," Meyer said. "I didn't tell her my specialty."

"What would that be?"

"Economics. I misled Mrs. Davis. Guilty. She was trying to interrupt the CPR."

"They say you knew what you were doing."

"We are DC Number Two Basic Rescuers, both of us,"

Meyer said proudly. He gave me a smug nod. I sighed. He had insisted. He had nagged at me until I agreed. What was the result? Two dreadful hours of hard labor on a drowned and dark blue girl before finally the professionals had shown up and told us we were wasting our time. She was gone. And now a dying old man whose ribs I had broken. Great.

A round, weary, red-faced man dressed in operating-theater green came scuffing in and collapsed into a wicker chair. There was a brown spatter of blood across his chest. His plastic mask dangled. He shoved his little green hat back, took his glasses off, and began cleaning them on a tissue. "Official time of death, Hack, make it nine twenty-five. Ten minutes ago. But he was dead as chopped liver the minute the car hit him. Busted all to hell inside. Ripped and ruptured. Liver, spleen, kidney, bowel. He was nearly torn in half. The certificate will say internal injuries."

The Sheriff introduced us, explaining that we were in town on business, seeking to arrange the purchase of some of the Lawless holdings.

The Sheriff said, "I told them up there I want a blood sample and urine sample to go to the lab. Damn fool ran right into traffic. Check for booze and foreign substances, I told them, and they'll tell my deputy when he gets over here."

Scudder got up and sighed. "My turn in the barrel. Four to midnight. I draw that one on Saturday night once every five weeks. Try to keep everything quiet for the rest of my tour, Hack."

"Try to."

We checked on Mr. Whittaker Davis again before leaving. No change. Because there was a fatality, possibly two, Ames wanted our statements on tape. He said they'd be typed up for signature in the next few days. Probably by Tuesday afternoon.

He made it sound like routine, but once he got me into his office and over at a small conference table at the side, with the tape all hooked up and tested, with me on record as saying I was giving the information of my own free will, he did more digging than I had anticipated. He covered my first encounter with Noyes, the absurd fight in the parking lot, the second encounter at the Cove, and what had been said back and forth on all occasions. And the third and final encounter. Very final for Nicky Noyes.

Hack Ames was good at his job. He had all the tricks. For a time I found myself going along in his rhythm, but then the alarm bells began to sound and I hauled back on my own reins. A good questioner will ask a question, get what sounds like a complete answer and sit there in silence, mildly quizzical, until you qualify or add to the answer. A good questioner will ask very simple questions requiring short and simple answers and slowly increase the pace until when he throws a curve, the silence seems to last too long, and you feel a compulsion to give an answer quickly. Any answer. A good questioner will ask a dozen questions about situation X, and then a dozen questions about situation Y, and finally he will start a series about situation Z, but the fifth question may be about Y and the seventh may be about X, questions you have already answered, but phrased just a bit differently. A good questioner will give you back your answers, twisted very slightly, and wait for the corrections. And he will ask you a question that is absurd, or grotesque, stop you before you can answer, and throw in a much better question while you are still off balance from the earlier one. There is always this problem. If you can know and anticipate and deal with the skilled questioner, you slowly begin to realize that you are doing so much bobbing and weaving that, in itself, it becomes significant. You cannot start refusing to answer. You cannot fake anger. You become aware of little inconsistencies here and there, and he gives you no chance to patch them up.

He turned off the recorder. He scratched at his dusty head, yawned, and said, "You're almost good enough, McGee."

"For what?"

"For playing games with tired old county sheriffs on a Saturday night."

"No games."

"Unless a fellow is trying to borrow money, Dev Boggs will just about believe anything you want to tell him."

"Meyer has a letter from—"

"I saw the letter he left with Boggs. I phoned that big man Friday afternoon, that Allbritton. Never could get him. Imagine if I got him, he'd back it up, but that letter, you know, doesn't really say much of anything. I checked back through your registration there at the North Bay Resort, and I called a friend over in Fort Lauderdale. He looked around and called me back. You two keep a low profile over there. This Meyer seems to make out doing talks at conferences and being a consultant once in a while."

"He's sort of an investor."

"Sure. And you are sort of a salvage consultant or some goddamn thing. And Billy Carter is a field hand."

"What are you trying to say to me, Sheriff?"

He cracked his knuckles and blinked his tired brown eyes. "What I am saying is that I get sick of being insulted. I've got a job here and I do it and I do it damn well, if statistics mean anything. For two months now I've had federal employees and state people coming into Dixie County and padding around, fumbling into this and that, screwing up the detail, living on travel and per diem, without the courtesy of checking in with me. A lot of them are supposed to be officers of the law, though what law and what office is often hard to tell. The general attitude is maybe I am involved in whatever it is they are overpaid to try to look into. Or I am some dummy barely competent to set up speed traps and arrest drunks. Hub Lawless is responsible for a whole batch of them coming in. I am getting tired of it, McGee. I am going to start throwing asses into the little slam here, and I can't see any special reason why I shouldn't start with yours. The way I read you, you are either U.S. or state level, and you are over here on the Lawless matter, or you are here on the new drug thing, and the one phone call I'm going to let you have, it better work out because you're not going to get two."

"Wrong on all guesses," I said.

"Bullshit, McGee! You think I don't know when a man is being evasive? You think I can't recognize fancy footwork?"

"Okay, okay. Van Harder asked me to come over and see if I could find out enough to get a rehearing on his license. He's bringing my houseboat around. I got a reservation for it at the Cedar Pass Marina."

He looked startled and incredulous. "You some kind of lawyer?"

"No."

"Licensed investigator?"

"No. It's just a favor for a friend."

"A friend? How come Harder is a friend of *yours?*"

"Because he fished charter out of Bahia Mar. He had the *Queen Bee Number Three.* He sold her to a man named Fazzo when he went into shrimping. Harder was already there when I began living there. All the permanent people around a marina know each other."

"Why did he ask *you?* What qualifications have *you* got?"

I waited a while on that one and finally said, "Indignation."

"All right! Okay! It's justified. It wasn't at the time. At

174

the time, McGee, it looked exactly like what it was supposed to look like, a reformed drunk who fell off."

"And his friendly Sheriff tried to kick him back up onto his drunken feet."

"I've been sorry about that ever since. I did it because I was angry, dammit. I like Van. It scalded me he should be such a jackass. Since then things have shaped up different. I'll go along with what he kept saying, that there had to be something in that drink Hub took up to him. All the rest of it was staged too perfect. Van could have come to me. I mean it. He can come to me and I can get that license give back to him, and I kindly think I'll go ahead and get it done anyway without his asking."

"Sheriff, if you really know Van, you know why he won't come to you."

For just an instant he looked puzzled, and then he nodded. "I know. I kicked him. Not hard or anything. But I kicked him. You don't kick a man like Van Harder. Those people that gave Hub a dollar and a half of work for every dollar of pay, they've certainly got cause to despise that man. Harder, Noyes, all of them."

We sat in silence. I wondered what on earth Meyer would be thinking, sitting out there waiting.

"I ought to chase your ass right out of my county," he said. "I really should."

"Mr. Boggs still has Meyer's letter."

"Don't try to keep conning me with that. Okay?"

"Okay."

"Maybe you decided to help Van Harder out because you knew about this case and thought you might run across some money."

"The thought crossed my mind, Sheriff."

He grinned for the first time. "Crossed a lot of minds. But it has all pretty much died down. It's pretty certain Hub is in Mexico and he took it with him, and got that lady architect with him too. Walking hand in hand into the Mexican sunset. Smiling a lot. Hard to believe Hub Lawless did that to his own town, to all of us. Wife, kids too. With them, of course, he told himself the insurance would take care of them. Except, on a big policy, they look for any loophole to keep from paying off."

"But you don't know all the answers yet, Sheriff. Things don't quite fit."

He tilted his chair back and stuck his thumbs inside his belt. He squinted at the desk top and said, "Now if I wasn't tied hand and foot by the restrictions of this office, I could churn around here and there, telling lies, making jokes, pushing buttons, hustling and scrambling. Maybe some pieces would fall out of the box and I'd get to know more. No! Don't tell me you understand a damned thing, because I don't want to hear anything about your understanding. There isn't any understanding. You might come back in here some day and have a chat, if you have some interesting conversation. I get bored a lot in here. I spent fourteen years in a car out on the roads. It gets tiresome in here."

"Before I go, it was kind of a shock to have Noyes trying very hard to kill me, or both of us."

"It knocked Nicky way off balance when Hub took off. He went away for a little while and came back with merchandise. We knew he was dealing, and we got a pretty good customer list. It's easier to keep your finger on a network you know than to try to unravel the next one that starts up. He got to hitting his own goods. Dr. Sam Stuart knows more about it than I do. He's worried all to hell lately. Something the kids are taking. We had a thirteen-year-old girl sit on a gravel pile last month and swallow gravel, a chunk at a time, until she had four pounds of rock in her belly. Weird. God only knows who'll take over where Nicky leaves off. Maybe the others we got will just start handling more."

"Meyer is waiting out there."

"Oh, sure. Send him in. It will only be a few minutes for him. I'll expect to see you around?"

I nodded. Meaning clear. See me around or he would come and get me. I went out and sent Meyer in. I sat and waited. A sturdy woman typed slowly. I could just hear the dispatcher. A gigantic deputy came in slowly and said to the woman, "What's it about?"

"You know what it's about."

"Not the damn charts again. Don't tell me it's the charts."

"You're sixteen over again, Rudy."

"But, damn it all, I'm not fat!"

"He says you got to be no more than two twenty-five. Weren't you in high school with Nick Noyes?"

"Junior and senior. Four years of him."

"He's dead."

"No shit, Marie! OD'd?"

"Hit by a tourist Cadillac while crossing the street."

"You've got to be kidding."

Meyer came out, and the deputy went in to take his chewing for being overweight. We went out and suddenly realized we had no transportation. After we phoned a taxi and stood waiting, Meyer said, "What took you so long in there?"

"He thought I was being cute about something, so he went around and around, coming in at me from new angles. He finally decided I was some kind of out-of-town law, so I told him why we're here."

"So he said go back to Lauderdale?"

"Almost. Not quite. Without saying so, he sort of appointed me official cat's-paw."

"How nice for you!"

"I didn't tell him what we've got so far."

"Which is next door to nothing at all. What we know changes nothing."

"It locates Lawless as of the next morning, ashore and alive."

"Which he is conceding anyway, Travis," Meyer said, opening the cab door.

We stopped at the Galley to make certain that it was really too late to get anything to eat, but it wasn't. Dave Bellamy said he was delighted to take care of old customers.

Good ol' Dave. He supervised the preparation of a pair of extra-dry Boodles gin martinis. Meyer looked beat. He beamed at the drink when it was placed in front of him. And, as on other occasions when the martini is badly needed, he quoted Bernard De Voto on that subject: "The rat stops gnawing in the wood, the dungeon walls withdraw, the weight is lifted. Your pulse steadies and the sun has found your heart. The day was not bad, the season has not been bad, and there is sense and even promise in going on. Prosit."

"Saved a life. Maybe," I said.

"And almost lost one or two. But didn't," he said.

"About that picnic tomorrow."

"Maybe that lithesome person hates picnics."

"She's living a picnic out there. I saw a deli next to the supermarket at Baygate Plaza Mall. I can get one of those big wicker hamper things, and a big cooler. I'll set up a picnic like she never saw before, from shrimp to champagne."

"What you're talking about is a Care package."

"What do you mean?"

"When you start hauling great quantities of food to a female person, it means you really care. It always has. I think it is some primal instinct. The hunter bringing spoils to the cave."

"Hmmm. Meyer, would it offend your sense of fitness if I called Gretel a girl?"

"Instead of a person or a woman or some such? You want to be patronizing and chauvinistic, eh? Look down upon her?"

"Cut it out, Meyer. I can go with all that approach right up to a point. When it doesn't mean much one way or another. You know. But here we have one of the truly great, all-time, record-breaking, incomparable girls. And I want to call her a girl."

"And take her a ton of food. Ah, me. Ah, so. And so it goes. Let's order before I faint from hunger. You are a child of your times, McGee. And so am I. Call *her* what you will, but call *me* a waiter."

CHAPTER

14

There are days you can't ever forget. It doesn't mean that anything really startling has to happen. It was a great glowing golden day in May. A Sunday numbered twenty-two. There you are in the midst of life, and one of those days comes rolling at you, and it is just like one of the magical days of childhood, like the first Monday after school is out.

We couldn't warn John Tuckerman and Gretel Howard we were coming. We had to hope they'd be glad to see us when we showed up an hour before noon. And they were. Demonstrably glad. She knew how to accept gifts. None of this "Aw, you shouldn't have." She went through the hamper and the cooler, giving little yelps of delight. "Hey! How about this? Wow! Look here, Johnny! Hey, you crazy guys. A jar of red caviar! Have you gone nuts, bonkers, utterly strange?"

I was glad that Meyer had realized it would be best not to bring any booze, or any beer. Tuckerman seemed slightly dazed. He wore a gentle smile. He rocked back and forth, heel to toe. You had to speak to him twice to get an answer.

"I said is the fishing any good?"

"Oh. Sure. I mean, I guess so. Haven't done much good. But they're out there, all right. They're out there."

He looked much better. It took me a few moments to realize that not only had he shaved; his mustache and hair had been trimmed back a little. He seemed to want to be part of the festivities, but he could not quite keep track of the chatter. We were not trying to dazzle him with repartee or profundities. It was just your normal picnic conversation, but it was as if he were a foreigner among us, looking back and forth with a slightly baffled expression, able to speak the language, only not all that well.

One odd little incident happened. Gretel stopped in the middle of a sentence and stared at John. He sat with his eyes squeezed shut and his jaw knotted. She put her hand on his rigid arm.

"Are you going to be all right?" she asked.

He nodded. And in a little while the tensions went out of him. I asked her about that later, after we had swum down the beach and were walking back, and she said that it was hallucinations. They happened now and again. Some sort of a cousin of delirium tremens, the result of the booze with which he had almost killed himself. She told me that was the reason she did not want to leave him alone. She didn't want to take him into town yet, or go in without him. Hence her magic washing machine. She thought that I had guessed the problem, and that was why I had brought enough food for fifteen people. By great exercise of character I made myself admit I hadn't guessed it.

We sat on the side of a dune. We could have been the only two people in the world. I wanted to kiss her. My heart was in my throat. I felt fifteen again. I looked into her eyes and saw her amused acceptance of us, and knew

I could. It was immediately intense, astonishing both of us, as was admitted later. We lay back against the slope of the dune, as closely enclasped as we could get, and it was all very delicious for a long time, and then it began to get a little bit too yeasty for the time and place. "Hey!" she said in a muffled voice. "Hey you! McGee!" And then, with a muscular squirm, she kicked us over far enough so that we began rolling, and we rolled over and over down to the bottom of the dune and had to go into the Gulf again to rinse off the sand that had caked on our sweaty bodies.

It was a great day. Eating and swimming and napping, walking and talking. A simple day. I can remember the precise pattern of the white grains of sand on the round tan meat of her shoulder, and the patterns of the droplets of seawater on her long thigh. Gretel filled my eyes. I learned her by heart, wrists and ankles, mouth corners and hairline, the high arches and slender feet, downy hollow of her back, tidy ears, flat to the good skull.

There would never be enough time in all the world for us to say to each other all the things that needed saying, time to tell all that had happened to each of us before the other had appeared—a sudden shining in the midst of life. In so many ways she was like a lady lost long ago, so astonishingly like her—not in appearance as much as in the climate of the heart—that it was like being given another chance after the gaming table had already been closed for good. She had a great laugh. It was a husky, full-throated bray, an explosion of laughter, uncontrolled. And she laughed at the right places.

The second strange incident happened in late afternoon when the four of us were up on the roofed deck of the cottage, sitting in the ragged old deck chairs and the unraveling wicker ones, squinting into the sun glare off the broad Gulf.

Meyer had talked a little bit about the odds and ends

we had unearthed, Mr. Wedley recovering his red Mazda, the items Kristin had left behind, DeeGee Walloway's guess as to what had happened. Things like that. I realized that Meyer was sidestepping the big dramatic incident. When he ran down I said, "Leaving it to me?"

"Why not?" he said.

"Leaving what?" Gretel asked.

"Nothing at all. Really." I became Lawrence of Arabia. "Chap tried to blow some large ugly shotgun holes in us last night. Number twelve. Range of fifteen feet. Missed. Wounded our vehicle."

"He missed," Meyer said, "because that slothful-looking beach bum sitting there with the rotten imitation accent has one of the most fantastic reaction times you would ever care to see. I heard a strange little clicking behind us and suddenly McGee slammed into me, and as I was tumbling along the asphalt I heard a deafening pair of explosions."

She had worn a half smile, anticipating some sort of joke. But when she realized Meyer was quite serious, her jaw dropped and her eyes went wide in consternation. "How terrible!" she said.

"He jumped up and ran over to the fellow and yanked the gun away from him before he could reload and aim again, and the fellow ran right out into the Bay Street traffic and got hit by a car. We saw him get hit. We knew no one could survive that kind of impact, especially a man that heavy. He died on the operating table."

"Who was it?" Tuckerman asked.

"Nick Noyes."

Tuckerman boggled at me. "Nick," he said. "Nick. Nick." It was not a sound of anguish or dismay. It was a puzzled expression he wore, as if he were trying to remember something about Noyes.

"He worked for Hub too, didn't he?" Gretel said. "In construction or something? Johnny, didn't the two of you hang around together after Hub left? Isn't that what you told me?"

I sat between Tuckerman and his sister. Tuckerman reached over and put his right hand on my forearm and clamped down. I would not have believed him that powerful. "Nicky is dead? Really?"

"Very dead, John."

The grip slowly softened and he took his hand away. His smile came slowly, and grew and grew. It was one of the contagious smiles of childhood, a big candy-apple, cotton-candy, roller-coaster smile.

"I won't have to kill him!" John Tuckerman said joyously.

Gretel inhaled sharply. "Johnny!"

"Well, I won't. You heard him, Gretel. Nicky is dead, and I won't have to even think about killing him any more. That's the best thing I've heard in a long time."

"Why would you think you had to kill him?"

"Oh, I've known I'd have to."

"But *why?*"

"Because he was after me."

"After you? How?"

"Just after me, dammit."

"But if he was after you, dear, wouldn't he have come out here?"

"Oh, he's been here. A lot. Sneaking around. You wouldn't know about it. I didn't tell you. I didn't want to worry you, that's all. Now he won't be around here any more. Unless . . ." He stopped and stared at me and began to glower.

"What's the matter, John?"

"You two could be helping him. You could be lying, to make it all easier for him."

We couldn't ease his suspicions until Meyer remembered he had the Sunday edition of the *Bay Journal* down in the car. He got it, and Tuckerman was at last willing to admit Noyes was dead. He went down to ground level and climbed the dune and sat just over the crest of it with his back to us, silhouetted against the sea glare.

"Let me apologize," Gretel said. "We've been through this before. I thought he was over it. So I asked about Nick Noyes, trying to lead John into it in . . . a less squirrelly fashion. From what I gather, Nick looked John up to commiserate with him, to get drunk together and cuss Hub Lawless and talk about their bad luck. That was while John was still living at the Vista, and before he had smashed up his car. I think Nick suspected that Hub's disappearance was planned and that my brother was in on it somehow. I think he was trying to pry information out of John. John is quite sure he did not reveal anything. He's not really sure, of course, but he thinks Nick Noyes was so angry at the whole thing, and so sure Hub had left with Miss Petersen, that if he thought John had any part in it, he would have blown the whistle. It *would* be actionable, wouldn't it?"

"Accessory to fraud, or conspiracy to defraud," Meyer said. "Something ominous at any rate."

"Also, that Wright Fletcher, the Sheriff's deputy, was out here prodding away at Johnny. He came several times after I was here, and I finally told him to make an arrest or stay away. He didn't seem to have anything to go on except the idea that, inasmuch as John was Hub's best friend, John had to know about anything Hub planned and did."

"He believes Noyes was out here prowling around?"

"Practically every night. He was very very sure one night. He said he could hear him. We'd had a hard rain earlier in the evening. It dappled the sand and took out footprints and tire tracks. There was just that one hard rain. The next morning I made him walk the perimeter with me. There wasn't a footprint or a tire track for a hundred yards in any direction. I almost convinced him

Nick hadn't been here. At noontime he told me that it was pretty obvious Nick had a special pair of shoes with soles which imitated the marks rain makes. He was serious. It breaks my heart. He was always so damned sane and practical and fun. At times—I don't know—I get the feeling he's putting me on, that it is all some kind of a weird game, and then I will realize he means it, he really means it all."

"Any idea why he thinks Noyes was after him?"

"No. None. It's an obsession. Nick was after him, just after him. No reason. Look at him out there! God only knows what sick thoughts are crawling through his head. He's better than he was. He let me trim his hair. You noticed? He finally got over the idea that if it was trimmed the hair ends would bleed. Yeck. Every day a little bit better, I keep telling myself."

Aside from those two incidents, it was one of your great days. We stayed into the night and built a fire of driftwood on the beach. A sea breeze kept the bugs away from us. We had stars by the billion. Meyer was in his best form. He came up with a tale I had never heard before, about a time years ago when he had attended a monetary conference in Tokyo. He was slated to deliver a paper he had written on the effect of interest rates on gross national product in the emerging nations. It was over an hour long. The taxi driver took him that morning to the hotel where he was to deliver his paper. Eager underlings led him to a big hall. He was pleased and surprised at the size of the audience. He gave his talk, shook hands with what seemed to be dozens of Japanese men, and left, still savoring the applause.

That afternoon he was called before the executive committee. They wanted to know why he had failed to appear and deliver his paper. He said he had. They proved he hadn't. He began to realize that he should have been made suspicious by the fact that the audience was entirely

Japanese, quite a few of them were women, and, of the men who shook his hand afterward, not one of them thanked him in English. And he remembered a small elderly Japanese man who stood in the wings while he talked and kept looking at his watch in a troubled way.

Meyer then told us of the lengths he went to to find the hotel again. He never found it. So he would never know whom he had talked to, or what they had expected. He had always remembered how their applause had warmed his heart. A polite people indeed.

He did it well. He had Gretel chuckling and groaning a long time after he finished. When it was late, she made some chicken sandwiches for us to take along, so we could collapse into bed at the Resort.

On the way back along the nine miles of lumps and potholes, I realized how ready I was for sleep.

"You and Gretel make an extraordinary couple," Meyer said, apropos of nothing at all.

"How?"

"Hard to describe, exactly. You give the impression of having been close for years. You are tuned to her in some fashion. The two of you look larger than life somehow. Of course, you *are* larger than couples one runs across every day. There is some sort of aura about you two. You had it in place when you came back down the beach that first day. I don't know why it should, but it makes me feel drab."

"For a drab man, you tell a funny Japanese story."

"I felt compelled to do my best. She makes you want to dig deeply into your bag of tricks. With no insistence at all, she seems to demand some kind of excellence."

"I don't happen to have any of that around."

"I think she thinks you do, or she wouldn't bother."

"How is she bothering?"

"Don't you know how she looks at you?"

"Okay, okay. Sure."

187

He sighed. "That fellow—what was his name?—Billy Howard. Billy must have been the prize damn fool of all the world."

"Maybe he couldn't stand the pressure of her expectations—the need to be as much better than the next guy as she was better than the next woman."

"Interesting idea. The retreat from excellence. But she isn't demanding excellence in that sense, Travis. All she demands is honesty, really."

"At this point in the life of McGee, how do I go about telling the truths from the lies? When I say something this time, how can I tell that I really mean it?"

"If you can't tell, we're all in trouble."

"How so?"

"In spite of your poses, old friend, you have a strange, tough, anachronistic sense of honor."

"Oh, sure."

"You bleed over your despicable acts. But like our friend Rust Hills, you tiptoe past the edge of corruption in a naughty world, and you genuinely suffer if you do not live up to your own images of your various selves."

"Are you telling me I need not fear meeting the lady's requirements?"

"Whatever they might be, Travis. Whatever they might be."

"Look at that hole. You could hide a coffee table in that hole."

"Be careful. We have no spare, remember."

I wandered the road, finding the smooth parts, feeling underneath the deepwater tan the heat of the long May day in the sun. I had a stack of those old-fashioned photographic plates in the back of my mind. The big camera had been made of brass and oak. I had spent a lot of the day ducking under the black cloth, raising high the T stick with the magnesium powder in the groove along the top of the bar, focusing the big lens, waiting until she held still, then triggering the powder. *Poom*. And a cloud of white smoke, and another image of Gretel tucked away forever.

Long ago a picture must have been an event. Capturing a living image has become too ordinary a miracle, perhaps. They go about with their automatic-drive Nikons and OM-2's and their Leicaflexes, and put their finger on the button, and the hand-held machinery makes a noise like a big toy cricket. *Reep, reep, reep, reep*. A billion billion slides, projected once, labeled, and filed forever. Windrows of empty yellow boxes blow across the Gobi, the Peruvian highlands, the temple steps at Chichicastenango. The clicking and whirring and clacking is the background sound at the Acropolis, at the beach at Cannes, on the slopes at Ville-franche. All the bright people, stopped in the midst of life, looking with forced smile into the lenses, then to be filed away, their colors fading as the years pass, caught there in slide trays, stack loads, view cubes, until one day the camera person dies and the grandchild says, "Mom, I don't know any of these people. Or where these were taken even. There are jillions of them here in this big box and more in the closet. What will I do with them anyway?"

"Throw them out, dear."

CHAPTER
15

I slept like a winter-bound bear and awoke refreshed to a morning of misty rain. Meyer was up and gone. He does not leave long chatty notes. This one said, *8:10. Bkfs dwnstrs. Then Dr. S.*

He was gone by the time I got downstairs. The waitress showed me to a table for two in a window corner of the small dining room. It looked out across the wet and empty courts. Between the far trees I could see segments of gray sea, almost flat calm.

I ordered, and as I was drinking coffee, waiting for the food to arrive, I saw Jack the Manager appear in the arched doorway to the lobby. He wore a black sport shirt and white slacks. The shirt was stained across the round front of him. He stared at me. He looked like an emperor penguin disapproving of a dead fish.

He came directly over to my table and said, "Mr. McGee!"

"Good morning. Join me?"

"I would like to point out—"

"Sit down and point out. Please."

He eased into the chair facing me. He looked nervous and uncomfortable. "There have been complaints," he said.

"About what?"

"Your group was very noisy Friday night. And there have been two altercations in the parking area."

I nodded. "Of course. Shots were fired. Then all those tires screaming, and then the sirens. Very upsetting."

He looked slightly relieved. "I'm glad you're taking this attitude. It makes it easier for me. Our guests are used to a—"

"Just one moment," I said, stopping him. I took out the pocket notebook which Meyer had convinced me was useful. I leafed through the pages, nodding to myself, frowning. When he started to speak, I stopped him with upraised hand.

I put the notebook away and smiled reassuringly at him. "I know what is basically bothering you. Right? And I am really not authorized to tell you anything at all. But you've been so pleasant, such a good host, that I am going to level with you, and I hope you appreciate what a rare thing that is."

"I don't know what—"

"From what I can guess, and from what I know of procedure, there is really very little chance of your being subpoenaed."

"Of being . . . for what . . . I don't . . ."

"And there is even *less* chance of the Resort here being either fined heavily or closed under the provisions of Chapter Twenty-one, Paragraph C-Six, Subparagraph *a*."

"But I don't—"

"So you don't have to *worry*. Right? You can relax! It isn't hanging over you any longer. At least, I am *reasonably* sure they won't come at you in that manner. But nobody knows, of course, until they have an executive session."

His face had turned red. He grasped the edge of the table and leaned toward me. "Mr. McGee, I haven't the faintest idea what the hell you are talking about!"

My food came. It looked very good indeed. I smiled at Jack the Manager, and I winked at him and said, "None of that now."

"NONE OF WHAT?"

"Shshsh. Please. You know I can't go any further with this. I shouldn't have mentioned it at all. I was only trying to do you a favor."

"But I want to know what this is all about!"

"Please forget I said anything to you. I violated a confidence. And for God's sake, don't say anything to anyone else, because if it was leaked out and got back to the Supervisor, there's no way in the *world* you could avoid a subpoena."

"I must insist—"

"Do you want to ruin everything for yourself? Have you got some kind of economic death wish?"

I chomped the good Canadian bacon. I beamed and winked and nodded at him. His choice was clear. Either I was certifiable as a maniac, or he and the Resort were in violation of the rules, somehow. In serious violation. I could guess his thoughts from his expression. It has all become regulation by blackmail, of course. Every small businessman lives with the knowledge that he is always in violation of some of the rules. Safety regulations, consumer protection laws, wage and hour laws, pure food and drug statutes, IRS regulations—and on top of all these are the interwoven, supplementary, conflicting regulations of the state, county, and city.

He fills out the forms and sends them in because he knows that, if the forms do not come back in, the computer flags him. He fills the blanks with lies because it would take more hours than there are in the week to fill in the forms arriving each week. He knows all these lies go on record somewhere, and that at any time a field inspector can happen along and check out the old lies and apply pressure. So all he can do is contribute to both political parties, support local, state, and national candidates, and hope for the best.

It was easier for him to believe he was in some kind of trouble than that I had lost my wits.

He got up and said, "Uh . . . thank you, Mr. McGee."

"Believe me, I was glad to do it."

"Uh . . . enjoy your breakfast," he said, and walked away. He turned in the archway, stopped, and stared back at me, his expression troubled, eyes clouded. He shrugged and walked on, out of sight.

It was a small and childish pleasure. I ate with appetite. Great eggs. Days of misty rain are fine. Jack the Manager would leave us alone. He would do a lot of wondering, but he would keep his mouth shut and stay out of the way. And we would refrain from chousing anyone out into traffic. And we would duck away from all shotgun blasts to avoid messing up the parking area.

Gretel was alive in this rain-mist day, in the same dimension, time sector, and hemisphere. She fitted in with any recitation of one of my lists of good words: pound sweet apples, song by Eydie, pine forests, spring water, old wool shirts, night silence, fresh Golden Bantam, first run of a hooked permit, Canadian geese, coral reefs, good leather, thunderstorms, wooden beams, beach walking, Gretel. We all have the lists. Different lists for different times of day and of life. Our little barometers of excellence, recording inner climate.

The first chore after breakfast was another call to the hospital to get the word on the old party we had restored to momentary life. They said that Whittaker Davis was in serious condition, but no longer in critical condition. I asked if his condition could be considered grave. She said they didn't use that word any more because people got it confused with being buried. She said if they did use it, Mr. Davis would be a little bit better than grave, that it sort of would come between critical and serious, but don't count on it.

Meyer points out that fewer and fewer people in this country speak English any more, and that the trend is toward the guttural grunt. As a case in point, he quotes the earnest newscaster he heard one time over WTVT Channel 2 in Utica, New York, speaking of an emergency operation performed upon the wife of one of the nation's most important citizens. With expression of concern he read from his script that she was being operated on because they had "found a noodle on her breast." The song lyrics, Meyer says, presage the future shape of the language.

I was glad the old party was hanging in there. At least we had provided time for the Davis clan to gather at the bedside, if there was a clan, and if the hospital permitted clans to gather.

While at the phone I found the number for Ralph Stennenmacher, General Agent, in the Coast National building. The girl said he was in, and tried to get my name and make an appointment, but I said I would wander on up and take my chances.

A neat little sign on the corner of her secretarial desk said, "Dora Danniker, Serf-Person." She was as tiny as B. J. Bailey, but had a lean pale little face, big glasses, and mouse-blond hair pulled back into a knot. You half expected a toothy actor to pull her to her feet, take away her glasses, fluff her hair out, and say, "But you are beautiful, Dora darling!" Then they would dance.

She looked me over with considerable speculative care, from my tan Eagle shirt to my green brushed-denim slacks and buff-colored After Hours shoes, and back up again.

She said, "It would be nice if you could at least say you'd seen me someplace before, McGee."

I thumped my forehead with the heel of my hand. "Friday night?"

She nodded and smiled an evil smile. "You called me your little pal for a while. You said I should fly away with you, and we would sail the seven seas, climb the highest mountains. And all that stuff."

"Have mercy."

"Even smashed as you were, friend, plotzed out of your wits, you were using your head. You were trying to sign me on to solve the big problem you were having with B.J. and Mishy. You weren't exactly what I would call some kind of a prize. I think it was because those two hate each other and needed an excuse. Do you get like that often?"

"Every night in the week, love."

She studied me, nodded to herself. "You couldn't look the way you look and do that. You were pretty funny for a long time. Life of the party. And finally, of course, you passed out."

"You were still there?"

"Because the guy I was with was still there and I was exhausted from trying to drag him away. You want to see my boss?"

"When convenient."

"He's got somebody in there with him now. Have a seat. Have a paper. I've got to get something done here or I'd spend a little more time working you over. How was your hangover?"

"Didn't your boyfriend object to this 'sail the seas and climb the mountains' routine?"

"Sure. But you finally got tired of him yapping at you. We were walking, the whole bunch of us. You threw Timmy up into a tree."

"I what?"

"You picked him up and threw him up into a tree. You

threw him pretty high. He's sort of a small guy. He grabbed a branch and you kept right on walking and talking. He really hates you."

"Please tell him I'm sorry."

"Don't worry. He hates everybody your size. It's just a general attitude—"

The office door opened and a man came out, speaking back over his shoulder, saying, "If they get any line on him, Ralph, like I said, I'll go on back down. But this ought to be enough for our purposes."

He smiled and nodded at Dora Danniker, gave me one quick flat glance, and went on out, a lean man in a wrinkled pale blue suit, carrying a gray tweed dispatch case. After he was gone I tried to fasten his face firmly in my memory, but it faded before I could begin to identify any distinctive feature. Ralph Stennenmacher stood in his office doorway and looked at me with a genuine smile of welcome.

Dora said, "This is Mr. Travis McGee. He hasn't had a chance to tell me what he wants to see you about."

He shook my hand and tugged me toward his office. He liked me. That is the secret. That's what had made Ralph a success. He was interested in me and he wanted to know more about me. He wanted to sit me down across his big blond desk and listen to my life story. When that genuine and unmistakable warmth is combined with good sense and good products, then you have a great salesman—and a happy man. One wall was hung with certificates, awards, commendations, and group photographs, hung frame to frame. He had white hair, big black-framed glasses, and a comfortable belly. He had little broken veins in his nose and cheeks, big knuckles, a resonant voice, and laugh lines around his eyes. He aimed a big finger at me and said, "Hey, I saw you and another man at the Cove having lunch with Walter Olivera. Excuse me, dammit, at the Galley. Mmmm. Friday?"

I said that was right. This Timber Bay had begun to give the impression of being a risky place for intrigue. Everybody seemed to keep an eye on everybody. I gave him the Devlin Boggs explanation of our presence in town, and he was glad to tell all.

"I wrote the coverage on all Hub's activities and on his personal life too. In the beginning we were thinking of having business insurance, of having insurance at his death go right into the company or corporation so that it could be used to buy out the widow's interest in the partnership or her stock interest, whatever. But I wasn't satisfied that it answered his problem, on account of the way he ran things. Understand, Hub was a good businessman, but he was a loner and a high roller. He wanted to run whatever show he was in, and he had an instinct about pushing his luck—right up until the end, of course. So it began to appear to me like there wouldn't be much of anything left of Hub-Law, Double L, Lawless Groves, or Hula Construction if Hub died. For one thing, nobody would know what was going on. He kept terrible records and he kept a lot of information in his head. And second, because of the way he liked to keep moving money and debt around, it might be that the businesses, each one of them, might have to be liquidated to pay off what was owed. So we started quite a while back with three hundred thousand ordinary life, with Julia the beneficiary, and built it to a half million, million, million and a half, two million, two million two hundred thousand as of the alleged date of death. The girls were contingent beneficiaries. We set the policies up with Julia as the owner, and we put them in her trust downstairs at the bank, the one her daddy Jake Herron set up for her when she turned eighteen. Her daddy helped me get started, by the way. A finer man never lived. . . .

"Where was I? Oh, the trust paid the premiums on the policies, and it left Julia in a pretty good condition. You could just about figure that after expenses and all, and knocking off the mortgage, she'd have anyway one point seven million, plus the little she gets from Jake's estate, which goes to the daughters, share alike, when Julie dies. That money could bring her in about ninety thousand a year tax free, more than enough right now to be mighty comfortable on in Timber Bay, but who can say if it will be enough tomorrow? Tomorrow it might cost ninety thousand a year to hire a truck driver. But it's all, like they say, academic. Hub Lawless is alive down there in Mexico somewhere, according to the report that freelance investigator that just left here gave me."

"I heard that a Mr. Frederic Tannoy was going down there with Deputy Fletcher to see if they could—"

"Gone and got back late last night. Tannoy was the one in the blue suit leaving as you came in. He gave me a copy of this thing he wrote up, which he now turns in to Planters Mutual General Insurance in Topeka. A good solid old-line company. Conservative investments, and they treat their policyholders right. I've worked with them a number of years, and this is the first sour one we've ever had. I'd give an arm if this hadn't have happened. Things like this hurt everybody. This says confidential, so I better not let you have it to look at, but I can read you off here what it says."

He frowned at the document, lips moving, and said, "What happened was that Tannoy and Wright Fletcher went down to Guadalajara with pictures of Hub, and they've got here a little list of five people swearing they saw Hub Lawless in Guadalajara after the twenty-second of March, the date Hub was supposed to have fallen off the boat. It also says here that they picked up Xerox copies of the office records from the Naderman-Santos Medical Clinic, where they had a set of presurgery pictures taken for the record and placed on file under the name Pickering. He made a firm date for Wednesday, March thirtieth, to sign himself in. He paid five hundred dollars down when he made the date in late February. He signed up for—these are hard words—rhinoplasty, rhytidectomy, and, uh, blepharoplasty. Nose job, face lift, and work on the eyes. He had used the name Steven Pickering, and he had a tourist card in that name and had signed as Pickering on the formal release for surgery. He didn't show up for his appointment. It doesn't matter, as far as the investigation is concerned. There's enough in this report so they can back off from paying the face amount of the policies. They can assume he went somewhere else to get the work done. It would be foolish to sue them. No chance of a recovery, or even any compromise. He's down there somewhere with that Petersen woman. I just wonder how he feels about what he's done to everybody around here."

"Maybe he doesn't care."

"Oh, no. Hub cares. That's how come people can't understand it, really. He's a good man. Everything just got to be too much for him. I've been thinking about it a lot. I think that if everything had worked out just fine for him in a business way—the new shopping plaza and that huge development nine miles south of the city—he would still have done something nobody would be able to understand. Maybe blown his own head off."

It surprised me. "Why?"

"Things aren't all that great. You play craps?"

"Once in a while. I'm no big fan."

"Imagine a man like Hub Lawless at a great big crap table. He's keeping a dozen bets going all the time. He's on the come line and the field. He's betting with fours and tens, against sixes and eights. He's bending over that table, sweating, changing bets, doubling up, drawing down, watching the dice and the stick man and the other players. He keeps winning because he is working harder than anybody else, and he's figuring the odds closer, and he's keeping track every minute. For a long time it's fun.

And one day he finds out that they've chained him to the table. That's it, his whole life, piling up counters. He can still keep going as hard as before, but it's different. Choice is gone."

It was a striking analogy. "He used to get away a lot."

"No. Not a lot, and not for long. Everybody thought he was such a happy guy, such good spirits, so friendly. I knew him real well, Mr. McGee, and in the last few years he seemed to me to be kind of . . . wistful. He was getting heavy and out of condition, and he smoked too much. He didn't have time to stay in shape. He didn't have time for much social life or home life, either. Nice home. Lovely wife and daughters. But he had chained himself to the table without realizing it. He knew, or had started to realize, that the rest of his life was going to be pretty much the same."

"One of those evaluations that come along at forty?"

"I suppose so. But he felt the weight of the people who depended on him for jobs. I guess he even felt my weight. I wrote all his coverage, and I don't mind saying I'll miss the business. I guess a man gets to feel the need to experience more lives than the one they give him a chance to lead, no matter how well he does at it."

"And along comes the lady architect."

"Sure thing. Ever shoot a sandhill crane?"

"No."

"I got talked into going over to Texas one time with some old buddies of mine and shooting crane. They put me in the tall grass downwind from this little sort of marshy pond. And after a time this big gawky old bird starts to soar in for a landing. They yelled to me to shoot it. So I stood up and shot it. It was about as tough a shot as standing on the end of a runway and shooting a seven-forty-seven. Blew most of his feathers off, and he landed thump dead about eight feet from me. Made me sick to my stomach. People will do some funny things in the name of sport. That's the way Kristin Petersen shot old Hub down. She blew all the feathers off him and he landed thump. He was ready for her. He was ready for anything that was going to change things around for him. Nothing tasted good to him any more. He stopped giving a damn what anybody thought of him. When the dice came to him, he wanted to show off for Kristin, so he bet the whole pile and lost it, and there was nothing left for him to do, if he wanted to keep her, but steal and run. And that is just what he did."

"He didn't do it very well."

"If he'd done it well, he'd have left Julia with her pride and with plenty of money. That was how he justified it, I guess."

"I certainly appreciate your being so open with me, Mr. Stennenmacher."

"Nobody in Timber Bay calls me that. It is too damned long a name. I'm Ralph to everybody. You come back any time you want to talk about Hub Lawless. I knew him about as well as anybody except John Tuckerman. Poor John."

"He's off the sauce. His sister has it under control."

"I heard she was taking care of him down there. I remember her when she was in high school here. Gretel was a beautiful girl."

"Still is."

"I get to know all the high-school kids. I do my magic shows."

"Magic?"

He smiled and pulled a long yellow pencil out of his ear, snapped it in half, threw the pieces up in the air, and caught the pencil as it came down whole. "When you think of magic, think of Ralph the magician. And think of insurance because it will be magic if you can get by without it."

"Oh."

"I get them in junior high, before they get too sophisti-cated. Levitation. Magic rings. Mystery fire. The multiply-ing rabbits. I practice one hour every morning of my life. I get up that extra hour to get the practice in." He stopped smiling as he thought of Tuckerman again. "John went downhill very very fast after Hub left. He drank himself into the hospital that first month, and that's where what little money he had left went to. I hope he works himself out of it. But I certainly don't know what will happen to him. He lived off Hub's energy and luck all his life. I can't think of anyone around here who'd hire him. There was something besides booze involved. Dr. Sam Stuart knows more about that than I would."

"Drugs?"

"Something like that. Something that bent his head out of shape."

I thanked him again, and I waved good-bye to Dora, the Serf-Person, as I left. I hesitated when I got off the elevator, then decided it was as good a time as any to see Devlin Boggs about Kristin Petersen's banking affairs.

I waited near his office. He was somewhere in the back of the bank. Soon I saw him striding across the carpeting, erect as a doorman, neat as an undertaker, lugubrious as a liberal in Scottsdale. I told him what I wanted to find out, expecting that he would turn the chore over to an un-derling, some pathetic little vice-president, but he wanted to handle it himself.

I sat and listened to him call the Atlanta Southern Bank and Trust and say those mystic words which en-abled him to pierce the secretarial barricades and get through to a certain Mr. Chance McKay. I thought that a dashing name for a banker—maybe not for an Atlanta banker. Finally Boggs made it through to him, and it is to be noted that the southern businessman and banker tends to relate to the telephone the way a four-wheeler relates to CB nineteen. Regardless of regional origin, he becomes just a bit mushmouth.

"Hey, Chance? Thishere's Dev Boggs down at Timber Bay, Florida. . . . Sure. . . . Just fine, mostly. . . . No, I couldn't make it this year. Surely missed it, too. . . . Old buddy, I need a small favor from you, won't cost you a dime. We're looking at a big loss down here on business and personal loans to a skip. Maybe it wouldn't look big to you, but it is king-size for Timber Bay, and it might could eat a hole in our loan-loss reserve that'll take a time to fill back. This skip took off, we think, with a girl friend who's one of your customers up there, and if we could get a clue on where checks are maybe coming in from on her account, or where the closeout balance was sent, it might help us find the skip. The name is Petersen, first name Kristin with a K. Account number four-four-eight, four-four-one. . . . Sure, take your time. . . . What? . . . Oh, okay."

Boggs kept the phone at his ear and covered the mouthpiece and said, "He thinks he had an earlier request on that. An official one."

"It would be likely."

"Right here, Chance. . . . Yes, go ahead." Boggs listened and wrote down numbers. "Yes. . . . I see. . . . Sure. Listen, I want to thank you. 'Preciate it. . . . What? . . . I do hope to make it this year for sure. Our best to Molly, hear? 'Bye."

He read to me from the scratch paper. "Her checking account balance is twenty-one hundred and twenty dollars and five cents. The last check was dated March twentieth, a check made out to cash for five hundred, and there has been no activity in the account since. She has passbook savings of about eleven hundred dollars. She has a one-year Certificate of Deposit at six and a quarter percent in the amount of seven thousand dollars, due in July, and two four-year CDs for fifteen thousand each, due year after next. She also has a safe-deposit box."

"A prudent lady. A tad over . . . what? Forty thousand? One assumes she's planning to return."

With mournful look he said, "If she's prudent, she wouldn't want to lump her money in with what Lawless absconded with. If anything went wrong, she could lose hers too. I imagine she's woman of the world enough to know that the affair can cool off at any time. She left herself a place to go back to."

CHAPTER

16

When I couldn't find Meyer, I decided it was a good time to locate Eleanor Ann Harder. I had the address and phone number Van had given me. She answered the phone and said she had just gotten off duty, but if I came right over, we could talk.

It was a small frame cottage on a small lot, with so many trees and bushes it was almost hidden from the street. She was a big woman, thick and solid rather than fat. She had a pale, rectangular face, small features, erect carriage. She could have been thirty or fifty. She wore her white uniform. We sat on the little screened porch at the side of the house and talked.

"We're so grateful to you, Mr. McGee, for anything you can do. Take Van's occupation away from him and he's lost. He's a very proud man. He's a very decent man."

"We should be able to work it all out. The Sheriff is cooperative. The whole situation looks different today, not like it looked two months ago."

"He phoned me yesterday afternoon from Sarasota and

said things were going well, and wanted to know if I'd seen you. I said not yet but that you would probably stop by. I told him about Nick Noyes and how the paper said he had fired shots at you and your friend before he was killed accidentally. Van was very upset about that. He couldn't understand why Nick would do such a thing. He hadn't thought there would be any danger involved in your coming over, or he would have warned you."

"He's making pretty fair time."

"He'll be here Thursday, he thinks. Should I tell the marina?"

"They're all set. No need. I would imagine you are certain Van didn't get drunk that night."

Her chin came up and her eyes got smaller. "Mr. McGee, I met my husband almost five years ago. I worked at Tampa General at that time. His shrimp boat was run down by an ore ship, and he spent four days out in the Gulf before they were rescued. He came down with pneumonia, and he was on my station. He is a fine man. We were married two weeks after he got out of the hospital. As an RN I know the symptoms of the abuse of alcohol. I knew of the ceremony of taking one drink aboard the *Julie* at the beginning of each cruise. It was his . . . I don't know how to say it."

"I know what you mean. Proving to himself each time he had whipped it."

"And he had. I know he was given something very strong to knock him out like that. He was fuzzy-minded for days. His memory was quite disorganized."

"But he didn't go to a doctor."

"I begged him to. A doctor might have detected something in specimens. Van is one of the world's most stubborn men. By the time he went to Dr. Stuart, it was too late for anything like that. He had three strikes on him around Timber Bay anyway. You see, he came from here."

"I didn't know that."

"It's hard to find out very much about Van from Van. As a young man he was a notorious drunk. He broke places up and was thrown in jail dozens of times. You knew him in Lauderdale after he'd sobered up and become a respectable citizen. A reputation hangs on. For example, when he lost his shrimp boat, there was talk around Timber Bay that he'd been at the helm, drunk, when it happened. When Hub hired him at Hula Marine, people said Hub would live to regret it. Hub Lawless enjoyed hiring . . . misfits. I think he enjoyed gratitude."

"Then it was pretty damned cruel to feed Van a mickey."

"It was wicked in the way that word is used in the Bible."

"It was part of the plot he dreamed up."

"So he could escape punishment as a thief and adulterer. His soul will scream in hell forever."

She meant it. She was not the mild lady I had thought. Her knuckles were white and a muscle under her eye twitched and leaped.

"Mrs. Harder, I wanted to make something clear to you. Van thinks that I am undertaking this venture for money. I'm not. I'll take expenses, if he insists. But no ten thousand. I pretended to go along with that because if I said I would do it as a favor, he wouldn't have wanted me to come over here at all."

"I know. He's planning to pay it. It might take three years, but he'll pay it. You can't stop him. If you do what you promised to try to do, then nothing on earth can stop him from paying you the money, as long as he is alive and working."

"Is there some way I could sneak it back to you?"

"I would never betray him like that. He'd walk right out of my life if he ever found out. I wouldn't blame him. I couldn't stand losing him."

When I told Meyer about her, when we met at the bar at the Galley, he said that when he had been little an elderly aunt had given him an image of the devil which had lasted all his life. "The traditional figure, of course. Lean, very white face, all in black, black goatee, cloven feet, bat wings, a tail with a strange pointy end like an arrowhead. And a pitchfork with little barbs on the tines. Whenever a wicked person dies, there is a final exhalation. The soul emerges on that final breath, looking a bit like a small graveyard spook, a little evanescent thing in a white sheet with black eyeholes. The soul tries to rise up to heaven, but the devil is right there, making his rounds of the dying wicked ones, and he spears it with his fork and stuffs it into a specimen bag he wears on his belt. When the bag is jammed full he turns it over to a messenger-type demon. That demon gives him an empty bag and takes the full one on down to hell. He goes down the nearest well, or mine shaft, or newly dug grave, and keeps right on going. He dumps the bag out and picks up an empty one. The resident in-house demons set upon the bagged souls and start all that frying, basting, slicing, and so on we hear about."

The bartender forced a laugh. Meyer stared at him. "You don't believe in hell?"

"Well, not *that* one, thank God." He wandered away, touching his throat.

"So what about Dr. Sam Stuart?"

"I'll tell you at the table, Travis."

As we finished our drink, awaiting the table call, I told him about Kristin's idle forty thousand. And I told him about how Tannoy and Deputy Fletcher had nailed down Hub's presence in Guadalajara subsequent to the supposed drowning.

At the table he told me about Dr. Stuart. "He's younger than I expected him to be. Sort of a jumpy, impatient, high-strung type. He has a crusade going. But he thinks it's lost before he can even get it off the ground. But he is going to try. He seems to be that sort of a person. What do you know about PCP?"

"Is that the name of his crusade?"

"It's an animal tranquilizer. Phencyclidine. It was developed for use in hypodermic guns to knock down grizzly bears in national parks and keep them down while they were transported to less accessible areas."

"If it's also called angel dust, I've heard of it. It makes a very rough trip, I've heard."

Meyer looked in his notebook. "It is known by different names in different areas. Hog, crystal, peace pill, blasting powder, and sugarino. Range of symptoms: it can produce a staggering walk, slurred speech, and slowed reaction times, imitating the effects of alcohol. It can produce bizarre sensations and hallucinations. People act out violent fantasies. It upsets the neural linkages in the brain. With repeated use it can cause permanent brain damage, with the lingering effects of paranoia, suspicion, anxiety, tendencies toward inexplicable violence, distorted memory, sporadic amnesia. It can duplicate acute schizophrenia."

"Nicky Noyes?"

"He's pretty sure of it. He thinks that it is the root cause of a lot more death and violence than people realize. One-car accidents, suicides, mass murders, sniping, stranglings. The effects are almost completely unpredictable, varying with each individual. He says the whole situation terrifies him."

"Isn't that just a little bit strong?"

"You should hear him, Travis. He made a believer out of me. He's had a couple of fifteen-year-old kids blind themselves with their fingernails."

I stared at him. "That made my stomach turn right over. They better stop that stuff at the source."

"That's the problem. Any college chemistry student

with four or five hundred dollars can set up production in a shed and be turning out phencyclidine in a few days out of easily available materials. They turn the liquid into a crystalline substance. A marijuana cigarette doctored with a pinch of angel dust goes on the street for ten dollars, and five or six little teenagers can turn on on one cigarette, and the chemists who set up the lab can make five figures a week wholesaling the stuff. He says there is an underground lab somewhere in the Timber Bay area. He says he thinks Noyes was one of the several local dealers."

"Oh, great."

"Dr. Stuart says Noyes wasn't too stable to begin with. He'd been in various kinds of trouble before Lawless ever hired him. Lawless straightened him out."

"I wonder if Nicky gave Tuckerman some of his free samples."

"I wondered about that too, and I asked Dr. Stuart if that could be possible. He thought it over and said that it would be impossible to separate the effects of angel dust and the effects of acute alcoholism. He said Tuckerman had been a heavy drinker for years, thinking of himself as a social drinker but getting ever nearer the edge, and in the process doing quite a bit of physical damage to himself. He said that after Lawless left, Tuckerman drank himself into a series of alcoholic spasms in April that destroyed a lot of brain tissue—maybe as much as a dozen series of electroshock treatments. Tuckerman has fatty degeneration of the heart, twenty percent liver function, coronary artery disease, and borderline diabetes."

"Does Gretel know all that?"

"He did mention that he had talked to her about John's condition, so I guess she was given all the bad news. He said he told her that John was erratic but probably not dangerous."

"She'll have to stay with him, then."

"There isn't anyone else," Meyer agreed.

And I knew that Gretel was not the sort of person to sidestep any obligation of the blood or the heart. Tuckerman would probably hang on for years. Nice timing, McGee. Your usual luck.

After lunch we went back to the suite at the Resort. I felt restless. I talked it all over again with Meyer. We had been up one side of it and down the other. We had done a lot more prying than our limited function warranted. We knew more about Timber Bay than we had wanted to know. Good ol' Hub Lawless was down there in Yucatan trying to turn his personal clock back to the steamy days of his young manhood.

I wandered around the sitting room, wishing I was on Gretel's beach with Gretel. I stopped at the windows and looked out, and saw a small familiar figure coming around the edge of the tennis courts, beyond the backstops, heading for the pool. By leaning close to the window, I saw her take up position on a chaise on the apron of the pool.

So I went down there and came up on her quietly, and sat cross-legged on the tile beside her chaise without invitation. Billy Jean wore giant sunglasses with rose-purple lenses, a yellow turban, yellow bikini, and a quart of coconut oil.

"I'm still supposed to stay the hell away?"

She shrugged. "Stay. Go. It doesn't matter, does it?"

"I was wondering if Nicky was on angel dust."

"You mean often, or just the other night?"

"Both."

"Okay, yes to both. He hit it pretty good, but like he said, it's okay for some people and it isn't okay for other people. I guess it wasn't so great for him either, shooting off a gun like that in the parking lot."

"B.J., he was trying to kill me."

"You say."

"Please believe me. He really tried, and if he hadn't been so unsteady, he would have done it."

She got up and pulled the back of the chaise out of the stops so she could lay it flat. She got back onto her towel face down.

"Okay," she said wearily. "So he really tried. And if he hadn't missed, I could have gone to your funeral. Just think."

"But it was an extreme reaction. It was crazy."

"Nicky was a crazy kind of person. Nobody ever really knew what he'd do next. He did whatever he felt like. You always knew things would be lively around Nicky. So the crystal rotted his head out. Okay, he's dead, isn't he? Why are you worrying about him? I thought the only person you ever worried about was Travis McGee."

"Did you try crystal?"

"Ha! Once, baby. Just once. That is a hit like you can't believe. Christ! There I am crawling around on my floor, and it keeps bending under me, and I'm scared shitless I'll fall through. I sit in a corner where I think it's safe and I look at my hands and my fingers had all grown together so my hands were like—you know—flippers. Like pink mittens. I saw a kid like that on television. His mother had taken the wrong kind of medicine when she was pregnant. I had these pink flippers instead of fingers and I started screaming and screaming and screaming. But they said afterward all I did was make a little mewly sound and I kept staring at my hands with the tears running down my face. No way I would ever try that crystal again. Nicky said I might get a real good ride out of it the next time, but it wasn't worth trying. I still dream about my hands looking like that. I'm at the piano and somebody asks for something that's tough to play, and I look down and there are those goddamn flippers again. No way. I stay with a little grass now and then, and not much of that either. And some hash when I'm on vacation."

She turned her head and looked at her hand and spread the fingers, worked them, closed the hand into a fist and put it under her cheek.

"B.J., I'm sorry I screwed up our friendship."

"I could certainly have done without you showing up with that pig Mishy, especially after the nice note you gave me when you left the lounge earlier."

"I apologize."

She rolled onto her side and plucked the purple glasses off and squinted intently at me.

"If you want to pick it up where we left off, forget it. You hurt me. You really hurt me, and the kind of person I am, I can't ever . . . you know . . . recapture a mood, not after I've been hurt. I thought you were a truly great person. It just goes to show."

I nodded. "You're right. It goes to show. I will cherish the memory of the little time we had."

"You will? Honest?"

"Yes, I will."

She grinned and put her glasses back on. "Okay. So will I. And that's the best way. A wonderful memory. Right?"

"One of the best."

"Maybe you're okay, McGee. Maybe you've got some heart after all. Listen, I'm sorry I got Nicky all worked up about you. I had no way of knowing he would do anything like he did. I mean, who could ever guess?"

I went back up to the suite. Meyer read me perfectly, and was amused I should take the trouble to placate Miss Bailey. I don't know why it should amuse him to have me try to get back in the good graces of people I have offended. It is just the sort of thing he does. But I offend more than he does. Oftener and more thoroughly.

I went into my bedroom and got the four-by-five color print of Lawless out of the nightstand drawer where I had put it. I straightened it out. It had cracked a little bit where I had folded it before. I took it to the bright light at the window and studied it.

Okay, so it was taken April eighth in Guadalajara, according to the accompanying message. And that would date it just seventeen days after a heart attack. He looked substantial, hearty, and cheerful, sitting there pouring his beer. So maybe it wasn't a heart attack. Maybe some kind of violent attack of flu. Or maybe he mended very quickly.

And Sheriff Hack Ames had received the slide in the mail just about one month later.

Probably, if it was a heart attack, he would not be anxious to undergo a lot of complicated surgery, and that was why he had never showed up at the Naderman-Santos Medical Clinic. So why hadn't he gotten his five hundred back, or at least rescheduled his appointment? Lawless could not have felt he had left a trail leading directly to Guadalajara. John Tuckerman knew where he was going, but John was loyal. But how loyal does a man remain when you take off and leave him penniless?

Some woman in Orlando had been projecting her Mexican slides and had recognized Lawless as being the man pictured in most of the newspapers in Florida, and featured on TV newscasts. And now Tannoy and Fletcher had nailed it down. Lawless had been seen in Guadalajara subsequent to the twenty-second of March.

The photograph wasn't telling me a thing. I looked at his clothing. The short-sleeved khaki jacket was bleached by sun and age to an off-white. I wondered what other clothing he had taken with him. Whatever he had decided to take, he had probably left packed in a suitcase in the jeep, down there under the cottage on stilts. It might be of some vague help to know what was missing from his wardrobe. It might be a clue to where he intended to hole up with the architect. Beach stuff would give one answer, and a lot of sweaters missing would give another.

I interrupted Meyer's somber inspection of the Monday *Barron's*. "I think maybe I'll go check something out with Julia Lawless."

"Do you owe her an apology too?"

"No. I thought it might make a difference to know what clothes he took with him."

"If you're that restless, Travis, why don't you drive down and see Gretel? I'm sure she'd be happy to see you."

"Am I being busy for the sake of being busy? Is that what you think?"

"All I know is you're making me nervous. Go somewhere. Please."

"Where will you be?"

"Right here. Asleep, if everything works out."

CHAPTER

17

When I arrived at 215 South Oak Lane, I saw that the garage-sale sign was still planted in the lawn. The sallow housewife with the dark blond hair and bitter smile sat in a folding chair in the shade just inside the overhead doors of the big garage. A very pretty young girl was standing at a table nearby, polishing a brass candlestick.

"Hey, McGee," the woman said. "We met the other day. I'm Freddy Ellis. Did you meet Tracy Lawless?"

The girl gave me a quick glance. "Hi," she said and turned her attention back to her chore.

"Looks as if you did well," I said.

"Damn well, considering. The gang of locusts came and went over the weekend. Several times. We're down to the dregs."

"Is Mrs. Lawless around?"

"She'll be back after a while," Tracy said. "What is it you want?"

"She told me I could stop back if I wanted to ask her anything else."

"About what?"

"Tracy!" Freddy Ellis said warningly.

"I'm sorry, but there've been enough people bothering her. This has been very hard for her. This sale and all. She's exhausted."

"When she gets back, if she doesn't want to talk to me, I won't push it."

She studied me and then nodded. She polished the last of the white residue from the candlestick and placed the pair on display. I looked around and noticed that all the guns and fishing tackle were gone. Most of the photographic equipment seemed to be gone. His ten-speed bike, rowing machine, and bowling ball were still there.

Tracy said, at my elbow, "I found out that they drill holes in a bowling ball to fit whoever buys it. I don't think my mother knew that either. I guess it won't sell. I don't know why the bicycle won't sell. It cost nearly six hundred dollars, and we've got it priced at two hundred, and it is practically new. He was going to get in really good shape. He was going to ride with me and Lynn every morning, and then he was going to ride it to work. I think we did that three times. Maybe even four." She did not sound especially bitter. Just factual.

A tall surfboard was propped against the wall. When I looked more closely at it, she said, "I'm holding that for a girl that has to ask her father if she can buy it. It used to be mine."

"It's a good one."

"I know. But it is dumb to have a surfboard here. When is there any surf to ride? Just in storms, sometimes. I didn't even ask for one. He just bought it as a surprise year before last. He threw away a lot of money that way."

"It's fun to buy things for people you love."

"That's one of the reasons, I guess," she said, and turned away. The bitterness had been visible for a moment.

Julia drove in and got out of her car, carrying a bag of

groceries. The daughter went to her and took it and apparently asked her if she wanted to talk to me. She nodded and smiled at me, and the girl went into the house with the bag.

We talked once again in the living room, with the coffee table between us. Yes, she had heard that the investigators had established that Hub was in Mexico subsequent to the twenty-second of March. She said that was nonsense. He was dead, and she knew it.

"Did Hack Ames show you a picture of Hub taken in Guadalajara on April eighth?"

"He tried to show it to me. I said it was impossible. It just couldn't be. I wouldn't even look at it. I said it was some kind of a trick. He got very annoyed with me. He really did."

"I've got a print of that picture here."

"Don't try to show it to me!"

"Julia, please. I was wondering what sort of clothing he planned to take with him. It could indicate *where* he was intending to go, whether he got there or not."

She hesitated, and then with a sigh of resignation she took the picture and turned it toward the light. She closed her eyes for a few moments, then studied it again, and handed it back.

"You can't learn much from that bush jacket," she said. "That's the last one of four he bought at Abercrombie and Fitch at least fifteen years ago. They were made out of their special Safari Cloth. They wore like iron. That was the last one. Shoulder straps. Four pleated pockets with buttons. I remember mending the left sleeve in front. You can see the mend. He ripped it on a branch."

"Do you know what other clothes he took?"

"I have no idea. He'd moved a lot of his stuff out to the ranch, you know. He was supposed to be sleeping out there."

"Could you tell by looking to see what's missing?"

She heaved a great sigh. "Well, I've got to go through that stuff sooner or later."

"Maybe it would be better to put it off for a while."

"No. I'll go look. Not that it will do any good."

She came back in five minutes, taking long strides for such a small person. She was bent forward, eyes glaring, jaw set.

"Here, damn you!" she yelled and hurled something at me. I got a hand up in time and caught the wadded cotton. Julie stood over me. "I told him and I told you that goddamn picture was nonsense. Look at it! Look at the sleeve! What did he do, smart man? Wear that to Mexico and sneak back after April eighth and slip it into his closet with the rest of his stuff? I *told* you. I told everyone. Hub is . . . is . . ." She collapsed onto the couch and began to weep.

"Julia? Julia!" I had to say her name very sharply to bring her back for a moment from the self-involvement of her tears. She stared at me, her face small, lined, and anguished.

"I agreed to tell you why I came here," I said.

"If it was to prove he's really dead . . ."

"To clear Van Harder. To get his license back. A favor for a friend. That's all."

Her stare showed she found it hard to believe. "Just for that? My God, you go plunging around, kicking and thumping, just for that? What kind of an idiot project is that?" Tears were drying.

"Your husband and his dear friend left Harder way up the creek. Harder was loyal to your husband. They gave him a very cheap shot."

"What do you think he gave me? And his daughters?"

"And his bank and his friends and his other employees too. I guess I stepped in just now because I didn't want to see some grown person crying for him."

"He was my husband!"

"When I was small there was a neighborhood kid who had a lot of toys. Whenever we played with him we all knew that whatever the game was, we had to let him win. If we didn't, he would pick up his toys and leave. He was kind of a fat kid."

"You've got some sort of adolescent infatuation with the idea of gallantry and fair play," she said. "He was doing what he thought was right. Damn you, why have you got me defending him? Would you leave? Please?"

Sheriff Haggermann Ames saw me in his little sterile windowless office at quarter to four that Monday afternoon.

He looked at the paper bag I brought in. "What have you got?"

"You won't like it."

"Would you like a list of the things that happen every day that I don't like and never expect to like?"

I sat opposite him and took the bush jacket out of the bag. I shoved the print he had given me in front of him, unfolded the bush jacket, and pointed to the mended rip in the front of the short left sleeve. His face did not reveal a thing. He told me to stay put. He came back with a slide projector, the kind which comes in a small tin suitcase which opens up into a tent-shaped ground-glass screen. The slide is projected onto the back of the ground glass. He plugged it in, turned it on, inserted the slide, turned it to sharp focus. Then he compared the shirt I'd handed him to the shirt in the photograph. He compared the shoulder straps, collar, mend, the buttons on the flap pockets. He turned the projection lamp off, tilted his head back, and stared at the ceiling.

"Get it from Julia?" he asked.

"Yes. She did the mending. He bought four of them a long time ago. This was the last one left."

"What the hell made you go ask?"

"I don't know. I began to wonder if too many trails led to Mexico. I wanted her to look and see what sort of things he took. I had the idea that if he took snowshoes and thermal underwear, it might mean people were looking in the wrong place. I sort of fell into this."

He looked at the shirt as if he wanted to set fire to it. "I fall into things too. They are like accidents, but not quite. Something in the back of a cop's head keeps nibbling away."

"I'm not a cop."

"Maybe you should consider it."

"I don't think so, Sheriff."

"Well . . . where the hell are we? As near as we can tell Hub was down in Mexico sometime in February. Maybe the woman took the picture then and got confused about the date. I don't like that. She was too positive."

"She was selling that date. She was selling the idea Hub is alive."

"And she was steering us toward Guadalajara," he said. "What if that architect lady wanted the whole pie? What if she was just using Hub? The way I read it, her career wasn't exactly climbing. Okay, so they meet the morning after he was supposed to drown. Maybe they meet at the place where he stashed the money. I don't think he jumped overboard with it. She knows the plan is to go to Mexico, get plastic surgery, hole up somewhere, and have a long happy life. But she doesn't like that kind of risk, being tied to him, maybe caught with him. So she pops him, buries him, and leaves with all the cash. To lay the false trail, she sends the slide to me."

"If she did that, Sheriff, the best and safest thing she could do would be go back to Atlanta, keep the money hidden away, and pick up the strings of the life she led up there. But there's been no transactions in checking or savings for two months, and she's got forty thousand dollars up there in the Atlanta Southern."

He gave me one of his mild, tired, dusty looks. He scratched the back of his head. "Dig, dig, dig."

"I was curious about her."

"Sure. So am I. The couple who subleased her apartment up there are curious too. And she took a leave of absence from the firm she was working with. They are wondering."

"Mr. Boggs was glad to make the inquiry."

"Sure. What else do you know you haven't got around to mentioning?"

"I brought that bush jacket right to you."

"Yes, you did. And sidestepped the question too."

"Can I ask a question?"

"Such as?"

"Who paid for Deputy Fletcher's trip to Guadalajara?"

He focused a bleak stare on the wall behind me and then turned and pushed a button on his intercom. "Pull Fletcher in from wherever, on the double, in my office."

He looked at me and said, "One thing about Wright Fletcher, he ain't too god-awful bright on the best of days. The script I'm going to try is that the body just now come ashore, positive ID from the dental work."

"He was going down to that shack where Tuckerman is staying and putting pressure on Tuckerman until the sister ran him off."

He smiled. I wouldn't want him smiling at me like that. "Now that's nice to know."

Ten minutes later I had my first look at Wright Fletcher. He was as big as the side of a house. He was as big as Walloway. He came creaking and jingling in, all leather and whipcord and the metallic necessities of office. At Ames's suggestion, I had moved back into a chair against the wall, almost behind the chair where Fletcher had to sit.

He looked uncomfortable. There were two rolls of un-baked fat on the back of his neck.

"That was a real nice break for you, flying down to Mexico like that with Mr. Tannoy. You know we could never have pried loose the money to send you down there. And we couldn't have sent you down official without probably an act of Congress, Wright."

"Well, Mr. Tannoy really needed me. He doesn't speak any Spanish at all. I'm not what you'd call fluent, but I was able to help him a lot."

"That's nice. I'm glad you were able to help him. And you are one thousand percent sure Hub Lawless is down here?"

"Well . . . I'm a thousand percent certain he *was* here. We found that sidewalk café place where that picture was taken, about three blocks from the main square, and I took another picture of it and gave it to you."

"That was a big help. Now let's say a body came drifting in and we just got a positive on the dental work, and is Hub Lawless, not looking too good after two months in the water."

"Honest to God? Did the body come in?"

"Wait a minute, Deputy! You seem pretty ready to believe that it did. I thought you had him all nailed down in Mexico. Is there something the matter with your investigation work down there?"

"N-no, Sheriff. No, there wasn't nothing wrong."

"It works out nice for Tannoy if the company doesn't have to pay off, doesn't it?"

"I think he gets some kind of a percentage commission."

"On two point two million! Must be a nice commission."

"I guess so."

"Now you had five people on the report you gave me, each ready to swear they saw Lawless down there after

223

March twenty-second. Five good sound reliable witnesse
People we could put on the stand?"

"Well . . . we didn't tell them they'd have to do that."

"Did Mr. Tannoy give them something for their trou
ble?"

"A couple of hundred pesos, Sheriff. Like about te
dollars. As, you know, a courtesy."

"I know. He put you up in a good hotel?"

"Very nice."

"Good food, good booze, a little night life?"

"Aw, Sheriff, like Mr. Tannoy said, it was kind of lik
a vacation anyway. Nobody should mind if we enjoye
ourselves, as long as we got the job done."

"Maybe there was a little bonus for you too?"

"Not really a bonus."

"Well, what?"

"Just a silver belt buckle, for a souvenir."

"And?"

"Well . . . a necklace for Madge."

"Silver?"

"Yes, sir."

"How many people did you talk to who remembere
Hub Lawless, but remembered him as being there back i
February?"

"Quite a few."

"Ten?"

"Well, more."

"I don't see their names on the report."

"Mr. Tannoy said they wouldn't do anybody any goo
He said it was all perfectly clear that Hub took off wit
the money, and it wasn't right he should get to rip off a
insurance company at the same time. He said that when
ever people rip off an insurance company, the rates go u
for all the rest of us."

"Get out of here!"

"Sir?"

"Get your fat sly ass out of here, Fletcher. It makes me feel sick to look at you. I'm going to think up an assignment for you you'll never forget. Git!"

After the door closed, he said, "So much for the Mexican connection. Can't blame Tannoy too much. A professional company man. Any company that'll pay him. Where are we now? It would be a pretty safe guess that Hub hasn't been to Mexico since February. Maybe he sent along the slide. False trail."

"After going to all the trouble to make it look like accidental drowning?"

"Okay, so then he realized it wasn't going to work. Remember I didn't get the note from Orlando with the slide until the tenth of this month, McGee."

"Nobody was talking about Guadalajara until you got it. So even if he knew what was going on around here, even if somebody was keeping him up to date, the escape route was still safe. And the complete change of appearance was still a good idea."

Ames thought in silence for a few moments. "We have to remember that he had already missed his appointment at the clinic by the time I got the picture of him." He pinched the bridge of his nose, squeezing his eyes shut. "Let's back up. Who would know about Guadalajara? Lawless, Kristin Petersen, and John Tuckerman. I put in a lot of hours back there toward the end of March, working on John Tuckerman. I couldn't move him an inch. He wasn't giving me the story word for word every time. That would have tipped me off. But it was damned close to word for word. All right, so he had to be in on the scheme. Those two were always close. I had to back off. I had nothing to go on. Harder was no help. Those two girls backed up Tuckerman's story. So if he was in on it, he certainly didn't get paid off. He had to give up his place. He wrecked his car. He was in the hospital screaming at the big polka-dot lobsters that were crawling all over him and up the walls. What would he get out of sending that slide to me? How would he manage it?"

He took the slide out of the projector. "Number eleven," he said. "Out of twenty or thirty-six. Developed by Kodak in April. Along with the thirty-nine billion other slides they processed in April." He looked at his watch. "We can make it to Ben's Camera House before it closes."

CHAPTER

18

Ben had a florid face and a curly red beard. He said, "Hack, there is absolutely no way to tell a thing about this slide. It is just about perfect exposure, but these days of automatic, through-the-lens, CD cells and all, the exception is when we get things through here that are over or under.

"Now because it has Hub Lawless in the picture, it could be like thousands of other slides and prints that have come through here with the Lawless family on them. They talk about other people having a hard time on account of Hub taking off the way he did—I am the one really hurting. I can't even guess the thousands and thousands of feet of Super Eight movie film he took of those girls and his wife. And every time Hub went off hunting or fishing or cruising, he'd be back in with a dozen rolls of color to be developed. And he was gadget-happy. I must have sold him forty different cameras over the years. And lenses and tripods and monopods. Flash attachments, viewers, projectors, screens. Name it and he'd buy it. I took back a lot in trade, of course, but I can tell you Julia had a lot left out there for that garage sale. I went out and helped her price it out to move it, and I hear they did well getting rid of it at the prices I suggested."

"Did John Tuckerman ever bring the film in and pick it up?" the Sheriff asked.

"John? Sure. He was Hub's errand boy. It would be more often John than Hub when it came to picking up film."

"Did John take any of his own?"

"You know, I don't think he owned a camera. I know he used to take some pictures sometimes, for Hub, when Hub wanted himself in the picture, like with a big fish, something like that. Snapshots. Aim and fire. Maybe he owned a camera. Maybe Hub gave him one. But John never seemed much interested."

"Did John pick up any film after Hub disappeared?"

"No. There wasn't any here. Hub stuck me for a hundred and something dollars on the books, on open account, when he took off."

"Did Hub get his pictures developed soon after he took them?"

Ben laughed. "Nearly always. But the man had too many cameras. And he had a habit of leaving exposed film in the cameras and forgetting what it was taken of. You can't do that with professional film and expect to get much. But you can leave amateur color film in a long time and not lose much. They know people tend to leave film in their cameras. They build it to last."

"So this slide here, developed in April, that could be a picture taken in February?"

"Or even last year sometime. I can tell you this wouldn't have come through my store here, seeing as how it is April, and assuming it was Hub's. It wouldn't have to go through any retail store, you know. A person can buy a slide mailer and send it to Kodak and get the slides back in the mail."

"Did Hub use those mailers?"

"Sometimes he bought some, when he was going to be away awhile. He'd mail in the film and then the slides would be waiting at home for him when he got home."

The Sheriff drove me back to the courthouse, where I had parked. I sat in his car with him for a few minutes. "What we've got so far, based on too damn many assumptions," he said, "we've got Hub in Guadalajara in early February, with John Tuckerman. We know they went down there hunting cat, but we didn't know they went to Guadalajara. We got Hub asking John to take a picture of the street there, with Hub over to the left. He isn't even looking into the camera, like a man does when his picture is being taken. What would make John want to sneak a picture way back then?"

"Maybe in the next slide, number twelve, Hub Lawless is smiling into the camera. Maybe John took it too soon."

"Why would there be any picture taking anyway?"

"You mean if they—if Hub—was planning the escape route, setting up the clinic appointment, and all? I suppose he was trying to stick with his normal routines. He always took pictures. He always came home from trips with pictures."

"Maybe you could see if he wants to talk any photogra- and Tuckerman got it developed and managed to mail one print from Orlando. Too much, McGee. Too damned thin. Too damned improbable. And why the hell would John Tuckerman want to screw up Hub's plans after helping him carry them out?"

"Because he didn't like getting the short end."

"You're getting along with him all right?"

"Pretty good."

"Maybe you could see if he wants to talk any photography or if he acts funny. Just to satisfy your own curiosity."

"Not yours?"

"No. If I wanted to learn anything about anything, all I have to do is have Deputy Fletcher saddle up and ride. Besides, I'm not permitted to deputize anybody unless we have a declared state of emergency."

"Sheriff, if I happen to find out anything I think you might want to know, I might want to tell you about it." I had my hand on the car door, ready to get out.

"Set quiet one minute longer, McGee."

"Yes, *sir!*"

"You could aggravate me pretty good if you put your mind to it, McGee. Be that as it may. I dropped by to see a man this morning, and he swore up and down you told him you were a lawyer."

"No way!"

"Stanley Moran."

"Oh. I told him I'd lay a subpoena on him if he didn't behave. I didn't pretend to be a lawyer. He asked me if I was a lawyer. I didn't answer the question."

"It bothers me, too, the way that architect lady up and left so sudden. Looked like she packed up and left and drove over to Orlando and flew out, never to come back. Meant to look like that, you think?"

"I don't know exactly what you mean."

"This morning I looked at the stuff she left behind. I wondered if it was anything worth taking with her. I borrowed the painting she left. Only so big. Hardly bigger than a legal-size piece of paper. Frame is light. It had the name of a gallery down in Clearwater on it, on the back. Can't pronounce the name of the artist. The title was *Tide Watch*. I phoned the gallery about it and they said it was purchased by a Miss Petersen in January of this year for seven hundred and fifty dollars, plus tax. It would fit in a suitcase easy, between clothes. A fifty-dollar painting, a hundred-dollar painting, a person could be so absentminded on account of wanting to leave in a hurry, they could overlook it. But seven hundred and fifty dollars?"

"And a person could pack her stuff, put it in her car, drive to Orlando, buy a cheap ticket, check the stuff aboard, leave the car at the airport, miss the flight, take a bus to practically anyplace, and the luggage would end up in an airline warehouse somewhere."

"Which fits nice with the information she hasn't touched her checking account since before the twenty-second of March, over two months."

"Or, if you are in a rush and traveling light, why bother with a seven-hundred-and-fifty-dollar painting when you are on the run with eight hundred thousand or so?"

"If somebody knew the entire scam, McGee, if they intercepted Hub and his new lady, took the money, buried them deep, then pulled that picture trick to steer everybody toward Mexico . . ."

"Somebody like?"

"I know. I know. Not like Tuckerman. Certainly not Julia Lawless."

For a moment, for one moment, I was tempted to tell him what I had learned from Gretel and John about the whole scheme as devised by Hub, and about the heart attack, the yellow jeep, the message John took to Kristin Petersen. But Gretel had trusted me, and she had induced John to trust me. If my luck ran really bad, one day this dusty dangerous little man would find out what I had held back and find out I had held it back. In a perfectly ordinary manner, with his ordinary face and gestures and tone of voice, he had a knack of creating a respect that bordered on dread.

In late afternoon I aimed the gray Dodge Dart southward, pretending I was intent on my mission of involving John Tuckerman in some small talk about photography. But Gretel filled my head, and I leafed through the hundred pictures of her, taken by a personal invisible

231

camera which had produced instant three-dimensional colored shots, vivid, never fading. I whistled. I decided that the unraveling of the Hubbard Lawless mystery was just a nervous reflex on my part. None of my business. Van Harder would be absolved and relicensed. The Sheriff was willing to arrange that without much further urging.

For all of me, the whole area could strangle in angel dust. All I wanted to do was find some way to pick up my woman and run, preferably in *The Busted Flush,* once Van Harder had turned her back over to me.

I steered around the deeper potholes. The sun was sliding down the sky, off to my right. A rabbit sat up and stopped munching as I drove slowly by. There was a small hawk perched on the mailbox, and it went arrowing off as I turned in. Soon the stilt house was in view, with the square green Fiat still parked under it. I popped the horn ring a couple of times as I drove into the yard. I got out and looked up, expecting to see her come out onto the veranda. Empty. There was not the slightest breath of a breeze. There was not the slightest stir of leaves or grass. Nor any bird sound.

The creak of the weathered stairs seemed loud as I went quickly up to the veranda deck.

"Hallo? Hey! Gretel? John?"

Nothing.

I walked around to the Gulf side of the deck, looking in the windows as I passed them. I tried the screen door and it opened. The table was set for two. There was driftwood and paper in the fireplace, ready to light against the possible evening chill.

"Hallo?"

I noticed the old ten-power binoculars. There were on the deck, looking as if they had fallen from the rough railing. I picked them up, thinking that probably Gretel and her brother were somewhere along the beach and I would be able to spot them. When I tried to look through them, it felt as if my left eye was being pulled out of the socket. Apparently they had fallen, and the prisms inside the left half had been knocked a little out of line.

There were clouds on the horizon, the sun moving down toward them. Squinting against the sun, I looked through the right half, adjusting it to my vision. I swept the beach off to the right and saw no one. I swept around to the left, looking south, and saw no one. I saw something against the concave seaward slope of a dune where the beach swung slightly westward. The sun made a bright glare against that angle of sand. I braced the binoculars against one of the uprights that supported the overhanging roof, made an additional adjustment to the focus, lost the object, found it again, and suddenly saw that it was a figure flattened against the sand, face down. It was a female, I thought. It was Gretel. It was too far away for anybody to be sure it was even female. I would have needed a forty-power spotting scope on a tripod to make it out properly. It could not be Gretel. But I was over the dune and on the beach and running hard on the packed sand, groaning as I ran, still telling myself it was not Gretel, running with no clear memory of ever having left the veranda.

It is curious how many things can go on in your mind simultaneously. If it was Gretel, she was sunbathing. She was upslope to present a better angle to the late sun. Of course. She would laugh when I came running at her like a maniac. (But she had looked too flat and too still.) A person can fall asleep in the sun. (Face down in the sand?)

When I was fifty yards from her, I heard that flat, sharp, lathe-snapping noise which a small-caliber high-velocity rifle shot makes in the open air. I had the general impression it was fired from somewhere in front of me, somewhere beyond where Gretel lay. I made two more long running strides before, simultaneously with the second crisp, abrupt sound, something tugged at the short sleeve of my sport shirt and burned my upper right arm. I plunged through soft sand, away from the wet packed beach sand, running as I had been taught long ago, moving without pattern from side to side, keeping low, and feeling once again that area of belly-coldness which seems to mark the spot where the whistling slug will impact. I dived and scrambled the last twenty feet, rolling fast to end up close to Gretel. There had been nobody on the beach, nobody visible on the dunes. The rifleman had to be up on the crest, just over the crest, peering over to aim and fire. Here the slope was so steep that when I looked up I could not see the crest, only a smooth round of sand partway up the slope.

Her dark hair was matted to a chocolate thickness at the crown of her head. Two green-bellied flies walked on her hair. Her face was turned slightly away from me. Her fingers were stubbed into the sand as though she had been trying to pull herself up the slope. She wore rust-colored shorts and a white T-shirt, dappled on the back with the brownish spots of dried blood. She wore one white boat shoe. On the left foot.

A great desolation chilled my heart. It was an emptiness stretching from here to infinity, from now to eternity.

Slowly, slowly the whole world was suffused with that strange orange glow which happens rarely toward sunset. The clouds turned to gold as the sun moved behind them, and the reflection of the clouds colored the earth. I have never seen the Gulf so quiet. There were no ripples, no birds, no sign of feeding fish, no offshore vessels moving across the horizon. I had seen this strange coppery light in Tahiti, in Ceylon (before it became Sri Lanka), and in Granada and the Grenadines. The world must have looked like that before the first creatures came crawling out of the salt water to spawn on the empty land. I turned my head and saw, beyond the shoulder of my beloved, the empty copper sea, hushed and waiting, as if the world had paused between breaths. Perhaps it was like this in the beginning, and will be like this again, after man has slain every living thing. Sand, heat, and water. And death.

A lone gull came winging in across the water, angling in, at a height just sufficient for him to clear the ridge of the dune.

The gull would have crossed the crest about two hundred feet ahead of me and to my right. When he neared the crest he suddenly squawked alarm and veered to the left of his line of flight and sharply upward before flying on.

So there he was. X. For unknown. The rifleman. I raised up very quickly and dropped flat again. If you lift slowly, you give them time to put a third eye in the center of your forehead. I retained the afterimage of the empty crest. Nothing. No glint of metal. No round shape of head or bulk of shoulders. Just the wind-smoothed tan sand. I took another look. And another. Nothing at all.

The terrain promised no advantage. I could not hope to run up the slope. I could get up there to the crest by churning and floundering and clawing my way up through the coarse sliding sand, as easy to shoot as a deer in deep snow. I could make good time down the slope, right down to the open beach, where I would make a pretty good target there as well. I could move laterally, but not very far. The slight concavity which hid me from the crest grew shallower to my left and was gone within twenty feet. Ten feet to my left I saw an object protruding from the sand, the end of something thrown up by a storm of long ago. It looked as if it might be wood, but it was difficult to tell in that golden-red glow. I wanted a stick, a stone, a switch—anything. It is an ancient instinct. Man is the tool user. Even as the saber-toothed tiger was disemboweling him, man was reaching for a branch to club the beast. It did not matter that nothing I could find on a beach would help me ward off the tiger or the bullet, I wanted something in hand. A tool. Comfort of a kind.

I edged over to it. Wood. A good shape and size for grasping. Was it too short or too long? Too short to use, too long to extricate from the sand? I worked it back and forth and pulled it free. It was the handle end of a canoe paddle. The piece was two feet long. I had grasped it near the break. On the other end, the end normally grasped, there were dead barnacles, tough, sharp, and firmly seated.

It had an incongruity like the red light that filled the beach. Canoes were summer lakes, frocks, big hats, and music coming across the water.

The initial panic had settled into a reliable flow of adrenaline. It is my fate and my flaw to have learned too long ago that this is what I am about. This is when I am alive and know it most completely. Every sense is honed by the knowledge of the imminence of death. The juices flow. In the back of my mind I tried to tell myself that I had been turned into a murderous machine by the sight of Gretel. But it was rationalization. There was a hard joy in this acceptance of a total risk. I knew that if he got me—whoever he might be—he was going to have to be very damned good at it, and even then I was going to create some astonishment in him. I would live totally on this thin edge until it was over, and then I would either be dead for good or partially dead until the next time.

The copper sea made no sound at all. I eeled slowly upslope, angling to my right, knowing that I would be exposed to him, would be in his line of fire before I could reach the crest. I worked it slowly, peering toward the area where the bird had veered. I kept muscles poised and bunched so that in an instant I could hurl myself back and to the left, hoping to fall back into the sanctuary of the concavity near Gretel. As I came closer to the crest, I diminished the chance of regaining the concavity undamaged. On the other hand, it was easier to watch for him. Or her. Or them. Or it. The dune was about fifty feet high, much higher than in front of the shack. Perhaps if someone suddenly appeared to fire at me again, at shorter range, it might be better to plunge over the crest, race and roll down the shaded side, taking a chance of finding some kind of cover.

At last I was close to the crest. The wind had given it a sharp, wandering edge. I was on about a fifty-degree slope. I dug my fingers into the sand just short of the ridge. My chin touched the sand. I was absolutely certain that somebody was waiting, alert, ready for the target to appear above the ridge, silhouetted against the slow-motion bonfire of the sky.

So I worked my legs up under me, adjusted my grip on the piece of paddle, and began to take slow, deep breaths. In the total silence of the world, my best way to get over was to bound over, letting out a yell which would shock the rifleman into a momentary rigidity, or into panicky unaimed shots. There was the hesitation much like that remembered from childhood, standing on the edge of the roof, a reluctance to make the first commitment.

In that great stillness a monstrous breathing sound began. A great snuffling intake, and then a long breathing sign. *Snuff-sigh. Snuff-sigh. Snuff-sigh.* As though a winded dragon lay beyond the ridge, slightly to my right and far down the landward side of the dune. It was very steady and regular. I tried to identify that sound. It seemed, somehow, very homely and familiar. Suddenly there was a metallic clank at the end of the snuffing sound, a hesitation before the sigh.

I knew then what the sound was. It had been unfamiliar only because it was so incongruous when compared with my state of tension. There could be two of them, of course. It was still a time for caution, but a time to discard the large bad idea of bounding over the rim and down the slope, yelling and waving my paddle.

I dropped back a little and then moved laterally until I was directly above that breathing sound. And then, instinctively holding my breath, I looked over the edge.

It was darker on the landward side of the dune. The red light that bathed the world was all shadows and wine.

There, below me, John Tuckerman shoveled the dry, loose sand. *Chuff* of the shovel blade into the sand, then the soft sound, like an exhalation, as he swung the sand out in an arc behind him. As he dug, the sand slid down the slope, rivulets filling some of the space he had shoveled. The muscles of his back and shoulders and upper arms slid and bulged under the sun-scorched flab. He worked with the metronomic energy of the demented. He was naked. It was a labor assigned in hell. From the blazing sunburn on his body, and from the look of the piles of sand he had shoveled, he had been at it all day.

He was excavating the yellow jeep. It was aimed south, parallel to the ridge. The wheels and fenders on the right side of the vehicle, in fact the whole right side of it, was still covered by the slide of brown coarse sand. There was a figure behind the steering wheel. It sat, arms in its lap, chin on its chest, looking like a crude sand sculpture made of a slightly darker shade of sand. An imperceptible movement of the air brought the faint, sweet, gassy stink of decay, and I nearly gagged as I realized that the sand was darker because it was clotted by the fluids released by the tissues. In the passenger seat a slight knob had begun to appear, in just the right place and the right size to be the back of a head.

I looked for the rifle, finally saw it about thirty feet beyond the front of the jeep, leaning against a leafless stunted bush.

He stopped shoveling. He spoke at conversational pitch, but in a strange tone of voice, a sweet wheedling tone pitched so much higher than his normal tone that he sounded almost like a woman.

"Now you shouldn't talk to me like that, Hub! I'll get you out of here and you can be on your way. Don't I always do what you want me to? Don't I?"

He waited, leaning forward, seeming to listen.

"No, it wasn't like that," he said. "What she was going to do was take all the money and leave all by herself. But I made her wait, Hub. I made Krissy-bitch wait, and she's right there beside you, isn't she? And that's proof. You and she can go on off together soon as I get you dug out and get the engine started."

Again he listened.

Again he answered. "Well, goddarn it, Hub, I forgot. That's all. I knew I had something to remember and I forgot. When I covered you up so you'd be safe, I just jammed it against the dune, put you in the driver's seat, climbed on up with the shovel, and spilled enough down to do it in ten minutes, no more. That's how I didn't know it would take me this long to get you out. You two will be fine in Mexico. They've about stopped hunting you. Now you stop complaining and let me work, will you?"

That high sweet tone of voice made the skin crawl on the back of my neck and the backs of my hands. And it was no longer a person-against-person conflict. He was a mechanical toy, and I had to get to him and turn him off. A mechanical man will walk into a wall and try to keep walking. He will fall down and his legs will still make walking motions, little gears and springs ticking as he winds down.

CHAPTER

19

He was working at the rear of the jeep, and as I tried to decide on my best and safest move, more sand spilled toward him, revealing the head and shoulders of the figure sitting next to the body of Hubbard Lawless. It was as dark and silent as he.

I moved to my right behind the crest, so no movement would catch his eye, and stopped when I was directly opposite the small-caliber rifle.

I timed my lunge so that it came just as he was lifting a full shovel of sand and beginning to pivot to throw it behind him. I came down the slope in giant plunging strides. The whirling shovel caught me just below the knees, whacking a leg out from under me in such a way that I landed face down on the hardpan at the bottom of the dune, losing my good canoe-paddle club in my effort to break my fall. I got up on what felt like two broken legs just as he whirled with the rifle in hand. I dived for my club, grasping it, rolling over and over toward him, heard the broken-stick sound of the shot, and felt both fire and numbness in the left cheek of my behind just before I rolled against his legs and knocked him down. He sprang up again with a rubbery monstrous agility, with a frightening strength. I'd grasped the gun barrel in my left hand, and I took a swing at him with the club as he was bounding at me, wresting the gun away from me. There was such a slight feeling of impact that I knew I had only grazed him with the club.

He backed away from me and aimed at the middle of my forehead. I could practically see the little round hole it would make where it went in, and the shattered suety ruin it would make where it came out.

"Johnny!" she cried, a long desperate wailing sound, full of an absolutely final despair. I was kneeling, as though in homage to my executioner. I looked back over my shoulder and saw her standing tall, teetering, on the crest of the dune, outlined against the burgundy light. He moved the sight from me to her, aiming up at her, as I threw the club at his face as hard as I could. He fired, and I turned again and saw her tumble toward us. She slid down the slope, creating a small avalanche of sand which almost covered her head when the sliding stopped.

With no thought of the gun, I went stumbling, crawling, floundering to her, and grasped her shoulders and pulled her head out of the brown sand. She made a dry spitting noise, trying to expel the sand caked in her mouth.

John Tuckerman was acting strangely. He seemed to be trying to aim the gun at us, holding it in one hand. With his other hand he was clutching at his own throat. As I leaped toward him to try to take away the rifle, he dropped it and put both hands to his throat. He was making a wet hissing sound. In what light was left I could see the sheen of the bright arterial blood which came out between his fingers and ran in a broad band down through the chest hair, down the belly, into the groin, and down both thighs.

He looked puzzled. Then he seemed to smile at me, one of those small shy smiles people use when they have committed some vulgar social blunder. A girl who had just lost her contact lens in her chicken chow mein once gave me a smile very like that.

He took two slow steps toward the jeep, then lowered himself gently to his hands and knees. He crawled a little farther, blood pumping out of the throat wound. He seemed to dwindle in size as I watched. He collapsed onto his face a yard from the jeep, with a final exhalation that made him smaller yet. There was a strange overlay of sentimentality about it. Faithful hound returns to master. I turned and hobbled back to Gretel. I had rolled her onto her back when I had pulled her face out of the sand. As I looked at her, the last of the red light went, leaving us in a darkening, gray-blue edge of night. Her face was so slack I could see what she had looked like asleep in her crib long ago. She was breathing, her respirations slow and shallow. Her pulse was heavy, steady, reassuring.

I checked my personal damage. The slug had gone at an angle through the right gluteus maximus, and it had been so undamaged in transit the exit wound was as small as the entrance wound. I could not get a very good look, of course. It was bleeding, but not inordinately. More of a seepage. And it had begun to hurt. A lot. That is the big walking muscle back there. Grab yourself a handful of right buttock—your own—and walk a few steps and feel what happens. A lot of clenching and unclenching goes on. I pulled my pants back up and fastened my belt. I looked around for a moment. Stillness. Stench. Hubbard Lawless and Kristin Petersen sat motionless in the jeep, heads bowed.

For a moment the world veered and tipped, and I had the ghastly conviction Hub would lift his head, give me a sandy and horrible smile, start the jeep, and go roaring down the rough track with the remaining sand spilling out.

The reserve gas can was chained and locked to the rear bracket on the jeep. I had the momentary image of myself using the shovel to break the lock, then checking the money and burying it in the sand where only I could find it.

But the lady was breathing, and the rental Dodge was one hundred million miles away. With an enormous effort, I scooped her up. I held her cradled in my arms. I began the long walk back to the car through the increasing blackness of the night, feeling the tickle of blood on the back of my right thigh, feeling the leaden ache of the wound plus the shrill yank of pain with each step. At last I made it and stretched her out on the back seat. I drove slowly to Timber Bay, sitting in a puddle of my own blood. I went directly to the hospital and into the archway reserved for ambulances.

As I clambered slowly out, an old man in uniform was dancing around me in utter fury, slapping the pistol holstered on his belt, telling me I could not park there. I smiled and nodded and started to try to pull Gretel out of the back seat. Then more people came. Helping hands. I did a lot of smiling and nodding, and they paid no attention to me until someone noticed that I was leaving bloody footprints on their shiny gray vinyl floor. . . .

They did not have to do much to me. Some suturing, antibiotics, observation. Keep me a few days. Find a tall enough crutch so I could take pressure off the ham muscles. It should have been routine. I had been in so many hospitals. I had been hurt so many times. But they disorient you. Their white lights burn all the time. They come by in the night. They change your habits, your hours, your diet, and the climate inside your head. You are an object, subject to their manipulations.

I wanted to see Gretel. I wanted to be with Gretel. I wanted to hold her hand. Their whole establishment seemed designed to keep me away from her. The red-faced, endlessly weary Dr. Ted Scudder had sutured my butt and had assisted in the emergency surgery on Gretel's skull. He was perfectly willing to tell me how Gretel was and what they had done.

The injury was consistent with someone's chasing her along the beach and clubbing her in the back of the skull, perhaps with the flat of the blade of a shovel. It had given her a depressed fracture of the occipital bone on the right side of the back of the skull. It seemed almost inconceivable to them that she could have been able to climb the dune.

"Extraordinary vitality," Scudder said. "We've got a very good man here. Townsend. I assisted. Two and a half hours of very careful work. Freeze those little bleeders. Tiny stitches in the tear in the dura. Fit the pieces where they belonged. Just three. Bit of wire. Considerable traumatic amnesia. Thinks she's in California. Thinks she's missing work. No visitors. Not until she gets herself sorted out better. Avoid emotional shocks. Also, it keeps Hack Ames from bugging her. My orders. Includes you, McGee."

When bluster doesn't work, when begging is useless, try guile. I lied my way right to her door and put my hand against it to push it open. Didn't. There was already one perilously deep black hole in the middle of my head. I had seen the flies and thought her dead. Never thought of checking. Made the worst possible assumption merely because that seemed to be the way my luck was running, and would run forever. Just one touch on the neck to find the pulse—that was all it would have taken. So, having made an almost fatal blunder of omission, I paused just before the blunder of commission, took my hand away, crutched myself back to the service stairway, and grunted my way down the stairs. I had thought of her . . . instead of my own dramas and concerns. Could I possibly be growing up? After so long?

On Friday at noon, with me sitting on my inflated rubber ring, Meyer drove slowly and carefully down to the Cedar Pass Marina. He had checked us out of the North Bay Yacht and Tennis Resort and moved our gear aboard *The Busted Flush*. Home is a good place to be when you hurt. I was so damned glad to see my old-crock houseboat squatting there that my eyes stung and misted. Van Harder was there, giving me that limp, dry, callused handshake so curiously typical of many men who spend their lives out of doors. We went to the lounge, and I got comfortable on the long yellow couch, rubber ring under my aching tail.

"I took my stuff off this morning," Harder said. "Had a talk with the Sheriff. Should have my license back middle of next month. Once I'm working again, I'll start payments on what I owe. Hack apologized for kicking me. He said he never should have done that, never. And I told him he was right, he never should have."

"You don't owe me anything," I said.

"A bargain is a bargain."

One long look at him was enough to convince me there was no point in argument. "Okay. Okay. But open a savings account here in your name. And when it gets up to the full amount, let me know."

He thought that over, nodded, and put some bills and change on the coffee table, along with a piece of yellow paper with figures written on it. "This here is what's left from the expense money bringing her over here. Forty-two seventy-five. It's all writ down. Eleanor Ann made sure the figures add up right."

"Thanks. She looks great. She really does."

"I had plenty of time to do this and that. Drains and screens and packing. Some splicing. Stuff like that. I'd rather be busy than setting around." He coughed. "She needs bottom work, and you got a soft spot on the transom, outboard, port. I chalk-marked it. Could be dry rot. Should be looked at."

I thanked him again and he said I'd be hearing from him, and off he went. Meyer brought me a cold beer and sat on the other side of the coffee table. "I saved the papers," he said. "Over there in the corner. Big sensation in the press."

"They tried to get to me. Hack Ames had the lid on. Walter Olivera was the only one who slipped by. I told him no comment. Hack's orders."

He went over and leafed through the stack and brought back a copy of the *Timber Bay Journal.* "Did you see this front page?"

I hadn't. It was a night shot, a floodlit picture of the jeep, the two occupants still in it, Tuckerman still on the ground beside the jeep. It had been taken by somebody who had squatted down in front of and to the left of the jeep, with wide-angle lens. Grisly and effective.

I had, of course, read and heard the news and the story of the official reconstruction. Hub Lawless's autopsy had shown plugged coronary arteries. Miss Petersen had died of suffocation under the sand after having been struck a terrible blow in the face which had fractured her jaw and cheek and most probably rendered her unconscious. In the original conspiracy, Lawless had gone overboard from the *Julie* at night opposite the shack. The jeep, with the $892,000 jammed into the big auxiliary gas can, was already there. Tuckerman went out the next morning and found Lawless dead of a heart attack brought on by struggling to get to shore. Either Miss Petersen was with Tuckerman or he went and got her. There was a quarrel about the money. Tuckerman killed the woman and put both bodies into the jeep after driving it to where the dune slope was high and steep. Covered it deep by avalanching enough sand down the slope. Two months later his sister came upon him when he was trying to dig the money out. He had struck her on the head, injuring her seriously. A Mr. McGee, a friend of Tuckerman and his sister, had arrived and had struggled with Tuckerman. In the struggle McGee had suffered a bullet wound, and Tuckerman had died of an injury sustained in a fall. McGee, wounded, had brought Mrs. Howard in to the hospital and had informed the Sheriff before undergoing treatment for his wound.

"I'm never around when things are going on," Meyer said.

"Be glad. This time, be glad."

"How lucky it was that John Tuckerman died of a fall."

"You remind me of the Sheriff."

"He keeps saying that?"

"We had four conferences in the hospital. He is a very diligent man. He is a very stubborn man."

Meyer peered out through the windows of the lounge. "And here he comes again."

Meyer went and invited him aboard and led him in. He was carrying the solid hunk of canoe paddle with the barnacles firmly fixed to that curved part which was supposed to fit into the palm of the hand of the paddler.

He sat down and sighed and smiled and accepted a beer. He bumped the paddle gently against his knee. "We got the lab report back, McGee. The tissue and blood they got off this thing, off the edges of these barnacles, match Tuckerman's type."

"So he must have fallen on it!" I said.

"You claim you missed him clean both times, when you swung at him and when you threw it at him."

"Startled him both times and missed him both times."

"From the shape and location of the wound, the lab people think that it struck the throat, moving from left to

right at high velocity, and tore a hole in the artery and a
hole in the windpipe. Are you sure there wasn't some
slight little impact when you swung at him?"

"Positive."

"McGee, you were defending your life against a mad
man with a gun. The booze and the PCP had turned hi
brain to hog slop. You thought the sister was dead and he
was going to kill you. And you could see the dead bodie
in the jeep. What the hell do you think I am trying to do'
Railroad you into Raiford, for Christ's sweet sake? I wan
to wrap this all up, all the way. I want a grand jury verdic'
of justifiable homicide. I don't want a file that says Tuck
erman fell down onto some barnacles, dammit."

"He fell down."

"What's wrong with my saying that you hit him a lucky
shot anyway, no matter what you say?"

"Sheriff," Meyer said mildly, "Travis McGee might fin
the attendant publicity somewhat constraining in hi
chosen profession of, shall we say, salvage expert. And he
would have to be charged, of course, to be exonerated
And in this computerized world, the charge would be a
part of his record. Secondly, of course, he is quite inter
ested in Mrs. Howard. If she should recover as fully a
they anticipate, she might find it awkward to feel any un
mixed emotion toward her brother's executioner. Lastly
sir, McGee and I are accustomed to exchanging confi
dences, and if there was any doubt at all in his mine
about whether or not he missed the deceased when he
swung or when he threw that object, I am certain he
would have told me. And you have my word of hono:
that such has not been the case. Oh, and one other possible solution. Were the object wedged into the ground at
about this angle, and were the deceased to fall, left side
first, he being a tall and heavy man, the wound migh
look as though—"

"All right, all *right!*" Hack Ames said. "You do go on

He fell. The most timely fall in the history of grand larceny and felony murder. You know what I am going to do with this half of a paddle? I am going to hang it on my office wall, and the moral is going to be for me to try not to get too cute." He finished the beer and stood up.

We both stared at him. I said, "Cute about what?"

"Remember the way we went around and around about that slide, once you found out the bush jacket was still in his closet at home? Hub's jacket?"

"It still bothers me," I said. "I can't see Tuckerman being sly enough to work something out like that, aiming the whole search toward Mexico, knowing Lawless was buried in the sand out there, in the yellow jeep."

"Stop worrying about it. The little lady that sent us the slide turned up. She came over to see us because she was absolutely certain the body we found couldn't have been Hub Lawless if the body had been under the sand ever since March twenty-third. She came over because she had broken up with her boyfriend and didn't have to be careful about talking about Mexico any more. And she wondered if she could cut in on any part of the reward for information in the case. Little bit of a thing. Very excitable and fast-talking. Hops around from this to that. Hard to follow her. Well, it took almost two hours to unravel it. She had gone down to Guadalajara twice. She went down in February with three other girls from the insurance office where she works. A winter vacation. One week. And she met a young Mexican there. An assistant manager of the hotel where they stayed. She went back to see him in April. She took pictures on only one day. Friday, April eighth, when her Roberto was busy and she walked around alone. She had the camera with her. A little Konica range-finder camera with automatic exposure. Had she taken the camera with her the first time she went? Yes. Taken pictures? Yes. Did they get mixed up together? No. Because they were dated. The date of development was stamped right into the cardboard. One batch said F-E-B, and one batch said A-P-R. Did you use the camera between trips to Mexico? No. So then came the key question. Did you take a part of a roll and leave it in the camera between trips? She got real still and stared at me, and those pretty eyes got bigger and bigger, and finally she hit the desk with her little fist and said, 'Boy, am I some kind of dumb!' We walked all around it, McGee. She felt terrible. She apologized and apologized. I told her she had been a big help, really. She had helped us unravel Hub's plan, the one he would have followed if he hadn't had a heart attack. The warning is clear. Don't get too cute. Always think of the simplest solution. Tricky stuff will snarl up your head."

"You do the tricky stuff pretty well, Sheriff," I said. "Like that expensive painting the Petersen woman left behind."

He shrugged again. "I'd counted her dead before that. John Tuckerman took her keys after he'd killed her, drove in after dark, packed her stuff, loaded it in the red car, and drove it to Orlando. That was before he was so far gone. His head was still working. Remember your guess? I think he bought a plane ticket to somewhere. Maybe Miami. Checked her baggage through and tore up the ticket. So it's in an airline warehouse somewhere. Left the car in a rental car space. Probably took a bus right back to Timber Bay."

After he left, Meyer said, "I don't think John Tuckerman was sane from the moment he came back with Kristin and found Hub Lawless dead or dying. He'd given his life to Hub. Clown, errand boy, hunting companion. And probably the woman turned her back on Hub lying there and demanded the jeep and the money. Or just the money. So he hit her and buried them both, and that was the end of him. Maybe on a half-conscious level his relationship to Hub was something he couldn't admit to him-

elf, something a good ol' boy is not *ever* supposed to
eel."

"Thanks for helping with the Sheriff."

"Just don't tell me whether you did or didn't."

"I don't plan to."

Epilogue

On a July afternoon, late, we came trundling down th
Gulf in *The Busted Flush,* just the two of us. We cam
down the length of Longboat Key, where the condo
miniums stand tall off Sarasota, and when we passed St
Armands Key, I told her about the famous shoppin
circle there and promised her I would take her to it an
buy her something ridiculously expensive. It would b
something useless and important and would have to d
with some of the slice of the recovery awarded me by th
committee headed by J. Devlin Boggs.

Some days we made good miles, some days zero. Sh
had fallen deeply in love with the old houseboat, ha
learned how to cope with the trickeries of the galley an
the cranky plumbing in the head. She wasted fresh wate
in long showers when we had it and did without when w
didn't. She learned how to read the charts and operate th
radio and the RDF, synchronize the diesels, and cook u
Chili Meyer.

On this uncounted day in July, we came into Big Pas

at dusk, on a tide so low I had to creep through the shoaling waters, bumping lightly twice. The charter boats were coming in off the Gulf. The sun was a forest fire in the west, and the distant downtown windows winked red in response. I chugged slowly by Sand Dollar Island and over to an anchorage area I had used before, happy to see no other craft there swinging on their hooks. We were well out of the channel, in about seven feet of water and about a hundred and fifty feet off a sandy beach, when I put down the two bigger Danforths, cut the power, swung on the lines, tested them, and found them firm.

While I made drinks, Gretel checked the larder and said she'd better make out a list in the morning. We had both spent all day in a sun so hot, so burning bright, that we radiated heat. Her brown hair had grown out to about an inch and a half. She had been shaved bald as an ostrich egg, and had given me no glimpse of her skull during the bristly time. Now it was revealed. Crowning glory, she called it. The constant sun was baking it lighter. I might end up with a blond person, she told me. She thought it made her look like a boy, hair that short. I told her that from the eyebrows up, in a certain light, at a certain angle, she might look somewhat like a boy. But include any other parts of her, and the illusion was lost. Smashed-all-to-hell-and-gone lost. That kind of lost. She asked if I was trying to call her hippy. I said she was hippy, busty, waisty, lippy, throaty, that she was all thighed, bellied, eyelashed, ankled, all ladied up just fine.

Today she had been quieter than usual, and I knew she had been thinking about the life I wanted for us.

After we ate and had tidied up, I went on deck to check the weather and the bugs. It was a splendid night, mild and sweet, frosted with stars. The western sky was black, where thunder bumped and muttered, and the breezes came from there. I got the inflatable mattresses out of the locker, put them side by side on the sun deck,

pumped them firm with the pedal pump, spread a blanke
over them.

There was a strawberry glow over the city. The light
winked out in the houses along the Siesta Key side of Bi
Pass. We lay on our backs and identified the constella
tions, and we both saw the same shooting star.

"Hey, do you wish on those?" she asked. "I forget."

"There's no rule against it. I wish you'd make up you
mind. That is, if I'm entitled to a wish."

"I think maybe I have. To review the proposition yo
made me, you want me to share your life on any basis
choose, just so long as I understand it's permanent."

"Properly stated."

"I think it is very probably exactly the right time i
your life for this to happen, maybe even the last chanc
you'll have."

"Something has been happening to me these last fe
years," I said. My voice sounded rough and uneven. "
bleakness. I don't know what to call it."

"No, darling. Don't go grasping at me. I'm not sayin
yes. Let go. There. Now listen to me. I really do love yo
And much as I love you and want you, I can't be . .
somebody's remedy. Some kind of medicine for the soul."

"But that isn't—"

"Listen to me, please. I have to be my own person.
have to take complete charge of my life. I did the hard
scrabble years for somebody else, for some idea that wa
never going to work anyway. I'm not talking about lib o
chauvinism. I've got kind of an alarming capacity fo
blind loyalty. Like my brother had. Fierce loyalty. I kno
that in some very final way, dear, we are all absolutel
alone. The relationships people have are an attempt t
deny that aloneness, but it doesn't go away. I want m
loyalty to be to me for a while, and maybe for all th
years I might have left. I have to be complete within my

254

elf and stand by myself in order to really become a person."

"You *are* a person, a damned wonderful—"

"Hush! I'm not going to run away. I love you. I want to stay near you, but if you won't accept my terms, I'll *have* to run away. I'll come to your town to live and work. We'll find me a place. I want demanding work that I can be good at and get better at. We will be friends, and from time to time, for as long as we both want, we'll be lovers. But nobody is going to try to manipulate or change or control or smother anybody else."

"But I don't—"

"Think about it, darling. Tell me tomorrow. I'm trying to be wise about myself. I can't be rushed. I have to reinvent myself. By myself. I don't want to sign on."

"But you'll be nearby."

She got up and went over to the rail. I followed and stood beside her, resting a hand on the warmth of her waist through the T-shirt. She moved to lean against me, head against my shoulder. She was a strong and accessible magic.

"I don't think he would have hit me," she said. "I've thought about him all day."

"You've been quiet."

"I know. I think there was somebody else there."

"There could have been," I lied. "We'll never know."

"No matter what that stuff did to his brain. I can remember up to the point where he sprang up out of bed in his room and went yelling outdoors as if he was answering somebody. I just can't remember past that."

"Don't keep trying."

She looked at the lights of Sarasota. "We don't know anyone here. We're not in their minds," she said. "So in some kind of funny way, we're dead. Nothing stopped in Timber Bay. They're stirring around up there tonight, laughing and hurting and hating and making love. Some are trying to live and some are trying to die. We're fading out of their minds. I'm fading out of the memories of the people I've known back in my other life. And as they are fading out of my memory, it is as if they were dying. Dying is all forgetting, maybe. Nothing more. You are not dead until there isn't a crumb of memory left anywhere in the world."

"You come up with some pretty strange stuff, lady."

"So why do you want me around for keeps anyway?"

"Two or three minor reasons. Nothing important."

"Settle for my being sort of a neighbor?"

"Like you said, I'll let you know tomorrow."

She turned into my arms. The thunder boomed closer. It was using up more of the sky.

It was clear that the rain would come. We went back to the mattresses. When the first big drops did come, they fell splatting unheeded and almost unnoticed upon my bare back and on her upturned face, vivid in the first stroke of lightning.